Keri Arthur

Killer's Kiss

A Lizzie Grace Novel

CHAPTER ONE

Evil brushed my psychic senses, a dark wind that pulled me from a deep sleep. The magic that protected the café above which I lived remained undisturbed, so whatever I sensed wasn't close. That didn't mean it wasn't a threat, however,

I tossed off the sheets and padded naked from my bedroom. The air was still and heavy with heat, and sweat prickled my skin. Though December wasn't usually the hottest month of summer, the last couple of days had been unbearably hot. Worse, the nights hadn't dropped below twenty-five degrees Celsius. I normally didn't mind the heat, but pregnancy seemed to have changed all that.

Moonlight filtered through the glass sliding doors at the far end of the living room, bright enough to sweep aside the shadows that normally held the room captive. The moon was full tonight, which meant the three werewolf packs that lived within the Faelan Reservation would be out and running.

Aiden would be with them.

The mere thought stirred the ache in my heart and

sharpened the longing in my soul. I loved the damn man, and I had no doubt he loved me, but pack politics continued to get in the way of our relationship. The fact that his mother—who remained pack alpha despite the death of her mate—hated witches in general and me in particular wasn't helping matters.

But werewolves weren't the only ones called by the full moon. Witches, particularly dark witches, often used her power and beauty to fuel their spells.

That dark wind had held an undercurrent of magic.

I had no idea whether it was connected to the evil I sensed, but I wouldn't be surprised if it was. The Faelan Reservation was regularly invaded by all manner of super-natural and demonic types, thanks to the largest of her two wellsprings being left without any sort of protections for well over a year. Wild magic—the raw, unbridled power that came from deep within the earth—was neither good nor bad, but, if left unguarded for any length of time, it always caught the interest of those wanting to claim its power for themselves. Sometimes those claimants were human, but mostly they were not.

I grabbed one of the hairbands sitting on the coffee table, then opened the sliding door and stepped out onto the balcony. A soft breeze stirred around me, but its touch was heated and did little to cool. I swept my hair up into a pony-tail, then walked over to the balcony and leaned on the top railing. This portion of Castle Rock was basically a retail area, so the street below was empty—probably a good thing, given my nakedness.

The moon rode high in the sky, and her power sang through me, fierce and bright. It made me itch to run, to feel the soil between my toes, the brush of leaves against bare skin, and to raise my voice with the rest of the pack in praise of the moon's glory.

But I wasn't a werewolf, even if I carried the child of one. I had no idea if it was her presence—however beanlike she might yet be—causing the need to run, or if it was simply a result of my deepening connection to the land and the wild magic—a magic that was now changing my DNA. And yet, for all the enhancements it was making, both physical and magical, it could never do the one thing that would truly make a difference to my life.

It could never make me a werewolf.

A gossamer thread of wild magic drifted toward me. I raised a hand, and it slipped around my wrist, a fragile moonbeam that pulsed with a deep sense of kinship and an even deeper sense of urgency, though I had no idea why. The thread belonged to the main wellspring—my wellspring, as I now thought of it—which was located within the O'Connor compound. Apparently, the wild magic had gotten fairly volatile during my absence, causing rockslides and minor quakes, but things appeared to have settled since I arrived back home.

But if the almost agitated pulsing coming from this thread was anything to go by, something was still going on, and I had no real way of uncovering what. The wellspring might well be gaining some form of sentience, but it wasn't like I could communicate with it, even if I could use and direct its power. And it wasn't as if I could approach the spring, given its location.

There was, rather unusually, another wellspring within the Faelan Werewolf reservation—a newly risen one that lay within the Marin pack's home ground. It was guarded by not only the soul of Katie O'Connor—Aiden's sister—but by the ghost of her witch husband, Gabe. Until recently, very few within the reservation had known of its existence, but that had all changed when I'd confronted the werewolf council and challenged Aiden's mother to a fight.

The fallout of *that* particular situation had yet to be decided, though I suspected it was partly responsible for the delay in Aiden's confirmation as pack alpha—a status that would allow him to confront their biases about wolves marrying outside their own kind, and the only real hope we had of a long-term relationship.

Not that he'd actually asked me to marry him, or even discussed his plans and intentions. The man could be remarkably tight-lipped when it came to such things. Hell, we weren't even *in* a relationship right now, and he certainly didn't know about my pregnancy. And wouldn't, not until I knew for sure what his intentions were. If he *did* intend to ask me to marry him, I wanted it to be because he loved me, not because I carried our child.

Of course, that was a secret I could only keep for a couple more months, at most, because he'd smell the hormonal changes once I neared the end of the first trimester.

The magic riding the night seemed to be coming from the direction of Émigré, the nightclub my psychotic ex had destroyed during his rampage of revenge against me and Belle. Said nightclub had been owned by a very old, very polite, but ultimately very scary vampire who had decades of murder and mayhem behind her. To say he'd gotten a brutal comeuppance for his actions would be an understatement.

The evil was more difficult to pin down, but maybe that would change once I headed out and looked around. I was briefly tempted to do so alone, rather than wake anyone I cared about over something that might amount to nothing, but given my track record of finding bloody chaos, it wasn't worth the risk.

I'm glad you came to that conclusion, because I was beginning to wonder if pregnancy had killed off a few brain cells.

The dry comment whispered into my mind, and I couldn't help laughing. One of the many benefits that came with Belle being not only my best friend but also my familiar was the ability to share thoughts and psychic abilities. It was a connection that had saved both our lives more than once over the years.

The only thing that's killing my brain cells at the moment is the heat. I pushed away from the railing and headed back inside. *What are you doing up at this hour? Or shouldn't I ask?*

It's far too hot for sex, if that's what you're implying.

I'm betting Monty would disagree with that.

Monty's a man, and we all know they have no brain cells when it comes to sex.

I laughed again. Monty wasn't only my cousin, but also the designated reservation witch, a position assigned by the High Witch Council and one that generally meant doing nothing more than passing on the occasional high council decree and providing the rangers with magical assistance if and when needed.

It had been needed a *lot* over the last year.

You've only been engaged for a couple of days, I said dryly. *Don't tell me the bloom has already started to fade.*

No, but it is why he's insisting the house we buy has a pool. He's planning sexy water times.

Of course he is. I pulled on some shorts and a boob-supporting crop top, then slipped on a pair of runners and headed downstairs. *Am I swinging around to pick you or Monty up?*

Monty. He is reservation witch, after all. Besides, if things play out the way they usually do, you'll be out all night and won't be in a fit state to open the café.

Maybe this will be the one time my psychic senses are wrong and there's nothing nasty happening.

Belle snorted, a sound that echoed sharply down the psychic lines. *The odds of that happening are about the same as Karleen having an epiphany and giving you and Aiden her blessing.*

Miracles do occasionally happen. Though I wasn't holding out for one in this particular case. Karleen's hatred of witches stemmed from the rape and subsequent death of her older sister when Karleen was barely fourteen, and Gabe's actions here with Katie had only reinforced that hatred.

I grabbed my keys and headed out the back door. *Be at your place in five.*

I'll roust Monty.

And would have great pleasure in doing so if the relish in her mental tone was anything to go by. Obviously, the heat was not affecting *his* ability to sleep.

I jumped into our SUV—which remained adorned with over a dozen bullet holes thanks to the very human, granny-killing creep we'd encountered almost a month ago now—and headed over to Monty's. He was waiting out the front of his townhouse, two travel mugs in hand. He was a typical royal witch in looks, with short crimson hair that gleamed like dark fire and bright silver eyes. He also looked entirely too alert for someone who'd been sound asleep only a few minutes ago. But then, Monty had taken to monster hunting like a duck to water. I suspected that, unlike the rest of us, he wasn't looking forward to the time when the influx of evil finally eased.

I stopped in front of him, then leaned across to open the door. He handed me the two mugs, then jumped in and did up his seat belt. I shoved the one that smelled like hot chocolate into the cup holder and handed him back the coffee.

He took a sip of his drink, then placed his mug next to mine. "So, what are we chasing this time?"

"Don't know. I'm sensing wisps of evil and magic, but I can't say whether the two are connected."

"Maybe your radar is sharpening and you're sensing trouble before it hits for a change."

I flicked on the blinker and swung right. "Or maybe whatever I'm sensing is simply too far away to get a handle on."

"I think I prefer my suspicion to yours."

So did I, but it probably wasn't realistic. The inner wild magic might be strengthening my psi skills, but there was a vast difference between psychometry and foresight. While I did sometimes have prophetic dreams, I hadn't yet suffered many waking ones—and hoped it was a situation that never changed.

I turned left a few streets up and followed the road around toward the old train station. But the closer I got to it, the stronger the caress of magic, and the more certain I became of its source.

And it certainly *wasn't* the old train station.

"I'm not liking the feel of *that*," Monty said, after a few seconds. "Though the magic does feel oddly familiar."

I glanced at him. "I suspect it's coming from Émigré."

"Neither the council nor—more importantly—the brigade have mentioned anything about Émigré reopening or Maelle returning, and they surely would have if either had happened."

The brigade was a group of retired ladies who met a couple of times a week in our café to gossip about local events. They rarely missed a juicy morsel of news and were usually aware of problems within the reservation well before the council or the local newspapers.

"The council never told anyone Maelle was a vampire either, so that's not entirely surprising."

"Yes, but given all the problems Clayton's murder caused, I'd have thought they'd be reluctant to allow her back in."

"I guess it would depend on the sort of contract she had with them."

Because there would be a contract. Maelle had invested too much time and money getting her business up and running not to protect it legally—especially when vampires generally weren't a welcome addition to most communities. She'd been upfront with the council about her "situation" from the beginning, however, and had sworn an oath that she would feed on only the willing while in the reservation.

It was an oath she magically *couldn't* break.

Which was why she'd taken Clayton *out* of the reservation before she'd slowly torn him apart, then danced through his bloody remains. I might not have witnessed the death or the dance, but I'd been told enough details, and knew Maelle well enough, to glean what had happened.

A tiny but extremely vicious part of me would always wish I'd witnessed it, if only because I'd dreamed for so long of seeing both him and my father pay for what they'd done.

And while I might not have seen Clayton's downfall, I had my father's. It was a glorious bit of justice that his underpowered disappointment of a daughter now had more magical capacity than him.

But no amount of bloody justice could negate the fact I'd probably never fully shake the mental scars caused by my forced marriage and the subsequent thirteen years on the run. This place, and the family we'd found within it, had certainly helped, as had being left the entirety of Clayton's estate in his will and walking away with not only a couple of beach properties but a million in my bank account.

And yet there always would be nights when past fears haunted my dreams.

I swept around the final corner and the SUV's headlights shone on the nightclub. Until only a few days ago, it had been nothing more than a broken shell.

That had definitely changed.

Though the roof over the front portion of the building—the section that had received the most damage in the explosions—was little more than a frame covered by that silver building wrap, walls had re-risen, and windows replaced. The weird, almost alien-looking biomechanical forms that usually decorated the matte black facade were missing, but the airlock-like front door was in place, as were the two rather sinister-looking security guards who usually guarded it. I wasn't sure why the latter were necessary, given the place obviously wasn't in any state to be open just yet, but maybe Maelle simply wanted to keep curious onlookers at bay.

"That building was a skeletal mess up until yesterday," Monty said. "How the fuck did it get to this stage so quickly?"

"Magic, I'm presuming."

"Even magic can't work miracles. Besides, there *are* such things as building codes and the like."

"Knowing Maelle, she probably has her fangs in someone who can fast-track approvals." I swung into a parking spot opposite and stopped. "I think we need to have a closer look."

"Should I ask why?" he asked. "Even if Maelle *is* using darker magic to rebuild her place, she can't be the source of evil. Not when she's made a vow to do no harm while within the reservation."

"Yes, but that doesn't mean she won't be aware of what else is out there. She was never really surprised about the other incursions of evil, remember. You coming in?"

He gave me the look—the one that said, "don't be daft." I grinned, grabbed my phone and keys, and climbed out. The two guards were obviously watching us, but hadn't yet moved. I could barely even see them breathe. But maybe they didn't need to. Maelle was capable of giving eternal life in exchange for eternal service, and these two should be dead, given one of the explosions had taken out the front portion of the building, right where they'd been—and still were—standing. They might not give off the same weird vibe as her thrall, Roger, but that didn't mean they were entirely human anymore, either.

Monty walked around the rear of the car and fell in step beside me. "Now that we're closer, is it possible to tell if the magic you're sensing is the same magic that's building this place?"

I hesitated, letting my senses run across the various spell threads that crisscrossed the building. None of the external ones were currently active, though the lingering glow of their power suggested they had been only a few minutes ago. I couldn't help but wonder whose blood was being used to fuel the renovation spells, then shivered and shoved the thought back into its box.

I did *not* want to know. She couldn't be using the unwilling and, right now, that's all that mattered.

"It has a similar feel," I said eventually.

"A statement I don't find comforting."

"And yet, in some ways, it actually is."

"I fail to see how."

"Well"—I waved a hand toward the venue we were approaching— "aside from the fact *similar* is not the same, the intricacy of the spells being used to rebuild this place so fast, and the amount of blood it must require, has to mean she couldn't possibly be creating havoc elsewhere."

"We're dealing with a very old vampire," he grumbled. "I'm thinking we have no idea what she is and isn't truly capable of."

"A truer statement has never been made."

"And yet you nevertheless believe she's not involved in whatever you're sensing."

"Not *directly* involved, but the similarity in the magic is troubling."

I stepped onto the footpath. One of the burly men immediately opened the door.

Maelle was expecting us.

That was never a good thing.

I did my best to ignore the rising wash of trepidation and walked into the foyer. This was the area where you checked coats and paid the occasional cover charge before heading into the main club area through a secondary set of airlock doors. Those doors no longer existed, but the framework was up and a heavy plastic curtain currently separated the two areas. I pushed the plastic aside and stepped through, holding it long enough for Monty to follow.

And discovered the magic that had been paused outside was active within. It filled the room with a dark electricity that had the hairs on my arms rising, even if the spells themselves were restrained to the reconstruction of the internal walls and didn't come anywhere near us.

I shivered and resisted the urge to rub my arms. I might not like the feel of the magic here, but I couldn't respond or show any sort of fear.

She would be watching.

The room itself was split into an upper and lower tier. On the upper tier and to the left, there were a series of seating "pods," which currently held tables but no seats, while the area to the right was dominated by a long bar that had once been made from twisted metal and glass but the top of which was now entirely black marble through which odd purple light pulsed. The lower tier was entirely devoted to the dance floor, though it currently was little more than pitted and blackened concrete.

I lifted my gaze to the ceiling. The silver Sisalation made the vast, black-painted arches that soared over the huge room look even more impressive, but they lacked the series of intricate and intriguing biomechanical and alien forms that had crawled over the originals. Maelle's lair—a dark glass and metal room built into the point where those arches met, giving her a 360-degree view of her venue while concealing her from casual sight—had been rebuilt and looked complete.

If the vague shadow visible through one of those panes of glass was anything to go by, our vampire was indeed in residence.

"Lizzie Grace," an effusive and familiar voice said, "how wonderful of you to visit so early in the reconstruction of our venue."

I turned and watched Roger emerge from the shadows clinging to the bar. I'd expected him to be here—Maelle would have considered dealing with the everyday problems and people that came with rebuilding beneath her. What I hadn't expected was for him to look so different, both facially and physically. He'd always been tall and thin, with pale skin, hair, and eyes, but right now, he was little more than a long streak of bones. Maelle had survived the explosion almost unharmed, but Roger had been so badly injured he'd been forced into a period of stasis so that his body could heal and recover. It was obviously taking a very long time for that to happen, even if he was now up and about.

"I'm afraid this visit isn't really a social one."

He sighed dramatically. "We had feared as much. Come, this way. My mistress awaits."

He motioned me forward, then pressed a hand against Monty's chest as he made to follow. "She does not await your presence. You may remain here."

"I *am* the reservation witch here, you know," Monty said, with a touch of amused annoyance.

"And is this reservation witch business?" Roger asked mildly. "Or is this visit more a 'there's trouble afoot, so we should therefore visit the local vampire' one?"

Monty rolled his eyes. "You're being pedantic, Roger."

"Indeed, I am, and thoroughly enjoying it." He pointed to the bar and the lone seat there—one that hadn't been there seconds ago. "I made you a coffee so that you can wait in comfort."

The fact Maelle could conjure a chair while controlling a multitude of other major spells was scary evidence that her magical prowess had increased.

I drew in a deeper breath to calm the rising fear and my

racing pulse, then touched Monty's arm lightly. "I'll be fine."

And I'll relay what's happening to him, Belle commented.

The brief shift in his expression said she'd included him in the conversation. He nodded and walked across to the bar. He didn't sit on the shadowy chair, however, and I can't say I would have, either.

I stepped down onto the bottom tier and walked across, my skin itching with the force of Roger's presence. He might look emaciated, but his magical aura was full—almost bloated. Maelle was obviously directing some of her magic through him.

The entrance to Maelle's lair was an inconspicuous-looking pod usually closed off by a wrought-iron door. That was missing, and the circular black glass staircase was now black marble that would have cost a fortune.

But then, a vampire who'd been alive for at least several centuries probably wasn't wanting for money.

Roger stopped at the base of the pod and motioned me on. "Be aware that she is in a bit of a mood tonight. Things have not gone well."

A comment that made me rethink how wise it had been to come here, but it was too late to back out now. Doing so would only annoy Maelle, and we couldn't afford to get her offside if there *was* a connection between her and the evil I was sensing.

Because that psychic bit of me was thinking it was no coincidence the two had turned up at the same time.

"If she gets mad and tries to bite me, things will go even worse for her."

Roger laughed and lightly touched my arm. His fingers were cold, almost clammy, and all I wanted to do was wrench free. I resisted. The shadows of Maelle's presence lurked in the pale depths of his eyes, and if she *was* in a mood then she'd probably see it as an insult.

"Ah, Lizzie Grace," he said, in a tone that was deeper, more accented, than his own. "How I have missed you."

"I'd love to say the same, Maelle, but it would, sadly, be a lie."

Roger laughed again, and this time when he spoke, his voice was his own. "Please, do go on up."

He removed his hand, but the unpleasant ghost of his touch remained. I did my best to ignore the revulsion and headed up, my footsteps echoing lightly on the black marble.

The metal door at the top was open and the room beyond filled with shadows. The black glass desk that usually dominated the rear portion of the room had been replaced by black marble shot with deep purple that matched the two plush-looking chairs in front of it and the one behind.

Maelle stood near the glass panel with her back to the door, but turned as I entered. She had a liking for wearing Regency-style clothing, though from what I could glean, she was far older than that era. Tonight, it was a deep red riding habit with a white lace, high-collar undershirt. Her rich chestnut hair had been plaited and curled around the top of her head and once again looked crown-like. Her skin was porcelain smooth, and her lips ruby red. Lipstick was *not* responsible for that color; it was an indicator that she'd recently fed.

Which was a relief, given her amused response to my warning about taking a sip. She'd always been rather deter- mined to taste the power in my blood, and I doubted that had changed any, especially after she'd witnessed just what

I was capable of when she'd helped me rescue Belle from Clayton.

"Do you wish for a drink? Tea, or perhaps something stronger?" Her voice held a soft French accent that hinted of her origins, though I suspected she'd been in Australia for more than a few decades now.

"No, but thank you." It never hurt to be polite when you were dealing with a very old vampire who had a penchant for dancing through the remains of her victims.

"Then what can I do for you, Elizabeth Grace?"

There was something in her expression—a soft gleam of amusement in eyes so pale there was only the slightest variation between her gray irises and sclera—that suggested she was well aware why I was here.

"I sensed evil tonight—"

"I hope you are not implying it is me."

The amusement was stronger, but tension nevertheless slithered through me. "Of course not. I came here because that evil ran with darker magic—"

"And it led you here."

"In a sense, yes."

She raised an eyebrow, the movement elegant. "In a sense?"

"What I'm sensing is not the magic you're using to build this place." I waved a hand around to indicate our surroundings. "But it does have a similar feel."

"The magic that arises from the fuel of blood—be it from the witch's own veins or that of others—often has a similar feel. It is the inescapable nature of such spells."

"Yes, but the similarity runs deeper than that."

She studied me for a moment, then motioned eloquently toward one of the plush chairs. "Please, sit. We two are well beyond the formality of standing in each other's presence."

I generally preferred to stand, because it made running easier if things went wrong, but it hadn't been a request, no matter how politely it had been said. I obeyed.

She pulled out her chair and sat down, her legs crossed and her fingers interlaced. She looked as relaxed as she ever did, and yet I could feel the tension in her. It fairly crackled around her body.

"What similarities do you sense?"

Instinct prickled again. She knew—or at the very least, suspected—who or what was out there, and that might mean the evil I sensed was another magic-capable vampire. It would be extremely unusual, though, because as a general rule, they did *not* like to share territories.

But if another vampire was out there, why wasn't she dealing with them? The vow of no harm wouldn't stop her—not when the presence of another vampire likely boded no good for the reservation's inhabitants. Besides, her actions with Clayton showed just how easily her vow could be skirted.

I hesitated, searching for the words to explain what instinct was perceiving. "It comes down to what is basically biological inheritance. In witch families, we not only inherit certain DNA traits from our parents, but also a similar magical resonance, even if there are vast variations in strength and capabilities between siblings. What I'm sensing out there has a resonance that echoes your magic."

"My bloodline died out a very long time ago."

It was calmly said, but the tension in her ramped up. It crawled across my senses, causing tiny sparks of energy to leap across my fingers—an automatic response I was incapable of fully controlling when confronted by the truly scary. "I wasn't talking about any relatives that might be alive today, Maelle."

Her answering smile was cool, but the awareness in her eyes sharpened. A response more to the sparks than my accelerated heart rate, I suspected. "And has this evil you sense done anything to attract your attention?"

"Not yet."

"Then why do you hunt it?"

"Because I'd really prefer to stop it before harm is caused." I studied her warily for several seconds. "You know —or suspect—who it is, don't you?"

A small smile tugged at her lips. "Yes."

I waited for her to continue, but she didn't. My unease increased, but I clenched against the responding sparks, hoping, somewhat futilely, to contain them. "Do you believe this person will cause any problems within the reservation?"

Her smile grew wider, colder. "If she *is* here, she will indeed be a problem. I fear—" She stopped and shrugged. "Her presence will not bode well for any of us."

If Maelle fears this other vamp or dark sorceress or whatever the hell else she might be, came Belle's comment, *then I am totally and utterly freaked out.*

So was I. We'd dealt with a lot of truly evil beings over the last year, and in all that time, Maelle had shown no real concern, whether she deigned to help us or not. That this other woman was giving her reason to pause meant we were probably about to deal with the biggest, baddest bogeyman —woman—yet.

"I need some help here, Maelle. I'd rather intercept her than wait for her to become too big a problem."

She sighed. "I cannot help you track her. Until she makes a move against me personally, I am unable to do anything to hinder her movements or to even hunt her. I can give you her name, though it is unlikely to mean anything, given there won't be any existing records of her."

Suggesting she'd probably come here illegally. I suspected that was the case for most vampires who'd immigrated here, as they generally weren't welcome passengers on commercial planes or ships.

And with good reason, Belle said. *Who hasn't heard the story about the vamp going on a blood bender at thirty-five thousand feet above the Pacific?*

That's an urban myth. There's never been any concrete evidence of it.

Because they never found the plane and the transit records mysteriously disappeared.

Planes can't just disappear, Belle. Not without people knowing about it.

Maybe it hit the Pacific equivalent of the Bermuda Triangle. Maybe authorities don't want us to know about it.

You and Monty have been watching old episodes of Unsolved Mysteries *again, haven't you?*

Her amusement drifted down the line. *How did you guess?*

I mentally snorted and returned my attention to Maelle. For the briefest moment, there was a glimpse of vulnerability—perhaps even uncertainty—in her expression.

Which only confirmed the growing tide of fear was justified.

"Her name is Marie Nicolete Bouchier." She made an odd, almost involuntary movement with one hand. "She is my maker."

Oh dear, Belle said.

Understatement of the year, I'm thinking. To Maelle, I added, "Why would your maker be here, let alone hunting you?"

"Presuming, of course, that is her reason for being here. It could be nothing more than coincidence."

"You don't believe that any more than I do." After all, it wasn't like vampires were well known for their cozy catch-ups with each other.

"In truth, I am unsure what to believe. I never thought she would venture beyond the remnants of our coven, let alone travel halfway around the world."

Vampires have covens? Belle said. *No wonder witch covens got such a bad fucking name.*

There're no vampire covens around today, I'm sure.

None that we know of, Belle corrected. *The High Witch Council might be aware of them, but they're unlikely to tell the rest of us.*

And that makes it a question to ask either Monty or Ashworth, I'm thinking.

Ira Ashworth—who now lived in the reservation with his partner Eli, and who over the course of the last year had become a grandfather to me in all ways except blood—still worked for the Regional Witch Association. Like Monty, he had full access to the High Council's main libraries and catalogues. If there was information to be had on vampire covens, one of them should be able to find it.

Why not just ask Maelle? Even if she refuses to answer, we're no worse off.

True, but it's still best if we check the archives, just in case Maelle is economical with the facts. She *did* have a tendency toward that.

I returned my attention to her. "I wasn't aware vampires had covens."

Her eyebrows rose. "Why does this surprise you? It's not as if there would be any benefit to your High Council—and others—becoming fully aware of them."

Suggesting the council might have at least *some* awareness of them, even if their knowledge was scant.

"What was the purpose of them?"

"What is the purpose of witch covens?" she countered.

"We gather for ceremonies, rituals, and/or celebrations." Though, in truth, few royal blood witches actually took part in such gatherings. It was mostly the province of the three lower witch houses—or commoners, as they were often rather disparagingly called by the three "royal" bloodlines—or half-bloods.

"In our case, it was also protection. A safe place in which the newly spawned could grow and learn control over both their bloodlust and their magic."

"Not all vampires are magic capable, though."

"Those born within covens were."

"Born" meaning their death as a human and their rising as a vampire, although the actual process of becoming a vamp started well before death. According to the information we'd gleaned from the library Belle had inherited from her grandmother, the process involved injecting the blood of a vampire into your system once a week over a course of five weeks and then letting said vampire drain you unto death.

In my opinion, you'd have to be extremely keen on eternal life to put yourself through such an ordeal. I knew from experience that a vampire's bite was decidedly unpleasant.

"That suggests covens deliberately sought out people who were either dark witches or blood sorcerers."

"They sought out those who were magic capable. It was never practical to seek out those well-versed in using magic —aside from the fact they were difficult to mold, very few would willingly give up their freedom or power for the greater good of the coven."

"You make it sound like some kind of cult."

"In some respects, I suppose it was."

"So, what happened?"

Her eyebrows winged upward again. "With my coven, or our covens in general?"

"Both."

"Ah, well." Her gaze moved to the dark glass, a cool smile touching her impossibly red lips. "In most cases, it came down to the nature of the beast."

Meaning, no doubt, that vampire covens were just as afflicted by egos and power seekers as witch councils, Belle said.

Where there is power, there is always corruption. The two seem to go hand in hand. Hell, my father was a good example. While he'd never been corrupt, per se, he'd also never been above manipulating people and situations for the good of the family. His days of doing that, however, appeared to be over. His magic had been ripped away by a wraith intent on bloody revenge, and the few people he'd consulted couldn't say if or when it would ever return.

I hoped it never did. Those who worked for—and with —the family's businesses would be far better off now that my mother was fully in charge.

"Meaning egos or the quest for overall power became a destructive force?"

"In most cases, yes."

"But not in the case of your coven?"

She smiled her unpleasant smile again. "In our case, I would say it came down more to a matter of direction."

Her expression suggested she wasn't going to explain what those directional differences were—not yet anyway— so I didn't bother asking. "Then why would your maker now be hunting you?"

"Because she was our coven's elder and because, for many centuries, she was also my lover." She paused, her gaze distant and her expression holding a warmth that often came when reflecting on fond memories. "I broke both."

I blinked. That statement did *not* go with her expression.

At all.

"Intentionally?"

Her gaze flicked to me. "I never do anything *un*intentionally."

"May I ask why?"

"You may not." She paused. "Unless of course, what you are sensing is indeed her, and she is indeed intent on revenge."

"Do you really think that possible?"

"Anything is possible."

Meaning, I suspected, she had no idea. "Would you be seeking revenge if the positions were reversed?"

Her smile said it all. Holy hell, we could be in real trouble here if this situation *did* erupt into a fight.

I did my best to contain my unease, but the glimmer in her pale eyes said she was not only well aware of it but enjoying it. "Will she have come here alone?"

"She is *never* alone."

"Meaning she will have the coven with her?"

"She would bring her lovers and whatever fledglings she might have." Maelle shrugged, the movement casual and yet not unconcerned. "That could mean somewhere between ten and twenty people. She has an appetite."

Oh great, Belle said. *A bunch of horny, hungry vampires is all we fucking need in the reservation.*

Especially if the evil I was sensing *wasn't* them. "Are

you able to provide a description so we know who to look for?"

She briefly paused, though I had no doubt it was done for effect more than any real need to think about it. "She is fair of face and hair. Her eyes are green, her build petite, and she is deceptively young looking."

The description brought to mind an image—a memory —I'd once caught when Maelle had touched me without warning. It had been a brief glimpse of a beautiful young woman wearing a crown in her golden hair and sitting on an intricately carved red velvet throne.

Had Maelle smashed the coven and her lover to claim that throne?

I suspected *that* was a question she would not answer. Not until we were certain the evil I sensed was Marie, and even then, not until there was evidence she intended bloody revenge.

"How young looking are we talking?"

Maelle's shrug was another of those impossibly graceful movements. "Sixteen, perhaps? Do not, however, be fooled by her projection of innocence. She is far older than even me."

"Thanks for your help, Maelle." I rose. "I'll keep you updated if we uncover anything. I'd appreciate it if you could do the same where possible."

She nodded regally, though I suspected it wasn't in any way an agreement to share information. "Just be warned that if it *is* Marie, she has a hunger for power and the means to sway even the stoutest soul. She will seek you out if she senses your vibrance."

Vibrance was an odd way of putting my magical output, especially since my use of a concealment spell was now second nature. It had successfully hidden the glow of power that came from the continuing growth of my native wild magic from the High Council in Canberra, so surely it should also work against a dark witch or sorcerer. The only reason Maelle knew of its existence was because she'd been here well before I'd learned to properly shield.

All the same, it might be worth ramping up the shield a bit more, Belle commented. *Better safe than sorry.*

And it was certainly a better option than being bit. "If she tries to taste me in any way, it will end no better for her than it would for you."

A slow smile stretched her rich lips. "That is a challenge many would not ignore."

"It's nothing more than a statement of truth. I'm no longer underpowered or unprotected."

"You never were."

I guess that was true, even if I hadn't realized it for a very long time.

I nodded politely and left at a measured pace, even though all I wanted to do was fucking run. Roger was nowhere to be seen, so I walked across the dance floor and bounded up the steps. Monty was already at the exit and swept aside the plastic sheeting, then waved me through ahead of him. The barely breathing guard had already opened the external door, which suggested Maelle was at least in contact with them even if she wasn't using them as her eyes, as she did with Roger.

I breathed a deep sigh of relief once I was clear of the building, but didn't say anything. Neither did Monty. Any conversation we had would have carried easily on the hot, still night, and I wasn't about to risk her people hearing and reporting back.

As I neared the SUV, the sense of danger—of wrongness

—hit so hard I stumbled and would have fallen had Monty not grabbed me.

"You okay? What's wrong?"

"Sensory hit." I swallowed heavily and held out the car keys. "Let's just get in the car and leave."

He grabbed the keys from my hand, then caught my arm and escorted me around to the passenger side. While the force of wrongness had eased, it nevertheless continued to wash across my skin, making it twitch and itch.

Something had happened.

Something bad.

I shivered and reached for the hot chocolate sitting in the middle console. It was delicious, even if no longer truly hot, but I couldn't help wishing it held something stronger. But alcohol of any kind was off my imbibe list for the next eight or so months.

Monty jumped into the driver's seat, started the engine, and then drove off. "Where are we headed?"

I ran my psi senses across the still strong wave, looking for some indication of a location. "We need to do a U-turn and head down to Blackwood."

Blackwood was a small but historic gold mining town that sat at the northern end of the Burennberg State Forest. It was a rural area, and had few facilities other than a pub, a couple of lovely cafés, and a holistic health provider. The four hundred or so people who lived there generally drove to Ballan for everything else—although according to a very chatty customer who came to our café on a weekly basis to collect his supply of cakes and slices, Ballan's bakery just didn't have the same range of cakes ours did.

Blackwood was also one of the reservation's border towns, and I didn't believe it was a coincidence that whatever I sensed had hit the one surefire place within the reservation there would be little chance of crossing paths with a werewolf. They certainly patrolled the area, especially in the summer months, as the Burennberg State Forest was a popular tourist and hiking destination, but it was after one in the morning, and most tourists weren't stupid enough to wander around a forest well known for its rugged features and deep gorge.

"Blackwood is a strange place for evil to be hiding," Monty commented.

"I don't think it's in the town. I think it's in the nearby forest."

"Of course it is. I mean, why would things be easy for a change?" He paused for a beat. "Should we call the rangers?"

I scrubbed a hand across my eyes. "Probably."

He glanced at me, expression sympathetic. "You want me to do it?"

"I'm tempted to say 'definitely' in answer to that."

"There's a chance Aiden won't answer. He did mention something about splitting the on-call hours tonight so that everyone could have some run time with their pack."

"Which doesn't mean he'd share the load evenly. The man is a workaholic, and he would have nominated for more than one shift."

"You can't keep avoiding him, Liz. It's not fair."

"I know. I just—"

"Want him to declare his feelings before he finds out about the pregnancy," Monty cut in quietly.

I shifted in my seat and stared at him. "Belle told you?"

"Not in so many words, but she did mention you puking several times during our phone calls while you were all up in Canberra. It's not hard to put two and two together."

"Here's hoping Aiden isn't so good with arithmetic,

then." I grimaced and added softly, "Is it really so bad to want a declaration of some kind before he finds out?"

"Of course not, but by the same token, you'll never actually get that declaration unless you're willing to meet with the man."

I sighed. "I know but—"

"You're worried the more you're with him, the bigger the chances of blurting it out."

I couldn't help smiling. "When did you become so damn clever?"

He laughed softly. "I've had a year to get reacquainted with the way your mind works, and it's been quite an eye-opener, let me tell you."

"That doesn't exactly sound like a compliment."

He grinned. "After being stuck in the stuffy halls of Canberra for so long, it was very refreshing. Life is never boring when you're around, my dear cousin."

"I'm betting Belle's presence in my life doesn't hurt either."

"Belle's presence is *definitely* a bonus. One I intend to cherish for the rest of *my* life."

He really is a sweetheart, I said to Belle.

Sometimes saccharinely so, she replied dryly.

And you love it.

I do. Just don't tell him that.

I laughed mentally but resisted the urge to tease any further. "I guess if I keep avoiding him, he'll suspect something is up anyway."

"The man might be a stubborn bastard, but he's definitely not stupid."

I pulled my phone out. There were at least two dozen unanswered calls from him sitting on it, and while he'd stopped short of charging into the café to confront me, he'd certainly bailed up Monty and Belle. They'd simply said I needed some time to digest and reflect on everything that had happened in Canberra. Which wasn't actually a lie. Discovering I was pregnant certainly *was* taking some getting used to.

My finger hovered briefly over his number before hitting it. It didn't ring for very long.

"Liz," he said softly. "As much as I might wish otherwise, I take it this isn't a social call."

His warm, familiar tone made my soul sing and heart ache. Monty was right. I really did need to talk to the man. Given his persistent calling, he obviously had something to say.

Whether it was something I wanted to hear or not was another matter, and yet another reason I'd been avoiding him. Apparently, I'd come back from Canberra a coward.

"I'm afraid not. Monty and I are currently heading down to Blackwood."

"Another incursion?"

"I'm not exactly sure what the problem is. I'm just sensing a deep wrongness."

"How far out are you from Blackwood?"

I glanced at Monty. He looked at the GPS and then said, "We've just passed Campbell's Creek, so probably fifty or so minutes."

Aiden grunted. "I'll be about ten behind you then. Keep me updated on your location, and if the trail leads into the forest, wait for me."

"Will do."

There was a brief pause. "See you soon."

"Yes." I hung up before the impulse to add something mushy got the better of me. I glanced at Monty. "Do you know if he's still staying with a friend in Maldoon?"

Monty quirked an eyebrow at me. "You mean the gossip brigade hasn't kept you updated with his day-to-day movements? I'm shocked."

I smiled. "I think the brigade knows better than to gossip about our head ranger."

Which didn't mean they didn't do so in private, of course.

"He moved back to the O'Connor compound not long after his father's funeral."

"Not into his family home though, surely? I can't imagine him and his mother coexisting peacefully in any way."

"That I don't know. The only time I've been there was when we gate-crashed the council meeting, and Aiden didn't exactly give us the tour on the way in."

I snorted softly, but didn't reply as the wave of wrongness briefly sharpened. It didn't have the same sort of feel as that of a vampire—even one as magically powerful as Maelle. It felt more along the lines of something demonic.

Of course, many sorcerers did make deals with demons—generally for power upgrades and/or demonic servitude—in exchange for their souls on death, but vampires were already dead, so I couldn't see many demons being interested. Unless, of course, it was the souls of her victims she was offering.

"I have no idea what is going on out there," I said, "but it's reaching flash point."

"A death-type flash point?"

"I guess. I mean, whether it's a demon or a vampire, death is usually their end game."

"At least when it comes to this reservation," he grumbled and flattened the accelerator, eking out every bit of speed from the engine that was possible.

It made for a noisy drive, given all the bullet holes.

He slowed as we swept into Blackwood. I sent a text to Aiden, then motioned Monty to continue on. Whatever it was, it wasn't in the trees surrounding the town, but deeper within the reservation's forested heart.

We swept out the other side of the town and began to climb. The waves of power increased the closer we got to it, and my skin itched. I still had no idea who or what the source of that wave was, but I was absolutely certain we were going to be too late to stop whatever was happening.

My phone pinged, and I glanced down. Aiden was now only a few minutes behind us.

The forest edged closer to the road, shutting out the moon's light and leaving deep divisions of darkness on either side of the headlights. We swept past multiple dirt roads, but as we neared the crest of another long rise, instinct twitched hard.

"Take the left just up ahead," I said.

Monty didn't stop or slow; he just wrenched the wheel down hard and all but spun onto the gravel road. The SUV fishtailed for several meters before he got it back under control.

I sent Aiden another text and then said, "You'd better slow. From the look of things, the road really narrows up ahead."

He did so, although that didn't mean we were actually going slow. If a kangaroo decided to jump out in front of us, it would be dead meat. The brakes in the SUV were good, but they couldn't perform miracles on a gravel road at this speed.

We flew past a track on our left and were soon approaching a fork in the road. The main track swung around to the right, but a narrower track went left and was steeply inclined.

"Let me guess," Monty said, voice dry, "we go left."

"Afraid so."

He slowed and swung onto the track. As the four-wheel drive system kicked in, I sent Aiden more directions. He might have said don't go into the forest, but he meant don't *walk* into the forest. We were perfectly safe as long as we kept to the main tracks.

I hoped like hell that I hadn't tempted fate with that thought.

We bumped up the rocky track, crashing past low-growing shrubs and overhanging branches. I hung on to the grab bar and stared blindly through the windscreen. The wrongness was now so sharp my skin burned, and every breath tasted of ash and darkness.

"We're close," I somehow said.

But so too was the culmination of whatever was happening out there.

We swung around the bend and discovered the road ended in a line of trees.

Monty swore and stopped the SUV. "What now?"

Before I could answer, the spell erupted, an explosion strong enough to physically push me back in my seat. I swore, undid the seat belt, and scrambled out.

It was then I smelled the blood and saw the darkly luminescent remnants of the spell.

But not any old spell. A blood summoning.

One that had called forth a demon.

CHAPTER TWO

"I'm not liking the feel of that," Monty said. "Which is the second time tonight I've made that statement. Third time's the charm, I'm thinking."

"Let's hope not."

I slammed the door shut and walked over to the edge of the forest. In the twin beams of the headlights, a very faint path was visible. There were no footprints in the dust, and there surely would have been had our sorcerer come this way. While it was possible to spell away telltale signs of passing, there was no reason why she'd have wasted energy. If she was aware of our presence, she'd also know that this forest was too far away for us to reach in time to prevent her spelling.

Monty stopped beside me, his hands in his jean pockets. "Given the amount and strength of fractured threads, I'm thinking the sacrifice site isn't too far away."

"No, but we can't go in until Aiden gets here. It's just too dangerous with all the mine remnants scattered about the place."

"Caution? From you?" He lightly touched my forehead. "I'm not feeling a temperature or anything—"

I laughed and knocked his hand away. "I don't suppose you can tell what sort of spell might have been performed?"

He raised a hand and caught a small stream of broken spell threads. Most of them disintegrated at his touch, but enough remained to at least get some feel for the spell's architecture.

"It's definitely a blood summoning," he said after a second, "but I'm not getting any indication of what sort of demon was called."

I raised my eyebrows. "Would you?"

"In a spell this fresh, generally yes."

"So why haven't you used this skill before?"

"Because we've never arrived so close to the spell culmination before. Not without being physically threatened by said demon or some other nasty, anyway."

"Let's hope whatever was summoned isn't waiting for us up ahead."

"You'd sense it if it was, wouldn't you?"

"My psi senses aren't infallible, Monty. Shit does get past them." I scanned the night again but couldn't hear anything other than the usual buzz of cicadas and the occasional ground-level rustle as possums and wombats moved through the scrub. "Why are the threads so fractured? That generally only happens if something goes wrong with the spell, doesn't it?"

"Summoning is a dangerous business, no matter how strong the witch or sorcerer. If the demon who answers is stronger than the summoner, then it's all over, red rover."

I motioned toward the quickly disintegrating spell thread. "Is it worth preserving that, just in case we can use it to track her."

"I can, but it's in such a poor state that it probably won't last more than an hour, even with assistance."

As his magic rose, the roar of an approaching engine snagged my attention, and I glanced around. Headlights glimmered through the trees, approaching at speed.

Aiden.

Anticipation rose, but I did my best to curb it. After all, this time it was my own fault that I hadn't seen the man.

Monty turned and raised a hand to protect his eyes. "That'll be our ranger. You going to be okay?"

I smiled and touched his arm lightly. "Of course I am."

But my heart nevertheless stuttered when Aiden climbed out of his truck and walked toward us. The man moved with a predator's grace, and it was just lovely to watch. Like most werewolves, he was tall and rangy, but his shoulders were wider than usual, and his arms and chest well defined without being over-the-top muscular. The moonlight played amongst the silver in his short, dark blond hair, and highlighted the sharp but pleasing planes of his face. His eyes—a deep blue, rather than the usual amber of a werewolf—showed as little emotion as his expression, but his aura fairly crackled with it.

The man was annoyed. At me. At my actions.

To be honest, I couldn't say I blamed him.

"What have we got?" It was said to Monty rather than me, even if his gaze was steadfast on mine.

"A blood sacrifice," Monty said. "The site is probably no more than 250 meters past this point."

Aiden stopped between us. His scent filled my nostrils, warm, musky, and familiar; it was all I could do not to lean into him.

"Any indication of what we might be dealing with?" he

35

asked. "I can smell the blood, but that in itself doesn't tell me much."

"A summoning sacrifice was performed, but at this point, we have no idea whether it was successful or not."

Aiden nodded. "That path leads up to the Tunnel, from memory."

"What's the Tunnel?" I asked.

His gaze met mine and, just for an instant, was filled with so much love and frustration it burned my senses.

"It's a short tunnel some miners in the 1850s cut through solid rock to divert the Burennberg River from one point of a horseshoe bend to the other to make accessing the gold in the riverbed easier."

I glanced at Monty. "A tunnel is a rather odd place for a sacrifice site to be set up, isn't it?"

He shrugged. "It would depend on its size, what condition it's in, and whether the diversion still exists."

"The sluice gate was permanently closed decades ago," Aiden said, "but the Tunnel remains intact and does still flood when the river runs high. I'll lead."

We followed him into the forest. Moonlight filtered through the overhead canopy in bright stripes, casting the shadows into deeper darkness while eradicating any lingering spell threads. Eventually, we came out of the trees to a small, grassed area that was—if the litter scattered about was anything to go by—used as a picnic spot. Beyond the grass was a rocky riverbed that was currently dry. The Tunnel lay to our right, and was a straight but not very wide cut in the rocky cliff face of the hill that towered above us. A couple of trees had recently fallen across the entrance—no doubt due to the storms we'd had last weekend—but they were positioned in such a way that an entry point remained.

Monty cast more light into his sphere and sent it

floating toward the Tunnel's entrance. "I'm not seeing anything that indicates a spell circle or sacrifice site."

"I doubt you would, given the blood scent is coming from inside." I glanced at Aiden. "Is the other exit point still open?"

Aiden nodded. "The Tunnel is probably a hundred or so meters long and comes out onto the riverbank on the other side."

"And you're not scenting anyone in the immediate area?"

He glanced at me, eyebrows raised. "Are you?"

I couldn't help a smile. "Your senses are a wee bit sharper than mine."

"I wouldn't be putting money on it. Not these days."

"They will never be werewolf strong, Aiden. Never."

Just as I would never be a werewolf.

I could see the echo of that thought in his eyes. He smiled, though it was a ghost of its usual self. "I think *that* is a primer for a discussion needing to be had elsewhere, in private. No offence, Monty."

"None taken, and I totally agree. Now, can we get moving before any damn hope of tracking our summoner disappears?"

I had a hunch that our chances of doing *that* had already gone, but kept it to myself. We moved forward in single file, Aiden once again in the lead, and Monty behind me. Once we'd climbed down the river's bank, we warily entered the Tunnel. It was narrower than it looked and smelled of moss and wet earth. Monty's light sphere bobbed along above our heads, enabling us to see where we were going without having to resort to flashlights.

The closer we got to the other exit, the stronger the blood scent became. But entwined within it now were two other scents—one that was sulfuric in nature, and one that was weirdly musky. The former was sometimes associated with demons, but I had no idea what caused the latter. I doubted it was anything "natural" though.

We squeezed through the exit and climbed over a couple more trees that had fallen across the sluice channel. Trees lined the bank to our left, but to our right was a small stony clearing. In the center of that clearing were several half-melted black candles. I knew without even approaching they'd be located at the cardinal points of a pentagram.

Inside that pentagram was a gutted sheep.

Aiden climbed out of the ditch, then turned to help me. "Is it usual to use such a large animal in summoning spells?"

I clasped his hand and let him pull me out, even though I didn't really need the help. It was just nice to touch him. Nice to have a reason to touch him.

I seriously, seriously, needed to stop stuffing around and just talk to the man. This was getting ridiculous.

"Depends on what they were summoning," I said.

He nodded and released my hand. I tried not to mourn the loss. I failed.

"So, the bigger the animal, the nastier the demon summoned?"

"Generally." Monty stopped several meters away from the pentagram and motioned toward what looked to be two circular scorch marks surrounding the sacrifice site, one inside the other. "He or she also used multiple protection circles, which is another indicator."

Aiden frowned. "What sort of protection circle leaves that sort of residue?"

"Black salt, which is a mix of salt and purified ash. It's fallen out of favor these days, but was often used in conjunction with spell stones as an additional layer of protection."

"Because demons can't cross salt lines?"

Monty nodded. "In this case, however, I doubt the ash used was purified wood. It's probably been sourced from the burned flesh and bones of the dead."

"Meaning I need to order a graveyard search for missing bodies?" Aiden asked.

"It couldn't hurt, though it takes a lot of heat to cinder bones, and someone would surely have reported it. We are in fire season, after all."

"Except," I said, "there's plenty of old mines around this area you could use and be in no danger of anyone seeing a column of smoke."

I followed the line of the outer ash circle to the opposite side of the ring and spotted an odd smudging across a foot-wide section. Smudging—or otherwise breaking—the continuation of a salt circle was one way of nulling its power. Given even the demon couldn't have broken past two rings, our sorceress must have done so from the safety of the other side of the circle—and probably from within the walls of a spell stone protection circle. When it came to demons, you could never be too careful.

I dropped onto my haunches to study the smudge, and it was then I noticed the faint track in the dust leading from the center of the pentagram, past the two circles, and into the scrub at the other side of the clearing.

It wasn't the type of trail caused by any kind of human or other mammal, but rather one by a reptile.

A snake, to be precise.

A fucking *large* snake.

I glanced up as Monty and Aidan approached.

"What have you found?" Aiden squatted opposite me.

"That looks like a snake trail, but there're no snakes that large in the state, let alone in the reservation."

"Given it's coming out of the pentagram's center, it's not likely to be a native snake." I glanced at Monty. "I know there's more than a few demon snakes, but the first one that comes to mind is—"

"A basilisk," he finished heavily. "God, I hope it's not—especially when it appears to be such a big mother."

Aiden frowned. "Why would anyone call a basilisk into being? It's not like we're lacking for big poisonous snakes in Australia."

Monty turned and followed the faint trail across to the tree line. "Yes, but this is an acid-spitting *demon* snake whose actions can be controlled."

"Acid rather than poison seems a little over the top," Aiden said.

"It's a rather over-the-top demon," I said.

"Meaning acid is not their only weapon?"

"No," Monty said. "Aside from the fact that if they're big enough, they can eat you, meeting their gaze is deadly, and their breath is so putrid it can wither vegetation." He waved a hand toward the undergrowth. "Which is what has happened here."

I pushed to my feet and walked across. The undergrowth a meter or so on either side of the faint path into the trees was beginning to wilt, but the die-off ended abruptly where the basilisk had entered the water.

"If this thing was called here by our sorceress intent on revenge," I said, "isn't it a rather odd demon to choose? There are plenty of other demons more capable of causing bloody havoc."

"That's presuming bloody havoc is what she intends,"

he said. "For all we know, Maelle might have a phobia about big, dangerous snakes."

"Maelle?" Aiden said sharply. "She's back?"

I glanced around. "We discovered her presence tonight. The council didn't tell you?"

He snorted. "The council are dragging their feet on a lot of matters right now."

Meaning his confirmation as the O'Connor pack alpha, no doubt.

"She's rebuilding the nightclub using magic," I said. "It's possible the sorcerer behind this summoning is, in fact, her former lover who might be here for a little revenge."

"Might?"

I shrugged. "Maelle's currently uncertain as to her purpose here."

Aiden snorted. "More likely, currently unwilling to help us *ascertain* her purpose here." He turned to face the pentagram. "Is it safe to step past the circles?"

"Should be, given the sorcerer would have broken them for the basilisk to leave, but let me check the pentagram."

"There's no life in it," Monty said, as he followed me across. "And the candles are snuffed out."

"Still best to check, especially given the tendency evil has to leave nasty little surprise packages for us."

I cautiously stepped over the two ash rings and approached the pentagram. It was larger than usual, as were what was left of the candles. But then, it was a basilisk being summoned, and apparently a big one at that. I sure as hell would have made sure there was plenty of protection between me and it. I went right while Monty went left, and we met at the top—or spirit—point. There was no magic or life in the pentagram's remnants.

I glanced at Aiden. "It's safe."

He and Monty entered, but I stayed where I was. Right now, my stomach was behaving itself, but I wasn't about to push it by getting any closer to that sheep.

Monty stopped abruptly a few meters shy of the center point and the carcass. "Is it my imagination, or is there blood soaking the ground here?"

Aiden walked over and studied the ground for several seconds, his nostrils flaring a little wider. "There's definitely blood, and quite a bit of it."

"Is it from the sheep?"

"I wouldn't think so—it seems to be concentrated in one area rather than being an arterial spray." He bent and examined the ground. "There're a couple of faint footprints in the center of the stain, and small bits of flesh and fiber threads as well."

"Flesh? Why would there be flesh here?"

Aiden glanced up, amusement evident. "You tell me. You're the expert on magic."

"Regular magic, not dark." Monty bent and examined the ground. "If that print was made by our sorcerer, it suggests she was barefoot, and that's unusual."

"Why?" Aiden asked.

"Because it's generally only white witches—witches who raise magic via the earth—who perform ceremonies barefoot."

"Not just barefoot," I said, "but naked. But it's also sometimes associated with darker rituals."

Mainly because it was easier to wash blood and gore from your body than it was your clothes.

Monty glanced back at me. "Which could be what happened here, but why would she stand inside the circle? Why put yourself in the path of possible harm like that?"

"I have no idea." I hesitated. "Are we sure it was our

sorceress standing there? Could it have been another sacrifice?"

"Possible, I guess, given the strength needed to summon a basilisk."

Aiden pushed to his feet. "If it wasn't the sorceress standing here, where is she likely to have stood?"

"Outside the pentagram, at one of the cardinal points. Hang on." I turned, stepped over the two salt circles, and studied the ground past the outer one. After a second, I spotted a partial print. "She stood here."

Aiden walked over and stopped beside me. Once again, I found myself resisting the urge to lean into him.

"They look more like a kid's footprints than an adult's."

"If Maelle is right and this is her lover, then that makes sense. She apparently only looks fifteen or sixteen years old."

He glanced at me. "Meaning she's also a vampire?"

"Afraid so."

He grunted. "If she's unleashed a basilisk, how do we capture it?"

"That I don't know."

"And the sorceress?"

"Maelle can't—won't—help us until she's personally attacked."

"No surprise there." He pulled his phone out and took some photos of the print. "What if it isn't Maelle's lover but someone else? Is there any way you can use this site or any remaining remnants of magic to track him or her?"

"Monty did preserve some of the spell threads we found. Whether it's still viable is another matter." I glanced at him, one eyebrow raised in question.

He immediately retrieved the sphere. The thread was little more than a faintly glowing spark now.

"I'm afraid there's not enough left to weave a tracker spell around," he said. "Though in all honesty, I doubt we would have succeeded. She's obviously covered her tracks very well."

"No doubt because she's aware there're five witches in the reservation," I said.

"A sorcerer strong enough to summon and control a basilisk isn't going to worry about five regular old witches," Monty commented, voice dry.

"Which would be a big mistake on her part, I'm thinking," Aiden said. "I'll rope off and record the area, then collect blood and skin samples. Until we get a body or an ID on whoever or whatever that bloodstain came from, there's nothing much else we can do at this point."

"We'll hang around while you do all that," Monty said. "Just in case the basilisk decides to come back."

Aiden unslung his backpack and pulled a roll of police tape from it. "If this thing is so deadly, can it be killed?"

"Everything can be killed," Monty said in a sage sort of tone. "It's just a matter of having the right implements."

"And those implements are?"

"If legends are to be believed, a mirror."

Aiden's gaze shot toward Monty, surprise evident. "Seriously?"

Monty nodded. "Its gaze is deadly, remember, so its own reflection will kill it."

"What about weasels?" I walked over to the rock Monty had perched on and sat beside him. "They're good at killing regular snakes, aren't they?"

"That's mongoose more than weasels, and we'd have to approach a specialist supplier to get one, as they're not native to Australia. But we could try a rooster. Apparently, basilisks don't like them."

I laughed, only to realize he was serious. "I can just imagine the response the council will have if we ask everyone to walk around with a rooster tucked under their arm until we catch this thing."

"I think I'll order my crew to carry mirrors and leave it at that," Aiden said.

His voice was dry, and I smiled. "Probably the easiest choice."

He nodded and continued taping off the area. Once he'd done that, he took all his photos and collected his samples, tucking them all carefully into his pack before slinging it over his shoulder.

By the time we got back to the cars, it was just after three. Monty opened the SUV's driver side and climbed in, but I followed Aiden across to his truck.

"I'm sorry I've been ignoring your calls," I said softly. "I just needed—"

"Time to think." He placed his pack on the rear seat, then slammed the door shut. The sound echoed across the stillness, and in the distance something stirred. "We've both needed that, at one point or another."

I glanced past him briefly, gaze sweeping the surrounding trees. I had no sense of evil, no sense that the basilisk was near, and yet I had the oddest feeling we were being watched.

Trepidation tripped lightly across my skin. I did my best to ignore it and said, "So what did you want?"

"It's way past time we sat down and had a serious discussion about our relationship and intentions, don't you think?"

His tone was dry, and I smiled, though my heart beat so fast it felt like it was about to escape my chest. This is what I'd wanted, but it was also what I feared.

"Definitely way past time." I hesitated again. "You could come back to the café. It's not like I'm going to sleep now anyway."

"You sure?" He touched my cheek, a light caress that felt like flame. "You look tired."

I stood my ground even though my muscles quivered with the need to step into his arms. To have him hold me, kiss me, like he used to. "I'm fine. Besides, I have to be up at six anyway to get things ready for the day."

He hesitated. "I need to log and store the samples first, so I probably wouldn't be there until five."

"That's fine. I'll make us both a bacon sandwich."

"Deal." He hesitated again, his gaze briefly dropping to my lips, then smiled and stepped back. "I'll see you soon."

I nodded, spun around, and quickly retreated.

"So," Monty said as I did up my seat belt. "What was that little tête-à-tête about?"

"You told me to talk to the man, so I did."

"You actually listened to a bit of advice from me? I'm shocked."

I rolled my eyes. "Idiot."

He chuckled softly, reversed around, and followed Aiden's truck out of the forest. It was a much slower—and saner—drive back, so by the time we arrived at Castle Rock, it was well after four. The faintest hint of color was just beginning to touch the fluffy undersides of the few clouds to be seen, but I nevertheless suspected it was going to be another wretchedly hot day.

Once we reached Monty's, I jumped into the driver's seat and headed home. The café felt stuffy and hot, so I opened all the windows to let some fresh air in. I'd close them down and turn the air-con on once the sun fully rose, but for now, that hint of a breeze was lovely. It wasn't like anyone could take advantage of the place being open—not even an ill-intentioned gnat could get through the basket weave of magical protections that surrounded this place.

I put the kettle on and then headed upstairs to grab the laptop. For at least the last six months, Belle and I had been electronically scanning the library her grandmother had left her, not only as a fail-safe against the High Council discovering we had it and subsequently confiscating it, but also against the possibility of fire. Castle Rock was located in a high-risk zone, and aside from the emotional attachment Belle had to the books, the library was too good a source of information to risk losing it in *any* way. We still had a good third of the library to convert, but we'd fully catalogued the indexes, which made searching for information a whole lot easier.

I'd barely made it back downstairs when my phone pinged. I tugged it out of my pocket and glanced at the screen. Aiden was on the way. My heart did a series of little skips that were part hope, part fear.

Which was silly, given he'd hardly need to talk to me if he was going to make our breakup permanent. Besides, his actions tonight were not those of a man intending to walk away. Aiden was many things, but he wasn't cruel, and he didn't tease. Not for something as serious as this.

I placed the laptop on the table and headed into the kitchen to make our breakfast. A little more than five minutes later, the small bell above the door chimed merrily, and the scent of musk and man brushed past my nose.

I plated up our bacon sandwiches, added them to the tray already holding his coffee and my tea, then picked it up and walked out.

He met me at our usual table and sat down opposite me. The cool breeze drifting in from the nearby window teased the back of my neck but failed to ease the heat washing my skin. It couldn't. Not when that heat was caused by the sheer force of Aiden's gaze.

I did my best to ignore the inner tremble and concentrated on emptying the tray. After resting it against the table leg, I sat down and picked up my sandwich, more to have something to do with my hands than for any real need to eat it right now.

Though I *was* hungry. I was always damn hungry these days.

He didn't say anything. Not for the longest of moments. He just stared into my eyes, his gaze hungry, determined, and yet also holding a touch of fear.

He was afraid of my reaction. Of me walking away yet again.

And that really did ease some of the inner turmoil.

This wasn't a break-up-forever meeting, even if what it *actually* was had yet to be defined.

"Eat," I said softly. "A bacon sandwich is always better hot than cold."

He laughed softly. "My taste buds are a little less refined than yours."

"Hardly," I said, rather impulsively. "You did choose me, after all."

"I did, didn't I? And then I went and stuffed it all up."

I didn't say anything. I couldn't. Not because my mouth was full of bacon, but because my gut was churning and my throat restricted. I could barely even swallow, let alone speak.

"But," he continued softly, "your trip to Canberra gave me plenty of time to experience just what my life would be like without you in it."

"And?"

It came out fainter than a whisper, but it didn't matter. He heard it. He would always hear it. Hear me.

"And I want you in my life. Not temporarily, but permanently." He paused briefly, and all the emotion, all the passion, and all the love and hope I could ever want was right there in his aura and his expression. "Elizabeth Grace, will you marry me?"

CHAPTER THREE

I stared at him for what seemed like ages, not daring to believe he'd finally said the words. Not daring to believe that he actually *meant* it.

"But your pack—"

"Will be a problem, there's no doubt about it." His voice was soft, but filled with determination. "But if I have to walk away from everything I ever wanted—everything I ever dreamed of—then I will. You are my heart, my soul, and my reason for being. Not seeing you every day hurt more than I could ever have imagined. I can't live without you by my side anymore, Liz. I won't."

I reached out and twined my fingers through his. "What you can't and won't do is walk away from everything you've ever known. It's not right, and it's not fair."

"There are many things in this world that aren't fair."

"I know, but you walking away from your pack is just as impossible as me walking away from magic. Either is unworkable in the long term."

"Don't get me wrong—I'll do everything in my power to have a life with you *as* a part of my pack, even if that means stepping down as alpha and living in the compound as a regular wolf. But if they decide to ostracize me because of my choice of mate, then I'll happily live within the reservation but outside the pack." His sudden smile was lopsided but tender. "I don't think I've ever been as happy as when we were together in Argyle. I want that—want *you*—for the rest of my life."

"Oh, Aiden—"

I rose and moved around the table. He met me halfway, slid his hands around my waist, his fingers so warm against my bare skin, and drew me into his powerful body. Our lips met and for the longest time, the only sound to be heard was the sharp tattoo of our hearts beating as one in rapid time.

He was mine, now and forever. No matter what.

Eventually he pulled back, though his breath continued to caress my lips and his eyes sparkled with delight and happiness. "I do note that you haven't actually answered my question yet."

I laughed and hugged him fiercely. "Of course I'll marry you, you idiot. But that doesn't solve the problem of your pack and your mom. We need to talk about that, Aiden. I need to know what you're planning—or at least hoping —to do."

"Having such a discussion right on the heels of such a momentous moment is very unromantic, you know." His voice was dry. "This obsessive need for details *is* one of your more annoying traits."

"The furnishing of details will lead to a much smoother, happier marriage, I can assure you of that."

He laughed. "Then I shall take note and endeavor to comply. Just be aware that oversharing is not an alpha tendency; allowances should be made for at least for the first few years."

"Then *I* shall take note and endeavor to be understanding." I sat down with a grin and picked up my sandwich. "I guess my first question has to be, where's my ring?"

He laughed again. "I figured it would be safer to go shopping together for one. I didn't think you'd want anything as ostentatious as Belle's, but you also wear so little in the way of jewelry that I had no idea what metal or style you might like."

"Well, it's safe to say silver is out." Aside from the fact he couldn't go near silver, I'd recently developed a werewolf-like sensitivity to it. While I could still handle both my athame and my plain-handled silver knife, I had no idea how much stronger the reaction would get. With all the other DNA changes happening, it was possible I could end up with a "touch it and die" condition as strong as any werewolf. "And I'm not keen on gold."

"Shame, because there's a ton of it in the compound. We could have dug a nugget or two up and gotten something specially made."

I smiled. "And no doubt your mother would have then accused me of marrying you for your wealth."

"That's actually the one point she has *never* raised."

"Give her time," I said, amused. "Are we announcing this engagement far and wide or keeping it under wraps until the council confirms your position as alpha? Which, by the way, I thought was nothing more than a formality."

"It generally is."

"Then why the delay? Your mom, or something else?"

"A bit of both, to be honest."

He grimaced and wolfed down the remains of his sandwich. The man was obviously hungry and, if the gleam in his eyes was anything to go by, not just for food. But as much as I wanted nothing more than to race him upstairs and have my wicked way with him, I couldn't let sex get in the way of this discussion—something that had happened too many times in the past.

"I'm afraid Mom's brought a motion before the council that the ancient ruling stating pack alphas cannot have relationships with witches or humans be reintroduced and enforced."

I raised my eyebrows. "That's an actual rule?"

He nodded. "It fell out of favor after the last war between witches and wolves was peacefully resolved, but it stems from even more ancient times."

"Peacefully resolved" was something of a misnomer, because many werewolves still resented witches and the restrictions enforced on them within their own lands.

"Do you think the origins of that ruling came from a time when witches used werewolves to create Fenna?"

Fenna were children created during a mating ritual held within the magical waters of a newly emerging wellspring. We'd initially thought werewolves were chosen simply because their healing capabilities helped the embryo survive the sheer force of the wild magic, but we'd since learned it was far more than that. The child created in that ritual became the living embodiment of that spring, with her own pool of magic inside that enabled her—as I'd recently discovered—to access the power of her wellspring from anywhere in the world.

I didn't have werewolf genes. I would never be able to use the full force of the power I could access. Not without it entirely consuming me.

But the child that grew within me probably *would* be able to. Her father was a werewolf, her mother's DNA ran with wild magic, and she'd been conceived in a reservation where the wellspring's luminous filaments floated around seemingly unhindered, despite the multiple rings of spells that not only protected it but should have prevented their forays outside the defined area. She would be a part of this land in ways that neither I nor the werewolves would or could ever be.

"There're no records from those times, but I wouldn't be surprised," Aiden answered. "There are many traditions and rulings whose source is lost thanks to the fact they were verbally passed from generation to generation rather than being written down."

Something witches were also guilty of, given the National Witch Archives only had one book on earth magic, which was what wild magic had once been called. Hell, we didn't even know *why* its name had been changed, though I guess it probably had something to do with the Fenna all but being wiped out and there being few people left who understood the process of linking witch to wellspring.

"Do you think there's any chance her petition will be successful?" I asked.

"No, actually, simply because the knock-on effect would restrict *any* pack alpha and their firstborns dallying with either witches *or* humans." His smile was decidedly wicked. "And you have firsthand experience of just how much we alphas like to dally."

I did indeed. Who'd have thought it would so quickly develop into something more serious? Certainly not me. Not initially—although as the months had passed, I'd certainly hoped for it.

"If that petition is only part of the problem, what's the other?"

"You, I'm afraid."

My eyebrows shot upwards. "*Me?*"

"More specifically, that magical display you and the gang put on in our great hall."

"Ah."

"Indeed." He picked up his coffee and took a sip. "There's a faction of the council—a minority faction, granted, but one that has a very loud voice—that were scared by the forces you brought to bear that day."

"I'm guessing that faction wants us banished?"

"Initially. But the wild magic's reaction to your absence certainly quelled much of that."

A comment that reminded me of the urgency I'd felt in the thread earlier. "Have the earth's rumblings eased now that I'm home?"

"Mostly." His eyebrows rose. "Why?"

"Just curious." I shrugged and let it go. Maybe I was worrying over nothing. Or maybe the power that had built up within the earth during my time in Canberra was simply taking time to disperse. "What do the dissenters actually want? Let's be honest here, they can't drive me out now, because of the wellspring, and they certainly can't petition the High Witch Council to do something about me, because that'll only bring unwanted attention." I paused to take a sip of tea. "I suppose they could revoke my trading license, but that's not going to achieve much more than pissing off our customers."

"I honestly don't think they know what they want. They're just... worried."

And no doubt his mother was busy behind the scenes fueling those worries. "Have you pointed out the fact that by marrying me, you're basically tying my allegiance to werewolves rather than the High Witch Council?"

"No, because I'm not party to council discussions thanks to the fact I'm not yet alpha."

"Then how do you know all the details?"

He smiled. "Rocco's been filling me in, probably against orders. He's of the opinion that you are now vital to the reservation's future security, and that you would be an asset to our pack."

Rocco was head alpha of the Marin pack, and one of the few wolves who'd known about the second wellspring on Marin pack ground before we'd announced it at that council meeting. There'd been no way I could keep its presence secret from him, as I'd needed his permission to access pack lands to see Katie.

"In many respects, he's not wrong," I said. "He's obviously not against you becoming alpha, but where does he stand with me as your mate?"

"He has no problems with us marrying, but he hasn't said where he stands in regard to the council position that would normally be yours." He reached out and twined his fingers through mine again. "But our marriage should have no bearing on the council's ratification of my position."

"I think you're being a little naïve there, Aiden. It has to be taken into consideration, if only because when it comes to pack matters, how comfortable are they going to be with someone *not* werewolf-born helping to make decisions?"

He somewhat lazily raised an eyebrow. "Are you trying to talk yourself out of marrying me? Because that would be the fastest case of cold feet ever."

I laughed. "You're stuck with me now, boyo, no matter what. But I can see their point when it comes to the council."

If I was being honest, in all the time I'd been wanting the man to declare his feelings, I hadn't thought beyond it. Hadn't really thought through the everyday practicalities of being a witch in a werewolf compound. All I'd wanted—

all I'd cared about—was to spend the rest of my life with him.

But the fact was, things were never going to be that simple.

"You have every right if you're living there."

"Living amongst wolves is very different to making decisions that will affect the direction of their lives. Many would resent it, Aiden, even if they don't give it voice."

He didn't argue, though it was pretty evident he also didn't see the problem. But then, alphas could often be rather single-minded.

"They'll have to reach a decision soon," he grumbled. "The council cannot legally proceed with everyday administration matters without the required two representatives from every pack."

I picked up my cup with my free hand, took another sip, and couldn't help a soft sigh of happiness. I'd unconsciously chosen a teacup whose history and presence vibrated with good times and deep happiness, and I wanted to believe it was an omen of things to come.

Though both instinct and common sense said we had a mountain of external shit to climb over first.

"Does the fact we've no real decision on your status also mean we'll have to hide the fact we're seeing each other again?"

"Fuck no," he growled. "I want you in my arms and in my bed from here on in."

"Your bed?" I replied, amused. "What about *my* bed?"

"Don't you have this whole 'no lovers upstairs' agreement going on with Belle?"

"We do indeed, but the important term there is 'lovers.' You're no longer just a 'lover,' so that rule no longer applies."

The heated, sensual glimmer in his eyes exploded, and waves of desire washed across my senses, so damn strong that for a moment, I could barely even breathe.

"Then how about we go upstairs and set about putting that rule to bed right now?"

"Sounds like a plan." I gulped down the rest of my tea and rose. "It's been so long since I saw any action, I think there might be cobwebs."

He laughed, caught my hand, and all but ran me toward the stairs. But as we started to climb, his phone rang. I groaned and crossed all mental appendages that it wasn't a callout.

He glanced at the screen and grimaced. "I have to take this."

Fate had no sympathy for my starved hormones, it seemed. "Meaning the cobwebs will remain for another day."

"Let's not get ahead of ourselves just yet." He hit the answer button and said, "Ranger Aiden O'Connor speaking. How can I help you?"

Though I couldn't hear everything that was said, the caller was a woman, and her voice was high pitched and frantic.

It *wasn't* "nothing."

I crossed my arms and leaned against the wall. From the snatches I could hear, someone had gone missing, and *that* made me wonder if they'd ended up on the wrong end of a blood summoning ritual. Fate did tend to do things like that in this reservation.

Aiden hung up on the promise to be there in forty minutes, suggesting whoever had gone missing lived a good distance away from Castle Rock. Maybe even as far out as Blackwood.

Meaning it was totally possible he or she were those bits of flesh we'd found.

"Do you need a hand?" I asked.

He hesitated. "I'm not sure what we're dealing with yet. It might be unrelated to earlier events."

"Very possibly not, but if you lose the scent trail, I could probably continue the search using psychometry. Besides, it at least gives us a bit more time together, even if not in the manner we'd been hoping."

"At this point, I'll take all the time with you that I can get." His quick smile was decidedly wicked. "But do be warned, I intend to spend as much time in bed with you as I can over the next few days."

"Just in bed?" I tsked. "Ranger, your imagination has slipped in the time we've been apart."

"Not that far, I can assure you."

I laughed, caught his face between my hands, and kissed him soundly. "I'll go grab my kit from the reading room."

"I left the truck at the station, so I'll go get that. I'll meet you out the front in five."

I nodded, kissed him again, this time more briefly, and then all but bounced down the steps. The air sparked briefly as I entered the reading room, a clear indication the spells encircling and protecting the room were active. The warm scent of cinnamon, clove, lemon, and sandalwood—all of which provided either protection or enhanced focus and concentration—lingered in the air, a leftover from the steady run of customers Belle had yesterday. It seemed a fast-approaching Christmas brought a melancholy need to seek comfort or forgiveness from the dead for many folks.

I walked over to the bookcase that covered the entire right-hand wall, shifted a pottery dragon, and placed my hand against the rear panel. Magic immediately crawled across my fingers. A heartbeat later, there was a soft click, and the wooden panel slipped to one side, revealing an eight-inch hidden compartment—one of thirty-six we'd had built behind the bookcase. A witch could never be too careful when it came to certain magical implements, even if it was very unlikely that anyone intending no good—be it witch, demon, or even a human—could cross the barriers that now protected this place.

I reached in, carefully retrieved my blessed silver knife, then closed the door and tugged my backpack free from the bottom shelf. Once the knife was securely tied in place, I grabbed a couple of cake slices, then closed all the windows before grabbing my keys and purse and heading out to wait for Aiden.

I didn't have to wait long. He stopped out the front of our building, then leaned across the seat to open the door for me. Once I'd belted up, he took off, doing a quick left at Barker Street and accelerating away. He put the lights on but left the siren off, thankfully.

I handed him a chocolate brownie—his favorite—then began to munch on my chocolate caramel slice. I normally would have considered it too rich for breakfast, but my hormones had other ideas.

"Where are we headed?" I asked round the mouthful of gooey deliciousness.

"Creswyn."

Which was almost as far away from Castle Rock as Blackwood was. "And who's missing?"

"Rosie Jackson. Connie said she woke up a few hours ago and discovered her gone."

"She just walked out?"

"Apparently. She left the back door open, but didn't take their car or her purse."

"Why is Connie only ringing you now?"

"Because she went looking for her first." The gaze he briefly cast my way was somewhat wry. "Connie's a werewolf, Rosie is human. The pair were ostracized from the Raines pack in the Northern Territory some fifty-odd years ago because of their relationship."

Them being from the Raines pack explained his wry expression. His former girlfriend—the one his mother had invited back not so long ago in the hopes she might pry his heart away from mine—had come from that pack.

"People weren't as accepting of gay relationships back then," I said. "Throw in the fact one of the pair was human and, well, it's not as bad as being a witch but it would have come damn close to it back in those days. They were probably better off elsewhere."

He nodded. "From what I understand, they traveled around for ten or so years before coming here to settle in Creswyn."

"Why there?"

He shrugged. "Connie's brother married into the Sinclair pack."

And Creswyn was the town that serviced the Sinclair pack. "Odd that she didn't petition the pack to allow them to live on the fringes of pack grounds."

They'd certainly done it before for outsiders, something I'd discovered during our recent hunt for the psycho granny killer.

He gave me a somewhat amused smile. "Remember your earlier comments re prejudices? Our reservation isn't immune to them, then or now."

As evidenced by his mom's reaction to *our* relationship,

even if the kernels of her hatred were based on past trauma. "Has Rosie ever gone walkabout like this before?"

"Not to my knowledge."

Which made the panic I'd heard in Connie's voice understandable. "Did she say why she lost the scent trail? Even if it was a few hours old, she still should have been able to track it, shouldn't she?"

It wasn't like there'd been any rain to wash it away.

"Apparently the scent just stopped. She said it was like someone had taken a knife to it and just sliced it from the ground. She nosed around but couldn't pick it up again."

Magic could conceal scents, and a werewolf certainly wouldn't have sensed its presence. It made the possibility of this being linked to our sorceress a little more likely.

"At least Creswyn is too far away from the sacrifice site for it to be our basilisk. They're fast mothers, but even they can't travel that distance so quickly. If it had happened tomorrow night, then it might have been a possibility."

"A snake wouldn't have lured Rosie out of her bed, though," Aiden commented. "And besides, Connie would have picked up the snake's scent."

"Unless the basilisk is using magic to conceal its scent and presence."

He glanced briefly at me. "And can it?"

"I wouldn't have thought so, but it *is* a demon, so who knows." I half shrugged and ate some more slice. It was warm enough that the chocolate on top was already beginning to melt.

We continued on in comfortable silence, the headlights sweeping away the shadows still clinging to the sides of the road while the wisps of pink grew stronger in the sky. The sun was close to peeking over the horizon by the time we reached Connie and Rosie's place. It was a pretty little white weatherboard cottage on the outskirts of Creswyn, with a white picket fence out front lined with roses. Their sweet scent filled my nostrils as I climbed out of the truck and followed Aiden through the gate then up the steps to the small veranda.

The door opened before Aiden could ring the bell. Connie was tall and stringy, with short white hair that contained a solitary streak of pale red in her slightly longer fringe, and deep golden eyes. Her face was weatherworn but pretty, and her aura a vibrant, churning mix of colors that were fear, anger, and sorrow combined.

She had the air of a woman who didn't suffer fools—or people in general—gladly.

"It took you long enough, Ranger." She pointed at me with her chin. "Who's that?"

"Liz Grace, she's—"

"A ranger? Because she don't smell like a wolf to me."

"I'm a psychic," I said. "And right now, my psi skills are your only fucking chance to find your partner, so stop being an ass and let us inside."

She blinked, surprise evident, then nodded. "I like you. Come in."

I hadn't read her wrong, which was a relief.

Aiden gave me a somewhat amused look and motioned me forward. I stepped into the hall and was immediately struck by the floweriness of it all—not only was there pale green and pink floral wallpaper, but also vases of roses on the nearby hallstand and several low hanging pots of flowering Christmas cactus hanging in the doorways. Given Connie's height, she obviously didn't mind ducking.

Connie motioned us into the living room. "What needs to be done?"

"I'll need something personal of hers—something that she wears close to her skin."

Connie hesitated. "I'm not sure there's anything that fits the bill. Rosie wasn't much into jewelry and the like."

"That's okay," I said. "Perhaps I can look around myself? My psychometry should be able to pick up something with a strong enough resonance."

"And if it doesn't?"

"Then," Aiden said, "we drop into plan B and organize a full search of the area."

Connie's expression remained dubious, which was frustrating given her early panic and the fact that every minute that passed was one less minute we had to find her partner alive.

And I didn't even want to examine that particular insight right now.

"Then she *is* a legit psychic?" she commented. "This isn't some weird means of casing the joint, is it?"

"Connie, if I wanted to case the joint and steal your valuables, I'd hardly be in the company of a ranger. Besides, I could simply magic my way in and take what I wanted, anytime I wanted, without you being any the wiser."

"She could," Aiden confirmed, the amusement so evident in his eyes and aura barely noticeable in his voice. "But thankfully for us all, the witches in this reservation are on the side of the angels rather than the sinners."

"She's a fucking witch, too? Damn, you keep some strange company, Ranger."

"You have no idea," he replied, and motioned me forward.

I stepped into the front bedroom and was again visually assaulted by flowers. While the scheme was pastel and should have been relaxing, there were simply too many clashing patterns for my taste. Which didn't matter, because I didn't have to live here.

I raised a hand and moved slowly around the room, gently skimming the various bits and bobs that were scattered across the tops of the dressing table and dress drawers. It wasn't until I reached the small chest of drawers on the far side of the bed that I got a strong response from the watch sitting there.

But not the type I wanted.

Rosie was dying.

I didn't know how or why, but if we wanted to save her, we had to find her.

Fast.

I turned and looked at Aiden. He didn't need to be told that things were bad. He silently handed me a glove, then turned to Connie.

"We need you to stay here—"

"I'm not fucking staying here while my wife is out there —" She flung a hand toward the rear of the house, but Aiden cut her off before she could say anything else.

"If you want us to find her, you stay here. Liz's psi talents can be overwhelmed by strong emotions, and you, my dear, are emoting quite strongly."

She harrumphed, but didn't argue any further. "Can you tell if she's okay? That's all I need to know."

"At this point in time, she's alive." Which definitely wasn't a lie, even if it wasn't the full truth, either. "More than that, I can't say. Not without going deeper, and that could be dangerous for both her and me. Where's the back door?"

"This way."

Connie spun and strode down the hall, her bare feet making little sound on the old floorboards. We entered a kitchen-diner that extended across the entire back width of the house, and which was, rather surprisingly, free of flowers. The glass doors that dominated the rear wall—they were the type that folded back on themselves to provide full access to the patio beyond—were partially open.

Connie stepped onto the patio, then stopped, hugging her arms across her chest. "She headed into the forest and went left. I lost the trail just past the uni's main cluster of buildings. I think she was headed toward Sawpit Road but, as I said, I couldn't find a scent or foot trail." She paused. "You don't think she's in the dam, do you?"

"At this point, we can't rule it out, but it is unlikely." Aiden touched her arm lightly. "We'll do our best to find her, Connie."

He didn't make it a promise. Didn't add "alive," but she didn't seem to notice. She simply nodded and leaned against the rear wall of the house, her expression a mix of hope and resignation.

I briefly tightened my grip on the gloved watch. Pain and bewilderment echoed through the silicon, and it tugged me forward. I stepped off the porch and ran across the rear yard. There was no fence—the only indication of the house's boundary was a very obvious dividing line between the lushness of the lawn and the drier undergrowth of the forest. As I ran through the trees, the melodious call of magpies greeting the new day filled the air, a cheery sound that belied the darkness building in the watch. It led me onto a dusty track that swept around to the left. Puffs of dirt rose with every step, but I was now moving so fast it had no chance to tickle my nose. Buildings loomed, but the watch's pulse led me past them and on again through the trees.

We reached another road, and I paused briefly, looking

left and right, more to check there were no vehicles rushing toward us than for any real need of direction.

I ran on, Aiden close on my heels. It wouldn't be the last time we'd run through a forest like this, but I couldn't help hoping that at least *some* of those future runs were because of the moon and the need to feel the soil under our feet, rather than a desperate race against time to save a life.

The pulsing in the watch sharpened so abruptly, it caught me by surprise and made me stumble. Aiden lunged forward, catching me before I hit the ground, and then placed me back on my feet.

His gaze swept me and came up relieved. "What happened?"

"Her heart—I think she's having a heart attack."

"Ah fuck."

"Yeah." I pulled free and ran on.

He followed, keeping even closer. "Is that what's killing her?"

"No. Whatever is killing her caused the heart attack."

Aiden swore. I didn't bother echoing it, though I wanted to. I leapt over a log and ran on, my steps sure and light over the forest floor. The pain echoing through the watch was now so strong that I had to flip the watch out of my palm and hold it by the very end. It eased the strength of the waves but didn't hinder my ability to track her.

Death remained closer than we were.

There was nothing I could do to stop it happening. Nothing other than run on and hope.

We crossed another dirt road and ran into a pine plantation. The soldier-straight lines allowed little in the way of undergrowth, which made running a whole lot easier, but didn't mean I increased speed. I was already at my limit.

The pulsing began to falter, but we were close to her now.

The watch didn't tell me that. The faint, flowery scent riding the air did.

Aiden made a low noise behind me, indicating he'd caught the scent. He didn't race past me, though the rush of anger and frustration that briefly caressed my senses said he very much wanted to.

We hit a fire track that divided one section of the pine forest from the other, and I slid to a halt.

On the other side of the road, lying in a small, semi-cleared byway, was Rosie.

She wore a pink nightie and fluffy slippers that were all but destroyed by her walk through the forest. She was fully clothed, lying on her back, with her arms crossed across her chest. At first glance, she looked to be asleep.

But she wasn't.

She was dead.

And the two small but very swollen red marks visible on the side of her neck said she'd been attacked by a vampire.

CHAPTER FOUR

"This is not the result I was hoping for." Aiden glanced at me grimly. "Is it worth trying to resuscitate her?"

I crossed my arms and briefly studied the dead woman. Her expression was one of pain and confusion—no surprise given a vampire's bite generally wasn't orgasmic, despite what fiction might say, though there were obvious exceptions. Maelle had a long list of lovers who were also willing blood suppliers, and I couldn't imagine that would be the case if the experience was nasty.

Unless, of course, they were into nasty.

But Maelle didn't drain her lovers to the point of death, and that was what had happened here. Rosie's soul had already departed, and that meant this death had been ordained.

"She's gone," I said softly. "Attempting resuscitation would be pointless."

Aiden swore softly. "Is it safe to approach her? There're no magical traps or whatnot around?"

I scanned the trees behind Rosie's body. There was no

magic, and no sense of movement or danger. Our vampire had fled.

Whether that vampire was Maelle's creator had yet to be discovered, but it was highly unlikely that two new vampires would enter the reservation at the same damn time.

But then, as I'd noted before, fate did like playing her games in this place.

"It's safe."

He nodded and moved closer. I followed, but stopped a meter or so away. Rosie had long copper hair that even in a tangled, sweaty state looked luxurious and, aside from the small dark freckle near the corner of her mouth, flawless skin. And while her face didn't have Maelle's perfection, put Rosie in Regency riding gear, and from a distance she could easily have been mistaken for her.

This *wasn't* an accident.

This was a warning.

The first shot across the bow, so to speak.

Despite the heat, I shivered. It wouldn't end here. There was no way it would end here.

Aiden took out his phone and recorded the scene, then pulled on a glove and carefully touched Rosie's chin, moving it to one side in order to get a closer look at the bite.

"The bite here is smaller than the one on Karen's neck," he commented.

Karen was the teenager I'd failed to save not long after we'd settled in the reservation, and the reason Aiden and I had met in the first place.

"She was bitten by an adult male. If what Maelle said is true, then this was done by a vampire who looks no more than sixteen in physical appearance." I hesitated. "I also don't think it's a coincidence that Rosie has the same physical characteristics as Maelle."

His gaze snapped back to the dead woman. "Damn it, you're right."

"And wish that I wasn't." The inner chill was growing stronger. I rubbed my arms and added, "The thing that doesn't make sense to me is, if she's going to leave nasty little messages like this all over the reservation, why would she call in a basilisk?"

"You say that like you expect me to have the answer." His tone was dry. "You'd think by now you'd know that, when it comes to magic, I never do."

I smiled, despite the seriousness of the situation. "And I'd think by now you'd realize that when I'm asking these questions, I'm simply thinking aloud."

His smile echoed mine, though it quickly faded when his gaze fell back to Rosie. "This is going to hit Connie hard. Even with Connie's brother living here, they kept pretty much to themselves."

"She must have thought it was worth it," I said softly.

His gaze came to mine, but for too many seconds, he didn't say anything. He didn't have to, because all that needed to be said was there in the gleaming depths of his lovely blue eyes.

Love *was* worth it. Love would *always* be worth it.

It might have taken him way too long to get around to thinking that, but damn it, now that he had, he was all in.

"I'll have to call out Ciara and Mac," he said eventually. "How likely is it that our vampire is hanging about?"

"With the day rising, very unlikely." Most vamps avoided any kind of sunlight, for the very simple reason that it was deadly to them. "Do you mind if I walk around and see if I can find anything?"

"Remain within shouting distance."

"I intended to, just in case I'm wrong and she attacks you."

He snorted. "When are you ever wrong about those sorts of things?"

"People keep saying that and yet my record is not one hundred percent."

"Yeah, but the one or two percent you do get wrong doesn't mean much in the scheme of things."

"That very much depends on whether you're the one or two percent."

Amusement flitted through his expression. "That is very true."

He got out his phone and began making calls. I dropped my gaze to his neck and was relieved to see he still wore the protection charm I'd given him. He was strong enough in his own right to fight off a vampire attack, and the charm would fight off most magical attacks, but I had no idea if it would work against a basilisk. Even if it wasn't a demon, the likely size of the thing suggested it could easily crush a man —or a woman—to death.

Still, the demon-repelling spell entwined within that charm should at least deter the basilisk, even if it didn't outright stop it. It would certainly work better than bullets, which, unless they were blessed or made of silver, were basically useless against most demonic creatures.

I dragged out my phone and took a photo of Rosie so that I could show Maelle later, then looked left and right. I wasn't picking up any scents that didn't belong, and there was no indication of magic—hell, even the luminous threads of wild magic were absent, which was very unusual indeed, given its penchant for roaming the entire reservation. The niggle of concern rose again, and again I shoved it back down and forced myself to concentrate on the problem at hand.

I mentally flipped a coin, and then went left. Dust puffed upwards with every step, which meant there should have been some evidence of tire tracks had they come this way via a car. I had no idea if they'd used another road or had simply walked in, but given it was likely there was more than one fire access road crisscrossing the plantation, the former was most likely. I couldn't imagine Maelle walking any great distance, so it was highly unlikely her maker would.

Despite the rising brightness of dawn, shadows still hugged the pines either side of the road. The forest floor was covered with a thick layer of needles, and while that layer might have been an arsonist's delight, it was too dry to hold anything in the way of prints. As the road began to sweep to the right, I paused, not wanting to risk going any further. That's when I caught the soft murmur of running water. If there were going to be any prints found, it would be on the softer banks of a creek, although given there hadn't been any rain for days and the ground was bone dry, that wasn't really likely.

I swung into the forest and followed the gentle murmur until I found the creek. It ran through the middle of a wide strip of cleared land separating two sections of plantation trees, which allowed the gathering brightness of the day to glitter off the trickle of water running along the creek bed. The erosion higher up the banks said that while the flow was currently light, in winter it was a very different story.

I studied the ground for several seconds but couldn't spot anything untoward, so I went right and followed the little stream back toward Aiden's position. It wasn't easy, thanks mainly to the gorse that had taken hold across much of this wider strip. Even at the best times, it was hard to move through that shit without getting snagged or scratched. In a crop top, it was next to impossible.

I was probably halfway there when I spotted the faintest furrow on my side of the riverbank.

Someone had slipped, and while they'd caught their balance relatively quickly, they hadn't bothered covering their tracks.

But it wasn't so much the slip that had my heart racing, but the tiny strip of material hanging from the end of a particularly nasty-looking gorse bush halfway down the bank. Sometimes, just sometimes, I could grab impressions from clothing, though I wasn't entirely sure that scrap would be big enough to be useful.

There was only one way to find out.

I backtracked a little to find a section of bank not covered by the nasty-looking gorse, then carefully went down and across. The slide marks weren't particularly deep, but whoever had slid had landed hard enough to leave a largish print. Maelle had said her maker was petite, and both the small print we'd found in the summoning circle and the bite on Rosie's neck backed that up, so this had to belong to someone else. Unless, of course, Marie was endowed with unusually large feet.

I bent and took a series of photos for Aiden and sent them across, adding a GPS location so he could find it later. Then I carefully walked up the steep incline to the spiky bush, taking a few more photos of the scrap before shoving my phone away and carefully—warily—pressing the scrap's edge between two fingers.

Images flicked rapidly across my psychometry senses, memory ghosts that were already fading into nothingness. In rapid succession I glimpsed the back of a woman wearing a pale, high-collared shirt, her golden hair caught up in a looped ponytail. Marie—of that I had no doubt. Ahead of her were two men, their short dark hair visible over the top of hers. The light sphere that bobbed along above the lead hiker's head cast a strange purplish glow across the trunks of the nearby pines and was very definitely a darker magic in nature. Then there was a sharp movement, an oddly eloquent but heavily accented curse, and the ghosts faded, leaving little more than a voice echoing through my mind.

The scrap of clothing belonged to a woman. A *French* woman who was part of Marie's entourage, possibly a fledgling rather than a lover.

I released the scrap, then turned and walked down to the creek. There were no further footprints visible, either on this side or the other. I nevertheless stepped over the water and walked up the opposite bank to double check, but there was nothing to find.

That didn't really surprise me. What *did* was the fact they'd made no attempt to cover that slip or bothered to retrieve the material. I doubted it was carelessness but rather that they were already covering their scent and didn't believe there was any danger in leaving such tiny traces when there was no trail to lead the rangers to this location.

I crossed the creek again and made my way back to Aiden. Ciara—who wasn't only the coroner but also his sister—squatted next to the body but glanced up as I stepped past the trees.

"Lizzie," she said, her expression and tone friendly. "I don't want to give offence or anything, but it would be nice to actually see you somewhere *other* than a murder scene."

"Well, you could always visit the café," I said, amused. "There're free brownies on offer for all rangers and coroners."

"With my waistline? Unlikely."

It was wryly said, and I couldn't help smiling. Ciara's build was pretty typical of most werewolves—she was tall and rangy, with hair that was on the browner side of the O'Connor pack's silvery blonde and a sharp but pretty face. She certainly *hadn't* put on any weight in the year I'd known her. Indeed, weight was something most wolves didn't have to worry about, thanks to their faster metabolic rate. Luckily for me, *that* was one of the DNA adaptations the wild magic was making, which was just as well given the copious amounts of cake I'd been eating recently.

"Received the images you sent," Aiden said. "Did you find anything else?"

"A scrap of material that came from the clothing of a woman in the company of another who matched the description Maelle gave me of her maker."

"That description being?"

I quickly told him and then added, "I wouldn't be putting out an APB though. She's not just a vampire, remember, but also a very old sorceress."

"Any way you and Monty can come up with a means of tracking her?"

I shook my head. "Not without Maelle's help, and right now, she's not in the mood."

Annoyance flickered through his expression. "And I'm guessing she's not likely to change her mind?"

"Not until Marie makes a direct attack on her."

"Oh, that's great news," Ciara muttered. "A vampire war is all we fucking need in the reservation."

"Look on the bright side," I said. "If they're picking off each other's people, they're not attacking Castle Rock inhabitants."

She gave me the sort of look that suggested she was in

no way comforted by this thought. "Rosie is *not* one of Maelle's people."

That was true. I glanced at the time and then at Aiden. "Can I borrow your truck? The gossip brigade are booked in for brunch, and I need to get back to help prepare everything."

He tugged his keys from his pocket and tossed them over. "Is there any reason they're hitting the cakes so early?"

"No one ever needs an excuse to hit cake early, Aiden, but in this case, I believe it's because they missed out on our Heaven on a Plate cake last Tuesday and are determined to avoid a repeat."

His eyebrows rose. "What on earth is Heaven on a Plate?"

I grinned. "It's layers of angel food cake, custard, cherry pie filling, and whipped cream."

"So, a simple trifle."

"There's nothing simple about it, dear sir, and there's been vast demand for it."

He snorted. "Nothing you or Belle make can beat those brownies."

"Which is why you eat her out of stock," Ciara said, amused.

"Eating is one of my favorite things to do," he replied, with a decidedly wicked smile.

The man was *not* talking about brownies or cakes, and my pulse rate did a happy little skip at the thought.

"Behave yourself, brother." Ciara glanced at me. "You should leave and stop distracting the man."

I raised an eyebrow at that, and Aiden shook his head in answer to my unspoken question. She didn't yet know he'd asked me to marry him—and probably wouldn't until he was confirmed as alpha. Which I guessed was sensible, given the fewer people knew, the less likely it was to get back to his mother's ears.

She *would* go ballistic when she found out, and there was a part of me that actually looked forward to the inevitable confrontation. An insane part, granted, but still...

The fact I'd already proven myself capable of holding my ground against her didn't mean much in the grander scheme of things, simply because the wider pack members *hadn't* witnessed it. If I was going to live within the O'Connor compound as his wife, then I had to prove to the entire pack that I was *physically* capable of doing so.

I saluted Ciara lightly and said, "Leaving now, ma'am."

"No, you're not. You're still standing there giving me sass."

I laughed and headed out, walking past Aiden and clenching my fingers against the need to brush them across his. The desire that ran through his aura seemed to chase me through the trees, but he was controlling the scent of it pretty well. I wasn't sure why, given that even if Ciara wasn't aware we were now engaged, she obviously knew the two of us remained madly attracted to each other.

It didn't take long to find my way back to his truck. Thankfully, I managed to jump in and drive off without running into Connie. As much as she had to be told the bad news, I didn't want to be the one doing it. Aside from the fact I really didn't have the time—or the emotional energy—right now, it was Aiden's job, not mine.

I parked out the back of our café, then dragged the back door key out of my backpack and headed in. Belle was already in the kitchen, singing softly to some tune on the radio. I dumped the pack in the reading room but hesitated as I reached in to grab and secure the knife. Bad luck tended to come in threes, and instinct was saying there might be one more event to go this morning.

I mentally crossed all things that instinct was wrong, left the knife where it was, and walked behind the serving counter to wash my hands and flick on the kettle. It was easier than fussing about with the coffee machine when you only wanted a quick cuppa. After grabbing a fresh apron from under the bench, I tied it on and went into the kitchen.

"Hey ho," Belle said. "What's been happening?"

"You haven't been following along telepathically?"

"Your mind has been locked down tighter than a cat's ass, which leads me to believe whatever happened had something to do with Aiden."

"Yes and no."

"Meaning?" She swept the cooked and cooled potatoes she'd been cutting into a large tub. With the heat of the last few days, we'd taken to offering potato salad with our meals rather than hot chips, although a surprising number of people were seriously offended by the idea.

"Meaning, two major events have happened since we discovered that summoning circle."

She gave me "the look." The one that said "stop the avoidance and just get on with it." The heat was not having a good effect on her usually sunny disposition.

Either that, or Monty had been too tired to do anything useful when he'd gotten home.

"As has been noted before, Monty is never too tired, too hot, or too sweaty to do something useful," she said wryly.

"You followed *that* thought pretty easily."

"Because you let it leak out. Your mind remains something of a steel trap. Which is annoying in cases like this."

And something that would have to continue now that we were both settling down. She couldn't continue living in the shadows of my thoughts—especially when she and Monty had a gaggle of kids to take care of.

"I'm not the one who has already started the gaggle, and if you're going to let thoughts leak, could it be useful ones?"

I laughed and tugged a cutting board out from under the bench. "Do you want the good news or the bad?"

"Good, because the bad will no doubt be something to do with Maelle's ex or the monster snake she called into being."

"Good guess." I tipped the bag of cucumbers onto the bench and began cutting them for the green salads. "I take it Monty told you I invited Aiden back here for breakfast so we could chat?"

"He did indeed." She paused, her gaze narrowing. "Did you tell him you were pregnant?"

"I did not."

"Why not?"

I hesitated. "I just need to keep the news to myself a bit longer. I mean, what if his mother is right about the child of a witch and a werewolf being deformed?"

"She isn't, and you know it."

"Yes, but—"

"You want to get past the miscarriage danger zone."

There *was* that. But there was also an inner voice telling me I needed to keep the pregnancy to myself for as long as possible. Of course, that voice might also be nothing more than a lingering echo of past habits, ones based on the necessity of hiding our true identities in fear of my parents finding us.

"This pregnancy is *my* secret. I will *not* have any whispers of entrapment happening."

"Then... did your willpower break and you had hot monkey sex upstairs?"

"Hot monkey sex is a really weird term to use when a werewolf is involved, but sadly, I did not."

"Then what?"

It was impatiently said, and I grinned. "The man asked me to marry him."

She blinked and, for several seconds, didn't react. Then she let out the biggest whoop I'd ever heard, slammed her knife down, and ran around the bench, enveloping me in the fiercest bear hug ever.

"That is the news I've been hoping for but never expected." She stood back and gave me a mock severe look. "You said yes, of course."

"Of course."

She glanced down at my hands. "No ring?"

"Not yet. He said he wasn't certain what style I'd like, although he did suggest digging a nugget or two out of the veins that run through the compound's mountain and getting something specially made."

She snorted. "I take it he hasn't informed his mother yet? Because I surely would have heard the ear-splitting howls of fury coming from their compound this morning."

I laughed. "He hasn't—and won't—tell anyone until he's confirmed as alpha."

"Meaning Katie was right—he *did* have a long-term plan."

"Apparently. I've already laid down some ground rules —going forward, he needs to include me in *all* plans made, be they long-term or short."

She laughed. "Good luck with that. I mean, Monty is the most verbal man I've ever met, and he still manages to keep secrets from me."

"Only one."

"Yes, but it was one hell of a big one." Her expression

became serious, although it was countered by the sparkle in her eyes. "I never actually asked—did you know he was planning all that?"

I picked up my knife and got to work. "No, although Aiden did. I tried to pry information about what Monty was up to during one of our calls when we were in Canberra, but he wouldn't budge. I'm glad, because the surprise was worth it."

"With that, I'll agree." She returned to her side of the bench and continued cutting potatoes. "What happened to prevent the aforementioned hot monkey sex?"

"A phone call about a missing person."

"And he didn't hand it over to someone else?" She shook her head. "The man obviously isn't yet sex-starved enough."

I snorted. "It was the full moon. Everyone else was out running."

She sniffed. It was a disbelieving sound. "I take it the missing woman turned up dead? Because that's how these things tend to go here."

"Sadly, yes." I swept the sliced cucumbers into the container and started the next batch. "She was drained by a vampire."

"*Maelle's* vampire?"

"If the images I pulled from a scrap of material I found are anything to go by, yes."

"Then you had best go talk to Maelle sometime today."

I raised my eyebrows. "That's not my job."

"It kinda is these days. I mean, you *are* the assistant reservation witch. Besides, she won't help Aiden—not when she's wet with wanting you—and she's obviously not interested in talking to Monty."

"She wants to taste my power rather than me," I

commented. "And if she ever *does* try to bite me, I suspect the wild magic will repel her. Hard."

"It didn't when the sorcerer imbibed."

"The sorcerer wasn't drinking my blood, and he caged my natural magic first. If Maelle even attempts that, I'll knock the bitch down."

"Somehow, I'm thinking that will not be so easy to do, magically or physically."

Undoubtedly, but if I could, in the end—and with a whole lot of help from Belle and the spirit of my dead sister —defeat a very powerful wraith and his demons, then I could certainly at least hold my own against a powerful vampire.

"It's the snake that bothers me—we just don't know enough about it to figure out how to find the thing."

"That can be said about all the demons or witchy entities that are lured into the reservation by the false promise of untapped power, but we generally muddle our way through."

The kettle began to whistle. "Coffee or tea?" I asked.

"Coffee, thanks."

I nodded and headed out to make it.

"I take it you didn't find anything in Gran's books?" she continued. "I saw you had the laptop out."

"Didn't get a chance to search before Aiden dropped in."

"I'll check later then. It might be worth asking Maelle about it when you talk to her, though. There has to be a reason that particular demon was called into being."

"Maybe Maelle is afraid of snakes."

It was said as a joke, but she was nodding as I walked back into the kitchen, my tea, and her coffee in hand. "It's totally possible, you know. A statistic I once read said

France only has two deadly types of snakes, whereas we have at least a dozen."

I still couldn't see it. Maelle just didn't seem the type. But it also never hurt to check.

"Did you ask Monty if he'd do an online search through Canberra's demonology archives to see what he could uncover about them?"

Belle nodded. "He said he'd pop in later with any information he finds."

"No doubt in time to snare some Heaven on a Plate cake before the brigade can grab it all."

"I was ordered to save him several slices."

I smiled. Monty loved cake almost as much as he loved Belle. "What's he doing that he can't drop by this morning and grab it?"

"Informing his parents of our recent engagement."

My eyebrows rose. "He hasn't told them yet?"

"No. His dad has been overseas on business." She waved a hand to indicate either who knew what that business was or who actually cared. Maybe even both. "He's set up a conference call with them this morning."

"Wouldn't I love to be a fly for that particular discussion." I paused. "Why aren't you there? You should be."

"He did want me there, but I thought it might be better if the initial announcement was made by him alone. You know how blue bloods are with Sarr witches. The mere sight of me might be enough to get their backs up."

Despite the amusement tugging her lips, there was a bitter note of acceptance glimmering in her silvery eyes. The high-and-mighty attitude held by most blue bloods when it came to those they considered "unworthy" magically hadn't evaporated in this so-called age of enlightenment. Not one little bit.

Mom, to her credit, had always treated Belle fairly, even if she did share those prejudices, and had in fact gotten on well with Belle's parents the few times they'd met.

My dad, on the other hand...

But his recent loss of magic meant he'd finally learn what it felt like to be considered an unpowered disappointment, and boy, did I feel good about that.

"I think you should have presented a united front, but I also understand why you're not."

She nodded. "They've basically ignored his existence since he moved here, and it's not like they're going to be involved in our lives going forward. It's more a courtesy call than anything else."

"There *is* one point you're both forgetting, though."

She raised her eyebrows, and I grinned. "We created something of a hullaballoo in Canberra tracking down that wraith, and people would have noted the jump in power output in us both. It might just be enough to sway opinions."

She snorted. "And tomorrow it might rain frogs."

"Hey, it has before."

"Not here, it hasn't."

I laughed, and we continued the prep work in a companionable silence only broken by random bouts of off-tune singing—at least on my part. Once Frank and Mike—our kitchen hand and chef—arrived to finish off, we moved into the café to get ready for the brigade's onslaught.

We were busy from the second we opened at eight and didn't get a break until almost two. As Penny—one of our waitresses—swept another order of cake and coffee over to one of the few remaining customers in the café, my phone rang loudly, the tone telling me it was Aiden.

"Maybe the man has freed up some time to do a little horizontal dancing," Belle said.

"One can hope." I hit the answer button and headed toward the reading room so I could talk without having to worry about customers overhearing something they shouldn't. None of them were near the counter, but werewolves could hear a surprising amount from a surprising distance. "Hey, what's up?"

"The snake, that's what."

"I take it that's not a euphemism for you feeling horny?"

"I wish." He sighed. "The basilisk has found its first victim. The man is now a fucking stone statue."

CHAPTER FIVE

"Stone?" I said, a little incredulously. "Seriously?"

"Apparently. Can't confirm because I haven't yet seen it. Monty's on his way over there to pick you up. I thought it would be wise to have two witches present in case this is some sort of trap."

"I take it you haven't already got people there?"

"Not yet, but I have ordered the woman who reported it to leave the forest and to keep her eyes down."

Which was always a good idea when it came to bush tracks anyway. There were plenty of regular old deadly snakes out and about in summer.

"Don't let anyone go in until we get there," I said. "And make sure everyone is armed with a mirror."

"Once I would have laughed at such a suggestion," he grumbled. "And I really do long for the days when I can do so again."

"It'll happen."

"I hope so, because I really don't want my wife risking her life traipsing around the bush after all manner of demons on a daily basis for the rest of our lives."

"You should be aware that said wife is never going to be a stay-at-home mom. She will always work, be it at the café or chasing the occasional supernatural invader."

"That is totally your choice and decision to make, one I'll support no matter what you decide. But I'm nevertheless putting it out there to the wider world that an easing of the risks everyone takes to protect this place would certainly be appreciated."

Amen to that. "You're just salty because we haven't had a minute to ourselves."

"I want *far* more than a mere minute." He paused, and then chuckled. "Though let's be honest here, the first time we get back into the swing of things might just be a little too quick for either of us."

"I shall temper my expectations for our first session, then." I glanced toward the front door as a car horn blasted out the front. "That'll be Monty. See you soon."

I hung up and grabbed my backpack, thankful now that I'd followed instinct and not tucked the knife back into its compartment. Belle handed me two paper bags as I whizzed by, though the luscious scents rising from them said neither contained Monty's requested Heaven on a Plate.

His old Ford was parked in the no-standing zone out the front of the café. I jumped in and handed him his slice before doing up my seat belt.

He opened his bag and peeked in. "A Clinkers slice. Not quite what I was hoping for."

"What you were hoping for isn't practical to eat while driving."

"Sadly true. Did she manage to save me some? Or did the locusts consume it all?"

I snorted. "She saved you a slice and had to fight off said locusts to do so. They are fierce when it comes to cake."

He laughed and took a bite, munching on it in appreciation as he one-handedly threw the car into gear and took off. Tires squealed in the process, and the whole car rattled. I resisted the urge to reach for the "oh shit" handle; the car was perfectly safe no matter how ready it sounded to fall apart. He'd even recently fixed the damn brakes.

He swung left and then said, "Did Belle tell you I was searching the demonology archives for any information on basilisks today?"

I nodded. "She also said you had a meeting with your parents to inform them of your impending nuptials—how did that go?"

He grimaced. "There wasn't what I'd call giddy excitement at the news, but they did accept it far better than I thought they might."

"Well, that's good, isn't it?"

"I guess." He shrugged. "To be honest, I think what swayed their opinion was the fact that, through Belle's connection to you, they now have a link to one of the highest profile families in Canberra."

"They've had that link since forever." I mean, he was my cousin after all.

"On paper? Yes. In reality? Our two families aren't exactly chummy." He shrugged. "But the recent hullaballoo in Canberra and Belle's part in it has them believing her deep connection to you gives them a greater chance of reconciliation."

"Wait until they find out said connection remains broken."

He glanced at me, eyebrows raised. "You've patched things up with your mom. That's something."

"Patching things up would be a more correct term. There's a long way to go." I took a bite of the slice. Mine was full of pink Clinkers from the look of things, which were my favorite. "Did you find anything on the basilisk?"

"Yeah, that there's not a whole lot out there." He grimaced again. "I did find one demonology text that said basilisks are rare demons and difficult to summon."

"Which makes it even more odd that Marie went to the trouble of doing so here. It has to have something to do with Maelle."

"I'd presume so, though I can't imagine either her or any of her people randomly roaming the woods."

Having previously seen a couple of her feeders, I certainly couldn't imagine it either. "Aside from the fact regular snakes *are* found in suburbia, I'm thinking the basilisk won't really be bothered by the location of its prey. Where was the body found?"

"On one of the walking tracks in the Fryers Ridge Nature Conservation Reserve, which is closer to Taradale than Fryers Town."

"Taradale is a midpoint between Blackwood and Castle Rock, isn't it?"

"As the crow flies, yes."

"As the snake slithers would be a more apt term," I said with a smile.

He rolled his eyes at me. "It does suggest it's heading for Castle Rock."

Because if it was already in the Taradale area, there were only two small towns now between it and Castle Rock —Louton and Campbell's Creek. Even if it had been called here to hunt Maelle's people, it was doubtful she'd allow them to live in either. I'd gotten the impression she liked to keep them close and generally did so by providing them with "appropriate" accommodation, usually in the most desirable locations in Castle Rock. Being a "fully kept" man or woman was one of the perks of being on call to a vampire's needs, apparently. Given Maelle seemed to have no trouble finding feeders, there were obviously plenty of people who had no qualms about becoming a blood bank for a blood sucker.

"Did you find anything further on killing a basilisk?"

"Nothing more than what we've already discussed, although you'd think that as a demon, what generally works on them would work on it."

"Don't know about you, but there is no way known I'm willingly getting close enough to a gigantic snake—or any kind of snake, for that matter—to stab it with a silver knife or throw holy water on it."

"I agree, but we have one advantage over the basilisk— we're capable of magic. It's not."

"The text said that?"

"Well, no, but it's a snake. It has no hands, and it can't speak."

"It's also a demon, and they can never be underestimated."

He glanced at me. "You're in one of your pessimistic funks today, aren't you?"

"When it comes to things going wrong at the worst possible moments, said funk is more often right than wrong. Did the text mention anything about turning victims to stone?"

"No, but it did mention freezing and instant death if you meet its stare, so that might be what the woman who found him meant."

"I guess we'll find out soon enough."

He nodded in agreement and finished off the rest of his slice. I did the same as I watched the scenery zoom past and tried to ignore the slivers of unease that rolled through me.

Slivers that were not caused by the possible presence of the snake but rather the sheer number of vibrations running through the old Ford. It was unnerving.

We finally turned right into a rather narrow and uninspiring road, and zoomed along until we neared an old bridge. A sign told us it was the "Main Channel," and parked off the road just beyond it was Aiden's truck and one other ranger vehicle. Monty stopped behind them, and we both climbed out.

Aiden was in the truck, talking on his phone, but Jaz—who'd not only become a very good friend but who was very much on my side when it came to my relationship with Aiden—leaned against the side of her SUV, her arms crossed as she watched us approach.

"I was hoping now that you were back from Canberra, things might settle down. Sadly, that hope was a rather foolish one."

"Well, technically, things *have* settled down," Monty replied, amusement evident. "The earth has stopped heaving, and rocks have stopped demolishing buildings and roads."

"The earth hasn't entirely stopped heaving if the reports I'm getting out of the O'Connor compound are anything to go by, but I meant creature-wise. Demons I can cope with, but a gigantic snake that kills flora as it slithers past? That would be a big fat no thanks."

"You don't like snakes?" Monty said, his amusement growing. "That must make things difficult, given all three wolf encampments are situated in heavy bush."

"There are such things as electronic snake deterrents, and I have a good dozen of them surrounding our house, trust me on that."

I wasn't sure such a deterrent would work on a demon

snake, but I thought it better not to mention that. "Has the woman who found our victim said anything?"

Jaz shook her head. "She went straight home, as ordered. Ric is over there now taking her statement. I don't expect we'll get much more than what she's already said, though."

Ricardo Pérez was the newest member of the ranger team and had transferred here via the reservation's exchange program—one designed to stop the problem of interbreeding—from a Spanish pack to be with his sister, who'd married into the Sinclair Pack. I'd yet to meet him, but he was, according to Jaz, the cheerful, unfazable sort.

I couldn't help but wonder if that cheerfulness would hold given the continuing threat of the supernatural. It wasn't like he'd come here expecting to be confronted by all manner of demons and mythical critters.

Aiden finished his call and climbed out of his truck. He had his "business" face on, but I nevertheless spotted the quick flick of excitement that ran through his gaze—one that echoed deeply through me. Even at the worst moments of our relationship—even when I'd walked away determined never to look back unless things changed—the deep connection that existed between us had never eased.

I doubted it ever would. There were some things that were meant to be. He and I were one of them.

Even if his mother refused to see or accept that fact.

That brief flash of excitement suggested something had happened. Something other than death.

Maybe the council had finally called a meeting.

Maybe, just maybe, they'd reached a decision.

For his sake, I hoped it was the one he wanted. I knew full well no matter what he said or promised, there would always be a distant cloud of discontent over our relationship if they stopped him fulfilling the destiny that had been his since birth.

He slung the pack he was holding over his shoulder and stopped beside Jaz. His gaze slid briefly down my length before rising to meet mine, and the bright flash of appreciation and desire that ran through his aura briefly muted the excitement.

"We have mirrors, salt, and holy water on hand," he said evenly, none of the turbulent emotions so evident to me remotely coloring his voice. "I'm hoping that'll be enough to protect us if this thing is still out there."

"It should be," Monty said, "but I'll nevertheless take the lead, with you directing me. Liz can bring up the rear."

I opened my mouth to object, then shut it again. Monty hadn't yet been updated on the recent developments between me and Aiden, so as far as he was concerned, we remained broken up. And while I had no problem letting him in on the secret, now was not the time. Though to be honest, I was surprised Belle hadn't mentioned it.

Aside from the fact it's not my secret to tell, you whisked him away before I could.

Monty is family—

And you can tell said family when you're ready.

Aiden motioned him toward the dusty track on the other side of the road and then, with a glance at me that held traces of annoyance at the obviously deliberate ploy to keep us separated, followed him in. Jaz picked her pack up off the ground and fell in step behind him, with me bringing up the rear. The trees closed in around us, but did little to ease the afternoon's heat. The flies swarmed, a black cloud desperate to get at the tiny beads of moisture dotting our skins, and the cicadas boldly belted out their songs to each other. The noise was deafening and made talking difficult, but it was also comforting. The insect world wouldn't be so loud if the basilisk remained in the area. They were generally too attuned to the danger snakes represented, given there were plenty around who didn't mind dining on them.

The track wound lazily through the trees, occasionally giving us glimpses of the nearly empty main drain before swinging away again. We were twenty minutes in when the scrub around us showed signs of dying off—and it wasn't the usual summer kind of die-off.

The basilisk had passed by here.

The path swept sharply left, and Monty and Aiden briefly disappeared. A heartbeat later, Monty swore.

They'd found the victim.

Jaz and I rounded the corner and then stopped either side of the two men. The victim stood in the middle of the path, wearing jeans, hiking shoes, and a singlet top. He'd been caught mid-stride but had obviously spotted the basilisk early enough to throw out a hand in denial. That was the moment he'd been frozen.

He didn't look to be stone, but he was obviously no longer mere flesh, either. Rigor mortis generally didn't set in until two or so hours after death, and that meant his arm should have dropped and his leg muscles given way.

Aiden glanced at Jaz. "You and Monty check the immediate area to see if we've any other casualties. The footprints indicate he might not have been walking alone."

Jaz nodded, and with a quick look at Monty, motioned him to follow her. Aiden skirted around the body, then stopped and sucked in a sharp breath.

"What?" I immediately said and moved around to join him.

The stranger's eyes had been burned away. There was

no blood, no gore, just blackened empty sockets where his eyes had been.

Horror curled through me, and my stomach briefly stirred. Thankfully, this time, the damn thing stayed put. "Well, the myths certainly didn't mention *that* happening."

"Which seems to be a theme with the entities we get here." He pulled several pairs of gloves from his pack and handed me one. "Can you sense any residual magic on or around him?"

I hesitated and scanned him carefully. "There doesn't appear to be anything, but let me touch him first, just to be safe."

I pulled on a glove then carefully reached out and touched one finger to his open palm. I might as well have been touching ice. In this heat, that was totally weird. But there was no reaction from the man's flesh magically.

"It's safe." I stepped back and hugged my arms across my chest in a vague attempt to control the tremors of unease rolling through me.

He pulled out his phone and began taking photos. Once he'd finished, I asked, "Have you any idea who he is?"

"No, but the woman who found him said his name was John Miller, the eldest son of one her neighbors. Apparently he'd only just returned home from a working holiday overseas."

I frowned. "That suggests he's not connected to Maelle."

"We won't know that until we discover more about him and talk to her."

He put his phone away and carefully patted our dead man down. There was no movement in John's clothes—no give. It appeared that not only had *he* frozen, but also anything connected to him. There was obviously a wallet in his front pocket and a phone in his rear pocket, but neither could be removed or checked.

I shivered again and hoped like hell that death had been instant. That he hadn't suffered, even if the state of his eyes suggested that likely wasn't the case.

"Ciara is going to have a hard time doing an autopsy on —" I stopped as the air around his body shimmered slightly. It wasn't the wind. It was a ghost. *His* ghost, if luck was with us.

"What?" Aiden asked sharply.

"I think his spirit is here. You want me to connect with Belle and see if we can uncover anything?"

"Worth a shot."

I nodded and immediately reached out. *You busy?*

I am if you call helping out Frank with the mountain of dishes busy. Her mental tones were amused. *What do you need?*

I think the victim's spirit might be here.

Think? Given your strengthening talents and the merging of ours, you should be able to see him if he was.

The air shimmered briefly, but I think he's too new for me to see.

Possible. Hang on while I go into the reading room and get comfortable. There was a long pause. *Righto, let's do this.*

I returned my attention to Aiden. "Start recording."

As he nodded and hit the record button on his phone, I deepened the connection between Belle and me, broadening it from a simple sharing of thoughts to one that was all-encompassing—a merging of metaphysical beings. There was no me here in this connection, and no her. There was simply us, even if her spirit remained anchored to her body via a tenuous ethereal thread—to do otherwise would mean her death.

John's spirit was indeed here, though he was little more than a hazy, almost glitchy figure that kept fading in and out of existence.

He's confused, Belle said, *and fighting the call to move on*.

A surprising number of spirits—especially the newer ones like John—did this. Sometimes Belle could help them move on, but there were always a few who had no desire to do so. Always a few who either refused to believe they were dead or simply had no desire to leave those they loved, even if it meant dooming their soul to never moving on once those loved ones *had*.

John, Belle said, her voice holding a slight whip of command, though more to gain his attention than any real need to force him to talk. Most ghosts were very happy to do so, if only to uncover what the hell was going on. *Tell us what happened*.

His spirit flickered, fractured, for several seconds before his reply came. *I don't know. I really don't know.*

I repeated everything that was being said for Aiden's benefit, though my attention remained mostly on the ghostly figure.

Why am I standing outside my body? he continued. *What's happened to me?*

You died—

No, he cut in. *I can't be dead. I'm here, talking to you.*

I'm a spirit talker, John. You're standing outside your flesh because you're currently refusing the call to move on.

I don't want to move on. I want to get back into my body. He paused, his insubstantial features turning toward us. The eyes that were black holes in his body shone blue in his death. *Can you help me get back into my body?*

You were killed, John. Your body is now incapable of

holding your spirit. You have two choices—remain here as a ghost or move on and be reborn.

I don't want to do either!

It was fiercely, angrily said. His form shivered as ghostly, half-formed fingers clenched. The man obviously had a temper, but thankfully, he was too new a ghost to be any sort of threat.

Tell us what you saw here today, John.

This time, that hint of command was meant to force obedience. John's figured shimmered briefly, as if in frustration, but he wasn't strong enough to deny her.

I saw a snake. A big fucking snake.

Describe it.

Four meters long, a head as big as a person's, and a thick torso. Its scales were so black they shone purple.

You didn't run?

Didn't get a chance. It reared up and hissed at me, and the next thing you know, I'm here, watching the thing slither past.

Were you here alone?

Julie was with me, but she ran into the forest the minute the snake rounded the corner.

Julie had good sense, obviously.

Did the snake go after her?

I don't know.

You didn't watch it leave?

I was too busy wondering what the fuck was going on. He paused, his ethereal body pulsing again. *Are you sure you can't shove me back into my skin?*

You died, John. Even if I could shove you back in, your body has already started the decaying process, and there is nothing I nor anyone else can do to change that.

Well, what fucking good are you?

No psychic or witch can force death to retreat once it has claimed its pound of flesh, John, no matter how powerful they are. She paused then asked me, *Anything else you need to know?*

Ask him if he knows Maelle?

She immediately did so.

He shrugged, the movement briefly tearing his filmy filament apart. *Don't think so, but I'm not good with names, so who knows.*

I don't think we're going to get much more out of him, Belle.

No. To John, she added, *Do you want to move on?*

What are my options?

Staying in this forest for eternity.

That doesn't sound very appealing. He hesitated, his wavering expression suggesting he wasn't happy, but grudgingly accepting of his fate. Which his words confirmed a few seconds later.

Belle immediately began the prayer spell that would help him accept the call and move on. His form shimmered again and then faded.

Belle sighed, a sound that whispered lightly through my being. *I don't think any of that was very useful.*

At least we now have a description of the basilisk.

Not sure how much good that'll do us right now. She grimaced. *Tell Monty to bring something home for tea. I'm not in the mood to cook.*

Will do.

Her being left mine. I took a deep, somewhat shuddery breath and then met Aiden's gaze. "You catch all that?"

He nodded. "At least we can put out a general warning about a large and aggressive black snake lurking around the outskirts of Castle Rock. The fewer people bushwalking at the moment, the better."

Werewolves—Jaz aside—were likely to scoff at the prospect of a black snake being dangerous, but humans might at least take some notice. I glanced around as Jaz and Monty reappeared.

"Find anything?" Aiden asked.

"No further bodies," Jaz replied. "And the scrub die-off stops at the channel."

"It obviously has a liking for water," Monty said. "How close will the channel get it to Castle Rock?"

"If it uses the Harcourt Channel—which flows into the Main Channel—it would be fairly easy to access Golden Point and the Campbell's Creek pine plantation."

"They run into Kalima Park, don't they?" Monty asked.

Aiden nodded. "And both would provide a plenty of areas for even the biggest snake to hide."

"Not to mention a good starting platform to go after its prey," I muttered.

"That would depend on who our sorceress has decided to send it after."

"And *if* she's decided to send it after anything," Jaz commented. "It could well be it was called here simply to cause chaos and keep us out of the sorceress's hair."

"Which is entirely possible if our sorceress *is* here for a little payback," Monty said. "I can't imagine either she or Maelle would welcome ranger interference if things get heated between them."

"I can't imagine they'd welcome our interference, either." My voice was dry. "But I'll go talk to Maelle—"

"Not alone," Aiden said sharply.

"I'm perfectly safe with her, Aiden. She can't magic me,

and the wild magic will prevent her biting me. Besides, she simply won't talk while you're there."

"She's cooperated with us before."

"This is different," I said. "It's personal—"

"It was personal last time," he cut in.

"That involved the murder of her feeders. This is all about her past and the woman who turned her. She won't share intimate details with you, Aiden."

"I can second that," Monty said. "They stopped me in my tracks when we talked to her yesterday. The only reason I knew what was happening was because Belle was cluing me in."

Aiden stared at me for a second and then slowly, reluctantly, nodded. "Fine. But keep Belle online, just in case."

"Always do when I've visiting a potential nasty." I dragged out my phone and took a photo. "I'll show her both victims and see if she knows either of them."

He nodded again. "I'll drop by for a report later this evening."

The sexy gleam in his eyes suggested he intended to be doing far more than simply getting a report, and my hormones did a happy little dance at the prospect.

I nodded calmly, though it was pretty obvious that Jaz had caught the undercurrents and wasn't buying said casualness, if the amusement evident in her expression was anything to go by. She kept her thoughts to herself, however. "Do you want me to escort you back to the car?"

And no doubt interrogate me on the way, I thought. I smiled and shook my head. "There's nothing out there that can hurt me right now."

And kept all things crossed that I hadn't just tempted fate as I said that.

"I'll stay here," Monty said, appearing oblivious to the

undercurrents. "It's unlikely our basilisk will do a U-turn, but it's better to be safe than sorry."

"I'll need to borrow the rattletrap's keys then, because I'm not walking home from here. Oh, and Belle said to bring something to eat back with you."

"You can borrow my truck," Aiden said. "The rattletrap isn't safe."

"I am offended on behalf of said rattletrap," Monty retorted, the annoyance in his tone countered by the twitch of his lips. "Her brakes were fixed a week ago."

"Good. Now fix all the other things wrong with her."

"Hey, she's street legal."

"Only just." Aiden tossed me the keys. "I'll walk around from the station to pick her up once I've written up the reports."

I nodded, pocketed the keys, and forced my feet to walk away from the man rather than toward him, as they wanted. It took me close to thirty minutes to get back to the road—it was too damn hot to hurry and there was no way I was going to risk heatstroke by doing so. Especially when the only water I had with me was holy water—something I'd have to remedy before I went out next time.

There *would* be a next time, and probably sooner than any of us wanted.

I tossed my pack onto the passenger seat, started up the truck to get the air-con going, then leaned across and opened the glove compartment. Aiden usually kept a selection of chocolates in there for me, but all I found were several small bottles of water and a dozen or so muesli bars. Which was better than nothing and no doubt due to the fact that the internal temperature inside any car or truck parked outside for very long generally skyrocketed, meaning chocolate would have melted within minutes.

I grabbed a bottle of water and a couple of bars to munch on the way, then threw the truck into gear and did a U-turn, carefully driving out of the forest before turning left onto the road back to Castle Rock.

I made my way through the backstreets to avoid some of the traffic, then once again parked outside Émigré. Magic buzzed around the building, the dark threads currently thick and easy to see—at least to those of us capable of doing so, anyway. The two guards remained at the door, neither of them sweating or even remotely looking uncomfortable, despite how oppressive the heat had become.

I grabbed my pack and climbed out of the truck. They watched me hurry across the melting tarmac and opened the door without comment.

It was so damn cold in the building that the sweat dotting my skin basically froze on the spot. I shivered and made my way through the plastic.

Maelle stood in the middle of the dance floor—which was no longer fire-stained concrete but overlaid instead with wood—frowning up at the ceiling. She was dressed in black, and it highlighted her paleness while emphasizing the deep richness of her lips. Vamps generally didn't need to feed any more than a few times a week—though I'd gotten the impression drinking small amounts from her feeders during their sexual encounters heightened the pleasure for her—so she'd either had an encounter very, *very* recently or she was "bulking" up her feeding regime in order to ensure she was strong enough to counter whatever Marie threw at her.

"I apologize for the temperature," she said, without looking at me. "It appears we have a problem with the thermostats. Would you like a coffee to take the chill off?"

"I'd prefer tea, if that's possible."

She nodded and continued to gaze at the ceiling. I

couldn't help looking up. A man hung precariously in midair working on the innards of what looked like some sort of control unit. He wasn't supported by harnesses, ropes, or even a metal platform. He was supported by Maelle. By her magic.

Magic I wasn't even feeling.

Fuck.

If she could hide her magic, then undoubtedly her maker could as well.

Fuck, fuck, *fuck.*

We were in an even bigger shitload of trouble than any of us had imagined.

So basically, it's business as usual came Belle's comment.

I snorted mentally, and the tension that had briefly risen eased. Which was a good thing, considering who I was standing next to. It was possible I might have misconstrued the reason for her lips' color, and a hangry vampire was not something I wanted to be getting on the wrong side of right now.

Or anytime, really.

The vibration of movement whispered through the floorboards—though I heard little in the way of footsteps—and I glanced around. Roger approached us, holding a tray that contained a teapot and a cup on a saucer, all of which were classic Royal Doulton, and a wineglass that contained a thick red liquid I very much suspected wasn't wine.

"Please, let us sit," Maelle said as Roger glided past us and headed for the only booth that was complete.

The electrician continued to hover. I hoped for his sake Maelle didn't get distracted.

I slid into one side of the booth, and she took the other. Roger then placed everything on the table and poured my tea. The sweet scents of jasmine and pear teased my nostrils. It was my favorite green tea, and while I hoped it was a lucky guess, I suspected it wasn't. She probably knew way more about me than I would ever discover about her.

Roger collected the tray and silently glided away. He didn't stop at the midpoint and look up at the floating contractor in order to act as her eyes, which made me even more nervous for his safety.

She raised her glass and took a sip of the thick liquid, her fangs extending to enable her to use them as a straw. It was a god-awful sight, and it took every ounce of control I had to not slide out of the booth and run far, far away.

"I take it something untoward has happened to bring you here again so soon."

I tore my gaze from her and warily picked up the cup. Thankfully, it hadn't been used enough to hold any sort of emotional echo.

"Three deaths in less than twenty-four hours," I replied evenly, "and I fear all of them will be linked back to you."

She raised an eyebrow, the movement eloquent and disbelieving.

"How so?"

"The first death was at a sacrifice site that called forth a basilisk."

"A demon snake," she murmured. "How appropriate."

"You fear snakes?"

"No. I conjured one that consumed many of her lovers."

"By mistake?"

"No."

Great. Just great. I took a sip of tea that did nothing to ease the growing tension in me. "The third was a man who'd come across the snake and was frozen on the spot. His name was John Miller—he's not one of your feeders, is he?"

"None of my current feeders are male, and I do not employ a man by that name."

"And never have?"

She paused, and the brief flicker of... not distraction but perhaps distance in her eyes said she was conferring with Roger. "No, we have not. What of the second victim? I take it this is the one you believe is connected most closely to me?"

I placed the teacup back on the saucer and got my phone, bringing up the photo I'd taken of Rosie.

"This is the second victim. You cannot deny the similarities in appearance to yourself."

She stared at the photo, her expression blank and her pupils pinpoints so small her eyes looked completely white.

It was yet another fucking awful sight.

After what seemed like forever, she raised her glass and took a sip. The blood briefly stained her canines before "melting" into the enamel. "I, of course, do not have a mole near my mouth, but I certainly know someone who did."

Did. Meaning they were dead. Given the few scraps of information she'd given me about her past, I wasn't sure whether that was a good thing or not.

Especially given that when it came to dealing with vampires—or at least those caught up in their webs of desire —dead *wasn't* strictly dead.

"Who, Maelle?" I asked softly.

Her gaze rose to mine, and the fury in them had me instinctively leaning back.

"My daughter."

CHAPTER SIX

"**Y**our daughter?" I said, shocked. "Do you mean a child you've given birth to or one reborn from your blood?"

"Fledglings are of our bloodline rather than our flesh, and they are never referred to as sons or daughters."

"But... how?"

Vampires *couldn't* reproduce. The changes their bodies underwent during the ceremony that gave them eternal life—unless someone stuck a stake through their bodies or they fried in sunlight, of course—not only rendered them incapable of eating, but also infertile. Which was a good thing considering how horny vampires seemed to become once undead.

Her smile was distant and fierce, all at the same time. "I was not born a vampire, remember. I was *re*born."

"Meaning your daughter was born before you turned?"

"She was my youngest. I had three in all, and two sons."

I hesitated, sensing I needed to tread warily, and yet at the same time, understanding that if I didn't push, she wouldn't answer. It was a fucking fine line to walk.

"Would they not have died long ago?"

"All except my youngest, Jaqueline, who followed me into this life and is a very powerful vampiric sorceress in her own right."

Is, not *was*.

As if we don't have enough family dramas to deal with already, Belle said.

I think every other family drama will pale into insignificance compared to this one. To Maelle, I added, "Did you turn her?"

"No. Marie did."

"With your approval?"

"Yes."

"And your daughter's consent?"

"Yes."

There was something in the way she said that—a slight abruptness and perhaps a whisper of... angst? ... that suggested consent might not have been one hundred percent. Perhaps her daughter had not fully understood the life she was stepping into, and that made me wonder just how old she'd been when Marie had turned her. The sexual age of consent was very different back then to what it was now, and these days, vampires tended to turn those close to —or older than—the legal age. At least from the little I'd seen and read about them.

"Was she one of Marie's lovers?"

"No. That I forbade. It was one of the conditions I placed on turning her."

I wondered what the others were and whether they were part of the current problem. But again, I doubted she'd tell me. "Then why would Marie be targeting women who look like your daughter?"

"Because my daughter was the only fledgling to survive my decimation of the coven."

"Why?"

It was a horrid thing to say, but nevertheless a valid question. One the saner part of me instantly regretted when her gaze snapped from my eyes to my neck, and she bared her teeth. Her anger was so damn fierce I could barely even breathe.

"Why would you even ask that?" Her tone was low and dangerous and my skin crawled.

"Because I wanted a real response rather than one that yet again skirted the truth."

"You are lucky I did not fly over this table and attack."

My answering smile was as fierce as the gleam in her eyes. This was a turning point. If I backed down now, if I apologized, she would no longer treat me as an equal. And that could get very, *very* dangerous.

I placed my hand on the table and let a couple of tiny sparks dance across my fingertips. I needed a reminder more than a threat.

The movement drew her gaze from the pulse at my neck, as it was meant to.

"Never forget, Maelle, that as deep, as dark, and as powerful as your magic is, I can and *will* counter any physical or magical attack on me."

She studied the dance of power for several very tense seconds, then smiled and leaned back, though the dangerous light in her eyes hadn't faded. One day she would test me. One day, it would be kill or be killed between us.

I had a bad, *bad* feeling that "one day" might be far closer than I might wish.

"My reaction was instinctive, and I apologize," she said

evenly. "But if you were a mother yourself, you would understand that no mother could or should ever contemplate killing their own flesh and blood, no matter who or what they had become."

I *was* about to become a mother, and it was interesting that Maelle didn't seem aware of that. But then, I was probably no more than five or six weeks gone, and there wouldn't yet be a heartbeat as much as electrical impulses she wouldn't pick up.

And even if you were further along, it is possible the wild magic would protect her, Belle said.

Protection is one thing, but nullifying sound?

Your wild magic has been reacting instinctively, and it's likely that will extend to your child, especially if she is destined to be Fenna. Maelle is a dual threat, remember, even if she has sworn not to drink from the unwilling or to kill within the reservation.

Unless she's attacked first. Which wasn't something I intended to do. Ever. And perhaps Marie had the same mindset, given that, at least for the moment, she hadn't gone on the bloody rampage Maelle and my instincts were expecting.

"If your daughter was Marie's sole surviving fledgling," I said, "why would Marie target a woman who looked like her? It seems an odd sort of warning."

"It isn't a warning as such. It is a statement of intent."

The penny dropped. "She intends to kill your daughter."

"I would presume so."

"Would your daughter have come here with Marie?"

"It is possible." Maelle paused and took another drink. Her canines had retreated slightly, but I felt no safer for it. "Very possible."

Getting information out of her was harder than pulling teeth. Not that I wanted to get anywhere near *those* teeth.

"Why would your daughter accompany the woman who is intent on not only killing her mother but also her? Surely she must suspect that is a possibility. I can't imagine any offspring of yours would be oblivious to the undercurrents and intrigues happening around her."

She nodded, regally accepting the compliment. "Unfortunately, as well as inheriting my abilities, she also inherited my nature—in particular, the ability to hold a grudge."

Suggesting she was every bit as powerful as her mother, and that was a scary thought. Two dark mages would be hard enough to deal with, but three might well break us.

"Does the grudge she holds stem from being turned without fully understanding the consequences?"

"More from the fact her lover was killed in the process of cleansing the coven." She half-shrugged, the movement eloquent. "I was unaware of their involvement, but it would not have mattered."

"If you had a problem with the coven or the way it was being run, why not just kill Marie?"

"Because, as I have already said, I could not until she attacked me personally."

Everyone else was fair game, however, Belle commented.

Obviously. I took another sip of tea. "Is your daughter capable of killing you?"

Surprise flickered across her expression. *That* was something she hadn't considered, and it made me wonder why, given her comment about grudges. "Perhaps. I've not seen Jaqueline since those long-ago events. She may have grown in strength."

"But?" Because there was one there, even if it wasn't

spoken out loud.

"I personally doubt it. She has too much of her father in her."

Was that overconfidence speaking? Perhaps, given Jaqueline was of her blood, and she'd had plenty of time to hone her skills.

"What prevents you from acting against Marie before she attacks you? Why isn't her invading your territory with obvious intent enough?"

"For those not born in covens, it probably would be. But it is a creed we agree to, a blood binding we must swear to, on rebirth. If we attack our maker without reason, we will be rendered undone. Forcing my hand is in fact the safest way to be rid of me, without Marie getting her hands bloody or risking defeat and death."

"Does that code go two ways? Can a maker kill her fledglings?"

Her smile was all the answer I needed. Which made me wonder if any of the fledglings she'd killed had been hers, and if not, what had happened to them. As far as I was aware, there were none here in Castle Rock, but maybe she simply kept them well hidden. Or maybe the bloody events of her past had for some reason dissuaded her from creating any more.

"Why did she call the snake, Maelle? Does she simply echo your past actions, or is there something deeper we should know about?"

"A snake featured prominently on my family's coat of arms, and it is a demon we can call at will. As I have said, it is what I used to cleanse the coven of her fledglings."

"Can you still call said snake?"

"If I wish."

"And will you wish?"

She laughed, a deep, almost sensual sound. I shivered, my fingers twitching as I resisted the temptation to rub my arms.

I didn't get an answer, however. All she said was, "She will not send a creature I can control against me. It is but a show of strength. I suspect it might also be a diversion, but not one aimed at me or mine."

Which was exactly what Jaz had suggested. "If your daughter attacks you or yours, we need to know, Maelle. The last thing this reservation needs is a war."

She studied me for a moment, then said. "If you or yours get involved in said war, it will not end well for any of you."

"Is that a threat?"

"No. A reality. Marie is not one to countenance any interference with her plans, and she is not bound by the same oath I am." She finished her drink and rose. "Be wary, Elizabeth Grace, because she craves power, and she will take what I do not."

Will, rather than attempt.

It was a statement of fact that chilled me to the core.

Maelle returned to her spot in the middle of the floor without a backward glance and once again gave her full attention to the contractor fixing the air-con.

I still couldn't feel or see the magic holding him aloft.

With a deeper sense of foreboding, I slid out of the booth and walked out. The air outside was so hot it hit like a fist in the stomach, and I was sweating in an instant. But as I hurried across the road, thunder rumbled ominously, and while it promised rain there was a part of me that couldn't help thinking it was a warning.

Things were about to get a whole lot worse.

I jumped into the truck, immediately started her up to

get the air-con blasting, then rang Ashworth.

"Darling girl," he said, his Scottish brogue a little stronger than usual, "what can I do for you on this shit of a day?"

I couldn't help smiling. "Not a fan of heat?"

"I live in Victoria for a reason, lass, and the predicted week of above average temperatures is five days too many in my opinion."

I laughed, even though I totally agreed with him. "Well, given the thunder I just heard, it's likely we'll get some relief tonight."

"From your lips to the weather entities' ears. Are you calling to see how two old men are coping with the heatwave, or is there something more sinister afoot?"

"The latter, I'm afraid."

"Ah well, you'd best come around and have a cup of tea with us."

"You're complaining about the heat, but still drinking tea?" I teased.

"It's a well-known fact that tea cools you down far better than a cold drink on a hot day. It regulates core temperature and keeps it at an even keel."

I laughed, delighted. He didn't often take the bait. "I'll see you both in a few minutes."

"I'll put the kettle on straight away, then."

I turned around and drove over. Ashworth and his partner, Eli—who had worked for the Regional Witch Association, but was now retired—lived in a gorgeous white weatherboard, red tin-roofed miners' cottage that still held all of its original features despite the fact it had been fully renovated and contained all the mod cons. I pulled up in front, then grabbed my backpack and walked down the path lined with flowers and roses. Despite the heat, none of them looked wilted. They were probably the only things in Castle Rock that weren't.

The door opened as I approached, and Ashworth ushered me in with a quick, "Hurry up before the cool air escapes."

I grinned and headed down the central corridor—the walls of which were a soft gray with white accents on all the fretwork—and entered the kitchen living area that dominated the entire rear of the house.

Eli swooped in, gave me a hug, then ushered me toward the table where scones and a pot of tea were already waiting.

"They may not be up to your café's standard, but they are pretty good all the same, if I do say so myself."

I laughed and sat down. "With Ashworth grumbling about the heat, I'm surprised you were even allowed to turn the oven on."

"Heat will never get between Ira and a scone." Eli cast a lovingly amused look his partner's way. "We all joke about the depth of Monty's love for cake, but Ira isn't that much behind him."

"No one could ever rival Monty when it comes to cake," I said. "Trust me on that."

A grinning Ashworth picked up the teapot and poured three cups, sliding one across to me before sitting down opposite. "So, what's your problem, lass? I take it we have another beastie infestation to take care of?"

"A basilisk, and the vampiric sorceress who summoned it."

Ashworth leaned back in his chair. "I'd heard Maelle was back in town, but why would she—"

"She didn't," I cut in, and quickly updated them both.

"All of which basically means we're about to be caught

in a bloody war between two crazy but powerful vampires," Eli said when I'd finished.

"Maelle isn't crazy," I said.

"That would depend on your definition," Ashworth said. "In my mind, anyone who bathes in the bloody remains of their victims falls on the wrong side of it."

He'd obviously read the reports on Clayton's death. While I hadn't, I'd all but witnessed Maelle doing that same thing with the remains of an attacker up in her crow's nest.

Did I feel any sort of guilt over the actions she'd taken to destroy Clayton? Not one solitary shred. Not after what he'd done to Belle. If I could have danced in his remains myself, I probably would have.

And no doubt would have been violently ill afterward.

"I don't suppose either of you have dealt with a basilisk before?"

"No," Ashworth said. "And thank God for that. They're nasty beasties by all accounts."

I sighed and reached for a scone. "Then have you any ideas on how we're going to track the thing?"

"We could try a weasel," Eli said. "From the little I've read, they're one of the few creatures a basilisk fears."

"Weasels aren't exactly large critters, though, and this snake is."

"Won't matter. If we can get hold of several, we could possibly drive the basilisk into a trap—one lined with mirrors."

"Which of course leads to the obvious question—how the hell are we going to get hold of weasels at such short notice?"

And even if we could, how were we going to ensure they went after the basilisk rather than regular snakes?

"I'll contact the association and see if they can give the

name of a wrangler able to take on the job at short notice."

Amusement twitched my lips. "A weasel wrangler? Such things exist?"

"Yes, indeed," Eli said. "Whether RWA has any on their books is another matter entirely."

"Why would they have a weasel wrangler on their books?" I asked, amusement growing.

"Because while RWA might be the government body charged with dealing with adverse situations involving witches, there are plenty of situations that arise that involve shifters and the like."

"I'm still not seeing why they'd be needed."

He laughed. "Weasels are very good at hunting smaller prey, and not all shifters are the majestic kind. I know for a fact the association has several rat shifters on their books. I'm not aware of any weasel shifters, but it's certainly a possibility and doesn't hurt to ask."

"Imagine being landed with either a rat, weasel, or, God forbid, a damn snake as your alternate form. Poor sods."

"In many cases," Ashworth said, amusement creasing the corners of his eyes, "a common rat, or indeed snake, can go places that a wolf or eagle could not."

I remembered the magpie shifter I'd met in Canberra and the ease with which he'd flown around. I guessed, given rodents and snakes could be found absolutely everywhere, right across the globe, it would make those shifters a valuable asset for any law enforcement entity.

"I still pity the rat or snake shifters," I said. "Their animal counterparts are almost universally hated, and that's got to be hard on them."

I grabbed the jam and cream, slathered both onto my scone, and took a bite. Eli might have claimed they weren't as good as ours, but one taste was enough to disprove that.

"Which is why not all shifters advertise their alternate forms." Ashworth glanced at his watch. "I'll contact the office once you leave and get the wheels turning. It might take a few days to get anyone here though."

"It might be worth seeing if we can map its movement in the meantime," Eli said. "Should be easy enough to do if it does kill foliage as the lessons say."

"Tracking it could be dangerous."

"Not if they keep their eyes down and run the minute they scent it getting close," Ashworth said. "A wolf should be able to do so long before it crosses into the danger zone."

I nodded. "I'll ask Aiden to get some of his people on to it."

Eli raised an eyebrow. "Does that mean you've finally stopped ignoring the man?"

"Indeed, it does."

"And?" Ashworth asked impatiently when I didn't go on.

"And he asked me to marry him."

With ecstatic whoops that put Belle's to shame, they leapt up, ran around the table, and wrapped me in fierce and loving hugs, their utter and very real joy for me forcing me to blink back tears.

I laughed and pushed them both back. "It's too damn hot to be hugging like that."

"I'm so pleased for you, lass." Ashworth dropped a kiss on my cheek before moving back around the table. "Have you set a date yet?"

"No, and we won't, not until the council has made its decision on him becoming alpha." I explained the situation and Aiden's intentions.

"You know," Eli said, in a wry sort of tone, "he could

have avoided so much angst and heartache if he'd just sat down and explained his plans to you initially."

"I know. More importantly, so does he. He's promised to do better in the future, but I'm not holding my breath hoping for an immediate miracle."

"I wouldn't be either. The lad's an alpha, and they come with certain traits that are very ingrained." He paused, gaze narrowing slightly. "Did you tell him about the pregnancy?"

"No, and I won't. Not until he's confirmed as alpha and our engagement is officially announced. I don't want it used against me. Us."

"Fair enough." He munched on his scone. "I shall treat the lad a bit more nicely, then, seeing as he finally came to his senses."

I laughed, and the conversation moved on. But just as I was about to leave, a tiny thread of sunlight peeking through one of the closed blinds reminded me of another problem. "Eli, did you ever finish the translation on that book?"

The book I meant was *Earth Magic: Its Uses and Dangers*, an obsolete and rather obscure book written in Latin that Monty had found in Canberra's archives. Earth magic was what the wild magic had originally been called, and it was through this book that we'd discovered the information about the Fenna and how they were created.

"No, sorry. What with all the Canberra business, it completely slipped my mind." He studied me shrewdly for a moment. "Why? Haven't the problems the wellspring was causing settled down now that you've returned?"

"To an extent," I said, "but there's not as many wild threads floating about as usual, and it worries me."

"It could simply be that all the protection and containment spells we've looped around it are finally having an effect."

I was shaking my head before he'd even finished. "It's more than that. There was an odd sense of urgency in the thread that came to me yesterday, and I've got a bad feeling there's something going on we need to know about."

"I'll get straight back to reading it, then," Eli said, "but have you tried talking to Katie?"

I shook my head. "Haven't had the time, to be honest."

"Might be worth finding the time," Ashworth said. "If there *is* something going on with the older wellspring, then surely she'd know about it, given her merger with the newer one."

"Make sure you take plenty of water with you," Ashworth said. "It's a hell of a walk getting to that place, and we don't want you getting heatstroke."

"Not that either of us actually know what sort of walk it is," Eli added wryly, "given we never really got that far."

That was because a Marin werewolf had heard them way before they'd ever gotten near the wellspring, despite the fact they'd been using a spell to cover their presence. Even if the wolf hadn't been near, I personally doubted either Katie or Gabe would have let them enter the clearing —the pair protected their haven fiercely.

I kissed them on the cheeks and then quickly scooted out the front door to avoid letting much cool air escape. Dark clouds were gathering, blown toward us by a strengthening wind, suggesting the storm would hit us later tonight.

I jumped into the truck and started her up to get the air-con going again, and then reached out to Belle. *How busy is the café? Do you need me there?*

It's calmed right down now that we've been eaten out of cake again. Her mental tones were dry. *Why? What do you want to do?*

Thought I might head up to see Katie. I want to talk to

her about the wild magic. Meaning I was totally ignoring the advice just given, but I couldn't escape the notion that it needed to be done sooner rather than later.

What's wrong with the wild magic?

There's not much of it about at the moment, and the stuff that is holds an undefined urgency.

Maybe it hates foliage-killing, flesh-freezing snakes as much as we do.

I laughed. *Well, anything with any sort of sentience would.*

Are you going to come back for the SUV?

You don't need it to go home?

Monty's picking me up in an hour. He's planning to let me run into the fish and chip shop while he keeps the rattle-trap and the air-con running.

I snorted. *How very generous of him.*

His words exactly.

I grinned. *Leave me a list of anything you don't get done, and I'll finish it tonight.*

I thought Aiden was coming around?

He is, but not until later, so I'll just head straight to the wellspring. It'll save a little time.

Ah, okay. Drive carefully on that damn road, though. Aiden won't be pleased if you write off his truck.

Surely even I couldn't be unfortunate enough to roll a vehicle off that road a third time.

She groaned. *Did you have to say that? You know fate can never resist a challenge.*

I laughed again. *Okay, so maybe I will drop by and grab the SUV. It's full of bullet holes anyway, so if I do roll it, it's not going to do too much more damage.*

Maybe not to the SUV, but you're a different matter. Please stop tempting fate.

With a deepening grin, I threw the truck into gear and then headed back to the café. I parked next to our SUV, ducked into the café long enough to grab a mirror, a bottle of cold water, and something to munch on—this time a simple lemon slice so I didn't have to worry about the chocolate melting—then jumped into the SUV and headed off again.

As I drove out of Castle Rock, I switched on my favorite Spotify playlist, flicked the volume up, and sang along, loudly and more than a little off-key. There was no better way to relax—well, there actually was, but Aiden wasn't here right now, and the SUV wasn't what I'd call comfortable for that sort of thing anyway, especially in this heat.

The turnoff leading to Katie's wellspring lay a few kilometers from the Castle Rock side of Maldoon. I slowed as I neared and swung onto it cautiously. The other times I'd gotten into trouble up here had been when it was pouring rain, but a dry and dusty road full of potholes could be just as dangerous. I did my best to keep away from the soft edges and the long drop into the heavily treed valley below, and managed to reach the narrow track leading up to the parking area on the edges of the Marin's boundary line without any problems. While this track didn't have the dangerous drop down into a heavily treed valley, the potholes were deep enough to lose a tire in. It was a relief when I was finally able to stop.

I grabbed my phone, keys, and the bottle of water, then tucked the backpack behind the back seat, where it'd be hidden from a casual glance. While it was unlikely anyone other than a werewolf would be wandering past, the last thing I needed was to lose the silver knife. The things were hard to come by, especially in a werewolf reservation.

I locked up, then began the long climb up the dusty

track. The bush was full of sounds, although the noise coming from the cicadas just about drowned everything else out. The scents lingering on the heated air told me I wasn't alone up here, but there were no wolves, just rabbits and snakes. Regular snakes, not the flesh-freezing demonic kind.

Not that *that* made me feel any safer. Snakes of any kind could stay the fuck away from me, thank you very much.

I was puffing badly by the time I reached the halfway point. I was reasonably fit these days, but the heat was strength-sapping. My damn crop top was dark with sweat, and my shorts were making my thighs feel like they were encased in an oven.

I hated summer, I really did.

I took a long drink and noticed for the first time that there wasn't much in the way of wild magic floating about. Usually, I'd be surrounded by the stuff by now.

I capped the water and continued on. It wasn't until I was a few minutes away from the clearing that the luminous threads appeared, filling the air with a song both alien and beautiful. It was a song I'd heard intermittently, if distantly, over the years but had never known its source. I'd always put it down to little more than my wild imagination, when it had in fact been the wild magic calling me, seeking me.

Or rather, seeking to unlock what had lain locked inside me.

This song did hold wisps of concern, but there was nothing that suggested Katie thought the reservation or her family were in immediate peril.

I made my way through the final few trees but paused at the edge of the clearing. It was small and strewn with rocks, thanks to the distant landslip that had taken out a good portion of the cliff directly opposite. At the base of the slip was an ankle-deep rock well. The water bubbling up from a seam near the cliff's base lapped over the edge of the basin, then wound down the gentle slope, eventually joining the larger streams farther down the mountain. Unlike many other tiny streams in the area, this one had not evaporated in the heat.

But that tiny well was the source of the wild magic, and the air above it shimmered with its force. Its output had increased while I'd been away in Canberra, and that made me wonder if the increasing power here had anything to do with the decreasing amount coming from the older well-spring. While they were separate entities, all wellsprings had the same source—the deep heart of the earth's outer core. No one alive today understood why it had developed into a collective force, or how it found its way to the surface through the springs, but the ancients certainly had—and just *why* we'd lost that knowledge was one of the great unanswerable mysteries.

It did seem natural that the increasing luminosity of one spring would decrease another, but that might be nothing more than wishful thinking on my part. Or, more possibly, a desperate attempt to explain a situation I didn't understand but feared would yet cause major problems.

I walked on, accompanied by the gentle song of the wellsprings' moonbeam-bright threads, a sound that was completely in tune with the bubbling water. Katie stood next to the spring, her form solid rather than ghostly, although if you looked hard enough, the wellspring's shimmer was faintly visible through her figure. She was a typical O'Connor in looks—tall and rangy, with short blonde-brown hair and a sharp but pretty face. She was, basically, a younger version of Ciara.

Standing beside her was a much wispier figure of a man

with scarlet hair. Her husband, Gabe, whose soul was destined to haunt this place forever.

"What brings you to our place of peace on a day as unpleasantly hot as this?" she asked, her voice soft and melodious.

I stopped several yards away, though it was still close enough to feel the caress of the wellspring's energy. The hairs on my arms and the back of my neck rose in response, and the power within me answered in kind. Sparks danced around me, bright and joyous.

"I was just wondering if you have any idea why there's an odd sense of urgency emanating from the older wellspring."

"No." She wrinkled her nose. "Its rumblings have eased, but the attack on our compound continues, even if they're now only minor."

"You can't do anything about it?"

She waved a hand, frustration evident. "No. While initially it seemed I might have some control over that spring, our merger has appeared to cease."

"I personally suspect it's due to your growing connection to that spring," Gabe said. "As it develops, ours fades."

I glanced at him. "Did you expect that to happen?"

"Her soul is bound to this wellspring rather than the older, so I was never under the impression we would totally control both. It would have been helpful, though, given neither of us know what will happen once your soul moves on from this life to another."

I frowned. "My link should bind me to it after death, shouldn't it?"

That's certainly what precognition was suggesting, but would that actually happen now that I was pregnant? Every instinct said my daughter would one day control it in ways I never could or would, so perhaps she would be the true heir.

Besides, from what Eli had read of the book so far, there'd been no mention of the binding being *soul* deep, and surely there would have been if the price of binding was future rebirths.

"I wouldn't have thought so," Gabe replied, all but echoing my thoughts. "The wild magic that resides in your DNA is strengthening the connection to the old spring, but only, I suspect, because it was unprotected when you arrived here, and your magic infused the area when you placed your protection spells around it."

I wrinkled my nose and sat down on one of the bigger rocks near the wellspring. Its power washed over me, warm and inviting. Just what it was inviting me to do, I had no idea. If Katie knew, she wasn't saying.

"It came to me when I was in Canberra."

"Did it?" He sat down opposite me and scratched his chin. "I guess, given you control it in ways no one has for hundreds if not thousands of years, that is not unexpected. There is so much we simply do not know about the springs these days."

"When you were researching the binding spell and came across the references to the Fenna, did it say *why* a binding spell was needed if that binding happened on conception?"

"Nothing at all. As I said, information was scattered and hard to find." He frowned, his silver gaze distant but luminous. "It's possible not all Fenna were conceived in a newly formed wellspring—there is, after all, only a very limited number of them emerging over the course of a century."

"Walking into an established wellspring to procreate would endanger both parents *and* child, though," Kate said.

"The two of us are a great example of what exactly can go wrong."

"But it didn't go wrong," I said. "Your spirit *is* bound, as intended."

"Yes," she answered, "but we certainly never intended for me to die straight away—we'd hoped the spell would simply ensure that on my death, my soul would remain here. And we certainly never intended for Gabe to die alongside me."

"I'd say that was due more to the fact he was working on gut instinct and scraps of spell information. Hate to say it, but the fact it was successful was probably due to good luck rather than meticulous groundwork."

He smiled. "Sometimes the best spells are those that rely on gut instincts."

That was a motto I lived by. I took a drink, more to keep my fluids up than because I was actually thirsty. The air around the wellspring's pool was surprisingly pleasant. Maybe Katie was using the wild magic to keep the worst of the heat out. While she was a soul ghost and he a regular one, and neither should in any way be affected by the heat, her comment when I arrived suggested they were at least aware of it.

But then, I knew as little about soul ghosts as I did Fenna.

"It is also possible," he went on, "that the spell went awry because neither of us have Fenna in our bloodstream."

"And yet wolves are used in the creation of the Fenna."

"Yes, but I found no mention of them surviving. Has Eli found any such note in the book he transcribes?"

"Not yet; he's still working his way through it."

"Then perhaps he'll eventually find the answers," Katie said. "In the meantime, I'll continue to keep an eye on the older wellspring and will notify you if I sense any sort of change."

"Was there a change before the previous attacks?"

She nodded. "There was a distinct buildup of power within the compound, but I had no means of counteracting it or warning anyone of the problem."

Because I was in Canberra dealing with fuckwits—both the murderous kind and the not.

"Does that mean it's not gathering right now?"

She paused, her expression briefly distant. "It doesn't build up in the compound, but there is a gathering within the wellspring's basin."

"Is that usual?"

"No." She frowned. "I'll keep an eye on it."

I took another drink and rose. "I'd better go."

"Yes, you should." Amused delight bubbled through her voice. "It never pays to keep your fiancé waiting, especially when the betrothal has not yet been christened."

I laughed. "You were spying?"

"I was."

"I didn't see any threads."

"It only takes one, and you were understandably more occupied with my brother." She reached out, briefly pressing her hand on my arm. Though her fingers were ghostly, the touch felt real. Warm. "I'm so pleased for you both. You are going to make a very fine alpha, even if you are no wolf."

I laughed again, the sound disbelieving more than amused. "I wish I shared your confidence."

"Mom will come around."

"No, Katie, she won't."

She raised an eyebrow. "Care to make a wager? She can hold a grudge, granted, and the past has had too much influence on her actions and decisions, but she will see beyond it and accept what is best for the pack. I'm sure of that, if nothing else."

"I don't share that confidence, Katie. More importantly, neither does my precognition."

She smiled. "Do note that I didn't mention how long it would take her to accept it."

"Meaning I could be old and gray before that actually happens."

"By the time you're old and gray, she'll be dead. It'll happen well before that, I'm sure."

I snorted, but didn't bother saying anything else. We'd find out eventually which of us was right. I said goodbye and headed back down the hill, accompanied much of the way down by the luminous threads. I was sweating profusely by the time I reached the SUV, and I was tempted —very tempted—to detour past one of the many swimming holes scattered about the area on my way home and take a dip. But once again, I'd spent way more time up at the well-spring than it had appeared, and it was now close to six. I needed to get home and have a shower before Aiden came over.

I turned the SUV around and headed back down the rutted, pot-holed track, then turned onto the road. Dust plumed behind the SUV, turning the sky behind me a dull shade of brown.

In the middle of that brown, a shape appeared.

A shape that was large and sinewy.

My heart leapt into my throat, and for a moment, I couldn't breathe.

The basilisk was behind me.

CHAPTER SEVEN

I was tempted to hit the accelerator and get the fuck out of the area as fast as I could, but I resisted. Aside from the fact that I'd most likely end up toppling down the steep hillside to my right again, the basilisk didn't appear to be gaining ground.

That it could even keep pace with the truck was fucking scary.

I flexed my fingers against the steering wheel, sending little sparks of energy flying, and then reached out to Belle.

You busy?

Nope. Why?

It would appear I've attracted the attention of the basilisk.

I glanced again at the rearview mirror. It was still there, getting no closer, but not falling away either. I wondered if that was intentional. It was a *demon* snake, after all, and demons weren't affected by the same constraints as the rest of us.

What? Fuck. Her thoughts went offline for a second, no doubt while she told Monty. *Where are you?*

On the old road that heads toward Katie's track, about a kilometer away from the Castlemaine—Maldoon Road.

Another pause. *Monty wants to know what the hell it is doing up there.*

I think the more pertinent question is, how has it gotten here without being seen? You can also tell him I have no intention of stopping to ask either question.

She snorted. *Is it threatening you in any way?*

Not yet.

Keep moving. We're on our way. Let me know if the situation changes.

Will do.

I looked behind me again. Between the shadows cast by the overhanging trees and the thick plumes of dust, it was barely visible, and yet the odd glimmer of luminescent purple flickered across the top of its coils as it moved. It would have been pretty on something other than a demonic creature hell-bent on destruction. Was that why it was up here? If we backtracked its movements from here—followed the line of dying foliage—would we find another frozen person?

Maybe, especially if Jaz was right and it had been called here to keep the rangers and the reservation witches occupied.

But what if Marie was also using it to keep tabs on us? Or, at the very least, me? If she'd somehow gotten a sense of my connection to the old wellspring, that was a distinct possibility, especially if, as Maelle had suggested, she was attracted to power.

I flicked another glance at the basilisk, but no insights were coming from my psychic senses. Which in itself wasn't unusual—they could be annoyingly mute at vital times.

We at least had one thing in our favor—there were five

of us. *How* we could use our numbers to greater effect when it came to our rogue vampire, I couldn't say. My psychometry skills couldn't come into play until I found something to trace Marie with, and I really didn't want to risk using the wild magic, especially if she was already aware of my connection to it.

I guessed I *could* act as a lure, though that would be an absolutely last resort. It wasn't only my life I'd be risking now.

Up ahead, the road between Maldoon and Castle Rock came into view. I glanced in the rearview mirror just in time to see the basilisk slither down the steep embankment and disappear into the bush. I stopped, but resisted the urge to lock all the doors—the snake was more likely to break in through the windows if it actually wanted to grab or kill me —and warily reversed back.

No sign of the snake, although the scrub die-off had already started. I reached into the glove compartment, grabbed the small flashlight I kept there, and shone it out through the driver side window. Just for an instant, iridescent purple glimmered in the distance, then it was gone. The basilisk had moved beyond the flashlight's capabilities.

I reached out to Belle. *The basilisk just stopped following me.*

I hope you're not now following it.

Silly, I am not.

Reckless, you can be.

I laughed. *I think it might be more beneficial to see exactly what it has been doing up here.*

There was a beat or two before she replied. *Monty agrees. Where are you?*

Still on the road to Katie's wellspring, just before the main road.

We're probably about ten minutes away. Have you called Aiden?

No.

Might be worth it, just in case he decides to drop by the café early.

As the mental line went down again, I carefully turned around so that the SUV was pointing the right way, then pulled off road as far as possible and killed the engine. Though sunset was still a good hour and a half away, heavy clouds were now visible through the breaks in the treetops. That generally meant there'd be a glorious sunset followed by a summer storm. I hoped the latter was strong enough—long enough—to clear the buildup of heat, otherwise it would just make things muggier.

I called Aiden, but he didn't answer straight away. When he finally did, he sounded on edge.

"Liz, sorry to keep you waiting, but I was on another call."

"A 'we've found a frozen person' type call?"

"No, a possible murder." He paused. "I take it this isn't a social call?"

"Wish it was, but no. I was up talking to Katie—"

"Why? What's wrong?"

"I just wanted to ask if she knew why the rumblings from the older wellspring hadn't entirely settled down now that I'm back."

"And?"

"She couldn't say, because it appears she's been locked out of the older spring. But that's not what I was ringing for." I quickly updated him and then added, "I think we need to see why it was up here."

"I agree. I'll assign the murder investigation to—"

"It's pointless for you or anyone else to come up here," I

cut in. "If we find anything, we'll call, but it might well be a wild-goose chase."

"You're not going to follow it?"

"At the speed it was moving, it's pointless. It could be anywhere by now."

He grunted. It was not a happy sound. "Be careful."

"You, too." I paused. "Come back to my place when you're done."

"If we're dealing with another vampire victim, it could be *very* late."

"Aside from the fact tomorrow is Monday and the café is closed, I don't care. I want you in my bed and your arms wrapped around me, even if we are both too stuffed to do anything else."

He laughed, the sound low and so very sexy. "I will never be too stuffed to make love to you."

I grinned. "I will remind you of that when we have dozens of kids running around our feet."

"Dozens?" He sounded amused. "Big families do run in my family, but I wasn't aware you wanted a boatload of them."

"Now you are." I paused. "Well, maybe not a boatload, but four is a nice even number."

He chuckled. "Maybe start off with a potential two and see how we both cope."

"Plan," I said with a grin. "See you tonight, then. Love you."

"Love you too, my dear witch."

The silly grin stayed on my face for a long time after he'd hung up. I scrolled through social media while I waited for Monty and Belle.

As Monty's beat-up Ford pulled up behind me, Belle said, *Monty suggests we continue down the road until we find somewhere more suitable for him to park the beast, then we can all jump in one car.*

Which will be mine, not his, thank you very much. I think the nearest spot is the track that goes up to Katie's wellspring.

That'll do.

I started the SUV and drove back down to the track that led up to Katie's parking area, then pulled over just a little further up from the turnoff to wait for the two of them. Monty hopped into the front seat and shoved his pack into the footwell, while Belle jumped into the back.

"Onwards we go," he said.

I threw the SUV back into gear, then gave him a wry glance. "You don't have to sound so excited by the prospect of finding death."

"It's not death, but rather the chance to find out more about this thing. Do you know how rare basilisks actually are?"

"He's been in contact with some bods up in Canberra in an attempt to get more information," Belle said, "They've asked him to write up a paper on it for the main archives."

"And this is good because...?"

"Because I can use it as a stepping stone to submit other papers on creatures past and present later on down the track, when the reservation finally stops getting infested by evil."

"And it'll also keep him occupied and out of our hair," Belle added. "This is a good thing for our bottom line, given the copious amounts of cake he'd otherwise eat."

I laughed, and we continued down the road, following the line of yellowing foliage until it led off the road.

I stopped. Monty undid his belt and leaned past me,

staring at the obvious trail that led deeper into the forest. "How close are we to Marin territory?"

"Within sniffing distance." I hesitated. "Might be worth contacting Rocco to let him know what we're up to."

He nodded and immediately made the call. I climbed out of the SUV, walked over to what looked to be some sort of native gorse, and carefully touched a couple of spiky leaves. My psi senses didn't stir, so I "reached" deeper. Just for a heartbeat, emotions rather than images flowed across the outer reaches of my psychometry, but they were alien and cold, full of fury, hate, and darkness.

They were also filled with death.

I shivered and released the leaves. "Monty, tell Rocco we might need him to identify a victim."

He gave me a thumbs-up from inside the car and kept talking. Belle joined me on the track, my pack slung over her shoulder. "Would a werewolf be silly enough to be caught by this thing? Aiden has put an alert out, hasn't he?"

"For people to avoid the bush, yes. But werewolves aren't likely to take much notice of it, especially when they're on home ground."

Belle made an exasperated sound. "You'd think that, after a year of being invaded by all sorts of nasties, they'd actually take an alert like that a little more seriously."

"Except the general population—wolf or human—don't really know about said invasions."

She cast me a wry glance. "If the gossip brigade suspects there's been an unusual number of supernatural incidents of late, surely the rest of the population would."

I laughed. "I think you'll find that for most people—gossip brigade aside, because they'd give Sherlock Holmes himself a run for his money—if it's not in the local papers or on media sites, then it didn't happen."

"A sad fact that actually plays to our benefit." Monty stopped just behind us. "The last thing we need is reservation-wide panic or even vigilantes. Rocco said he knows roughly where we are and will find us."

"You've told him to ignore the scent of snake if he comes across it?"

He nodded. "Whether he heeds the advice is another matter entirely."

"He will. He's one of the more practical ones."

Besides, he'd had firsthand experience with the violence that came with the influx of evil and wasn't likely to go against advice. In this case, anyway.

"Technically," Belle grumbled, "they've all had firsthand experience, given the banishment we did during their last council meeting."

"I think you'll find many consider that a one-off."

"Then many of them are blinkered fools."

"I think most people could be considered blinkered when it comes to this sort of stuff," I replied. "Even witches."

"Especially those witches living and plotting against each other in the cozy little capital that is Canberra." Monty motioned toward the trail ahead. "Now, can we get moving? There is a possible dead person out there needing to be found."

I immediately headed off. "And yet again he sounds entirely *too* happy about the prospect."

"Hey, if my spirit was out here, confused and alone, I'd be wanting us to find me ASAP."

"If you get dead, you can be damn sure I will be giving your spirit the sharp end of a tongue-lashing." Though her voice was sharp, amusement ran through Belle's thoughts, which I knew without even looking at her meant her eyes would be dancing with mirth. "Your spirit, my dear fiancé, is not allowed to move on until we've had a long and happy life together and we're too feeble to do anything interesting."

"I will never be too feeble to do anything interesting with you, that I promise."

She laughed. "Oh, you can be sure I'll remind you of that when you *are* old and feeble."

"I look forward to it."

She snorted. "I'll remind you of that comment, too."

I grinned and kept moving through the scrub. While the die-off made the basilisk's trail easy to follow, heading up the steep and rocky mountainside was not. The air was thick and heavy with heat, and the sharp scent of eucalyptus hung in the air. I hoped the oncoming storm held off on the lightning. These forests were primed and ready to explode, and a strike could well have disastrous results.

The scent of sweat soon replaced the eucalyptus as the dominant force in the air, however. Even if Rocco couldn't hear us—and really, he'd have to be deaf not to—he'd surely smell us. I wasn't entirely surprised when he showed up a few minutes later, his expression bemused.

"With the racket you lot are making, your chances of catching *any* sort of snake are next to zero."

He was shorter and stockier than most werewolves, but a typical Marin otherwise—black hair that was currently cropped short, dark eyes, and brown skin.

"The basilisk has already left the area," I said. "We just need to see what sort of damage it has left behind."

He swung into step beside me. "Is it possible it was just passing through?"

"Possible, but unlikely," Monty said. "We believe it was

called here with the aim of keeping us and the rangers occupied."

Rocco nodded. "Aiden mentioned the new vampire in his recent update. I warned the council it was a grave mistake to let Maelle back in, but I was outvoted."

I glanced at him, surprised. "Maelle caused no problems until my psycho ex came on to the scene."

He grimaced. "I don't believe any predator can coexist with its prey for any length of time without problems arising."

"Werewolves are predators," Monty pointed out.

Rocco's snort was contemptuous. "Aside from the occasional rogue, we've never considered humans prey. Hollywood and literature are responsible for that belief, not our actions."

"Then why sign the agreement allowing her to set up business here in the first place?" Monty asked.

"*I* did not. Again, I was overruled." He half shrugged. "I grant that her venue provided the reservation with a sorely needed nightclub and has become a tourist attraction. I just fear the eventual cost."

I rather suspected he *wasn't* referring to the current situation.

Silence fell as the incline steepened, although it was only us witches who struggled. Rocco wasn't even breathing heavily, and he certainly wasn't sweating.

As the hints of a storm-clad sky became more visible through the leafy canopy lining the mountain's crest above us, we found death.

This time it was a werewolf, in wolf form. Her teeth were bared, her body twisted, suggesting she'd been trying to turn away from the basilisk when she'd somehow caught its gaze.

"Ah, fuck." Rocco stopped abruptly. "It's Suzanne."

I glanced at him sharply. "How can you tell?"

"Aside from the fact she was on patrol in this area, the scar on her cheek." He scrubbed a hand across his bristly chin. "Do you know why she remains in wolf form? Death usually triggers the change back."

"It might have something to do with being frozen." Monty stepped past me and approached the woman, taking care to avoid anything that might be considered evidence. Not that there was a lot more than the woman and dying foliage. "Belle, are you sensing a soul this time?"

She hesitated, gaze narrowing slightly. "No, but that might simply mean her death was ordained and she moved on quickly."

Monty squatted in front of Suzanne and frowned. "Well, there's at least one major difference between this death and the first—unlike John, her eyes aren't burned out. There's a bit of opaqueness in one half of her left eye, but that's it."

"Maybe she didn't catch its full gaze," I said.

He glanced at me. "If that's the case, why was she frozen?"

"Are you sure she's actually dead?" Belle asked. "Has she still got a pulse?"

"I don't know enough about wolf anatomy to check that." He glanced at Rocco. "Can you?"

Rocco stepped forward and placed his middle and index finger just behind her left elbow, close to her ribs.

"There *is* a pulse, but it's slow and irregular." He stepped back and grabbed his phone. "I'll call an ambulance —what's her breathing like?"

Monty raised a hand, placing it close to her mouth. "Barely there. Tell them to hurry."

As Rocco nodded and moved away to make the call, I said, "How the hell is she even alive? There's nothing in the mythology that suggests that's possible, is there?"

"Not as far as I'm aware," he replied. "But, again, we know so little about them. Perhaps her saving grace was the fact she only partially caught its gaze."

"Surely it would be aware of that, though," Belle said. "So why wouldn't it finish her off? Why leave her like this?"

"Why did it leave the other victim?"

"The other victim was dead," Belle replied. "Totally different."

Monty rose. "Is it though? Both victims are frozen, even if one is dead, and neither were consumed. If its sole task here is to cause mayhem, I can't think of a better way than to leave a trail of frozen bodies behind it."

"Even a demon needs to eat, though," she said.

And so do vampires. I glanced past Monty for a second, studying the tree line above. Instinct stirred, though I wasn't entirely sure why. I wasn't going to ignore it, however. "You and Belle stay here with Rocco. I'll head up to the top and see if there's anything—or anyone—else."

"You shouldn't go alone," Belle said.

"If the basilisk comes back, or our vampire attacks, it may well take two of you to counter her and protect Rocco and Suzanne."

"All the more reason for you not to go alone," Monty said.

I rolled my eyes. "Aside from the fact I have the wild magic on my side, I'll have Belle riding my mind. Which, in case you've forgotten, is almost as good as her being physically by my side."

He sniffed. It was a very unimpressed sound. I grinned, moved around our impossibly alive victim, and continued up to the crest. To say I was puffing and seriously regretting my decision by the time I reached the top would be a monumental understatement.

I stopped and bent over, my hands on my knees as I sucked air into my burning lungs. Pregnancy seemed to have made me even unfitter.

Is unfitter even a word? Belle commented, mental tones amused.

It is now. I pushed upright.

That was when I saw the woman in the shadows of the trees not twenty feet below me.

A woman with copper hair and pale, flawless skin.

A woman who looked, aside from the color of her eyes, an exact replica of Maelle.

That's impossible, Belle said. *Vampires can't move about in daylight. It's the one rule that can't be broken, no matter how strong the vampire is physically or magically.*

And yet, here she stands.

Are you sure she's real? It's not a projection of some kind?

She looks real... And yet, despite the fact she was upwind, her scent was absent on the breeze. It was, of course, totally possible she was using magic to disguise it but, this close, there should have been some indication of a spell, even if it was little more than a wisp of foul energy.

I cautiously moved closer. Belle's tension flowed through me, as sharp as my own. I flexed my fingers, then formed a repelling spell around them.

Jaqueline didn't react. Not in any way.

Was she real? Or was she simply a vision? A daytime dream that was little more than a warning of what might be?

I stopped two meters away. Even this close, she looked real, but her expression was vacant; there was no hint of life in her blue eyes. My psi senses were now suggesting that, despite the evidence of my eyes, no one *physically* stood in the shadow of the tree.

She was either a ghost or a projection of some kind.

I flexed my fingers again and felt the repelling spell expanding and contracting with the movement. "Why are you here, Jaqueline? What do you want?"

For several heartbeats there was no response, then she blinked, and her expression came to life. Her gaze swept me and came up... derisive?

"So, you are the witch who dances with the wilder magic of this place?"

My heart lurched. They knew. This was not a good development.

"Dancing with wild magic is never a wise thing," I replied as evenly as I could. She wasn't here and couldn't physically threaten me, but who knew what she was capable of magically. Not annoying her into retaliation was probably the best path to take, and one that had worked so far with her mother. "I repeat, why are you here?"

She waved a hand, an elegant movement that held echoes of Maelle. "I came with a warning."

"How did you know I'd even be here?"

"Through the basilisk, of course."

Meaning they were using the basilisk to keep an eye on things during the day.

It would certainly explain why it's only moving about during the day, Belle said. *They'd have no need for its eyes at night.*

Especially if Marie did have a number of fledglings with her.

"I was nowhere near this place when your demon saw me," I replied.

"No, but we knew you, like all good little witches, could not resist retracing its movements and ensuring there was no human detritus left in its wake."

Nothing like respecting your food source, Belle growled.

Jaqueline's attitude is probably a result of spending too much time with her maker and whatever coven remains, rather than mingling with the wider world like her mother.

I'm not sure the wider world or even Maelle's presence would have made much of a difference. She did destroy the original coven, after all. That's some pretty heavy attitude right there.

Yes, but why did she do it? I think if we get an answer to that, we'll also know why Marie is now so determined to return the favor.

Maybe not. As has been said, with great power comes great corruption.

I had no doubt Maelle's destruction had been a power play, but there had to be something else behind it—something *other* than simply deciding she didn't like the direction Marie was taking the coven.

Of course, I might also be giving Maelle far more credit than she was due.

I crossed my arms and stared at the unmoving figure for a second. She watched me implacably, and it took me a moment to realize she was waiting for me to say something.

"What is your warning?"

"You are not to interfere with what comes. If you do, you will be erased."

It was the way she said it—so casual and matter-of-fact—that chilled me more than the threat itself. "If what comes is a war between you, your mother, and Marie, then I'll not only interfere, but stop you all."

Her smile was derisive. "You can try. You will not succeed."

"It's never a good thing to underestimate your opponents, Jaqueline."

"I neither underestimate nor care what you think. I'm simply here to advise you of our intent. Concentrate your efforts on the basilisk, stay away from my mother, and do not interfere with what comes."

"Warning heeded." My smile was every bit as cold and as dangerous as hers. "Now, let me give you one. You need to walk away now, Jaqueline, while you still can. Because I promise you, if you start this, I *will* finish it."

She laughed. "Challenge accepted, little witch. Victory will taste sweet." Her gaze swept me. "Wildly sweet, in fact."

My skin crawled, but I somehow held back the shudder of revulsion. She bowed her head, a regal movement that reminded me of her mother, and then her image disintegrated. All that was left under the tree were the lingering remnants of her disdain. I sucked in a deeper breath that failed to calm either my pulse rate or my unease, then released the repelling spell and resolutely made my way back up the hill. The instincts that had led me to Jaqueline had once again fallen silent, and I doubted there'd be any point in following the basilisk's trail any further into the compound.

Was issuing such a threat actually wise? Belle said.

Probably not.

Then why do it?

Because when it comes to power, I suspect neither she nor Marie will respect anything less than utter confidence verging on vanity.

And I suspect neither she nor Marie have any respect for

witches at all. Hell, it's possible she doesn't even respect the wild magic, given her reference to the wildness in your blood.

That might be nothing more than ignorance speaking. Hell, we barely understand what is going on with the wild magic in my DNA, so they couldn't be expected to.

That doesn't alter the fact that they should at least be wary of your control over the wild magic and they're obviously not, Belle replied.

And giving them any sort of demonstration would only increase the danger. While Jaqueline might mock my connection to the wild magic, I doubted Marie shared that view.

We needed to find them. Fast. The longer they were out there, the greater the risk of war.

Maybe we should make use of the gossip brigade's superpowers, Belle said, *and ask them if they've noticed a large group moving into the area recently.*

Worth a shot, I said, *but you'd need to enforce the need not to go snooping too close to any large group they might find.*

Easy enough to do.

For someone as gifted in telepathy as she was, that was certainly true. *I might contact Katie and see if she can give the wild magic a similar task.*

Can't hurt.

No, especially when the wild magic could cover the entire reservation easier than any of us could. Werewolves might in the end cover ground faster—especially given the wild magic didn't appear to understand urgency in any form —but that would also place them in the path of danger, and that wasn't an option.

I silently called the wild magic, and, after a few seconds, several glowing threads drifted toward me. They were all from Katie's wellspring, rather than my own, which was somewhat worrying given it had always answered my call previously.

I really did need to find out what the hell was going on with it.

Several glowing threads wrapped themselves around my wrist. While I really didn't need the wild magic to converse with Katie outside her wellspring these days, doing so took less of a toll on my strength and possibly hers.

Katie, I asked, *is it possible for you to track the basilisk? We need to know if its movements are random, or if there's some sort of pattern happening.*

The creature moves too fast for the wild magic to give us up-to-date data.

Yes, but knowing whether we're dealing with random or systematic movements will at least give us a means of predicting where it will be next.

And *that* would make setting a trap a whole lot easier, especially if Ashworth wasn't able to get hold of any weasels to herd this thing.

And the vampire you spoke to?

Meaning her threads had been near enough for her to witness the exchange even if I hadn't seen them. *If possible, yes, but you'd need to be careful. They're obviously aware of my connection to the wild magic, but we don't need them realizing there's a second wellspring here.*

Their magic could not corrupt or break that which protects my spring.

Maybe not, but they could cause a whole lot of damage to the surrounding areas if they did make such an attempt.

True. I'll be in contact.

Her wild magic unwound from my wrist and floated away. I reached the top of the hill, paused for a breather, and then continued down the other side. Two paramedics were now on the scene, and one of them had placed a bag breathing mask—which had obviously been designed to fit the snout of a wolf—on Suzanne and was assisting her breathing.

I stopped beside Monty and Belle and crossed my arms, watching as Rocco and the other paramedic carefully shifted Suzanne onto the stretcher, strapped her in, and then picked it up and carried her down the hill.

"How is she?" I asked, as we followed them.

"Still alive," Belle said. "I tried to see if her soul remained or had moved on, but couldn't risk going too deep in case the magic bled over and trapped me."

"If her spirit does remain, how long do you think she can stay in that condition before death seeps in?"

"Impossible to tell." She rubbed her arms, her expression perturbed. "But to be trapped in one's own body, unable to move, unable to even scream for help, would be the closest thing to hell I could imagine."

Monty wrapped an arm around her shoulders and pulled her closer. "It won't ever happen to you. You have Liz to pull you out of such a hell."

She let her head rest against his shoulder for a second. "I know. It's just the thought."

"And here's another one." He slipped his arm from her shoulders to her right hand, twining his fingers through hers. "Maybe we should all start wearing those mirror sunglasses."

"Seriously?"

He grinned. "Of course. Totally."

"You know," I said slowly, "it's not such a bad idea. The myth doesn't actually say what size the mirror has to be, and some sunglasses these days are highly reflective."

"I guess it would be easier than whipping out a mirror every time we hear a rustle through the undergrowth," Belle commented. "Though there'll be some seriously raised eyebrows if we tell our rangers to put out a reservation-wide demand for people to start wearing the things."

"I would think the locals are getting used to strange requests from our rangers and council by now." He paused to navigate a particularly steep section of the path. "Belle and I can grab a few pairs on the way home if you like. The chemist should still be open."

I nodded. "I'll mention it to Aiden tonight."

And hope like hell nothing else happened in the meantime so that we could finally have some time together.

Although even putting *that* thought out there undoubtedly meant the shit would continue to hit the fan.

The ambulance had left by the time we got back to the road, and Rocco was nowhere to be seen, which meant he'd probably gone to the hospital with Suzanne. Aiden would have, had a member of his pack been caught in the same situation.

We climbed into the SUV, and after doing a careful U-turn, I drove Belle and Monty back to their car and then headed home.

To discover the magic that protected the café aflame.

CHAPTER EIGHT

There was no obvious cause for its activation out front, so I swung into the side lane and sped down to the parking area. I braked hard as I reached it, slewing the SUV sideways before coming to a rocking halt.

Someone lay on the ground in front of the café's rear entrance.

I had no idea whether he or she was alive or dead, but they certainly weren't moving. They were also completely covered from head to toe. Even their hands were covered.

Vampire, instincts whispered.

And, given the wild reaction of the spells protecting the café, he or she had probably been attempting to either break them *or* break in.

Had my magic killed them?

It shouldn't have—not in theory, anyway. But I guess it depended on what, exactly, the vampire had intended and how forcefully my magic had rebounded theirs.

I turned off the engine, climbed out of the SUV, and cautiously approached. The figure didn't move, but I couldn't discount the possibility that this was a trap. I had no sense of anyone else nearby, but that might not mean anything. This person couldn't have walked here so bulkily dressed because they'd have attracted too much attention. There were a couple of cars parked behind the shops to my left, but I recognized them both—they belonged to the couple running the vintage clothing store on the other side of the lane.

Maybe whoever had driven the person here had skedaddled when the magic reacted. Or maybe he or she had been magicked in while I'd been busy talking to Jaqueline. That *had* to be the reason she'd appeared to give her warning—it was a diversion.

You want us over there? came Belle's thought.

No, I'm fine.

Heard that before.

I couldn't help smiling, although it didn't do a lot to ease the inner tension. *Seriously, the café's magic has taken out the threat, and if anyone does jump out, all I have to do is run inside.*

Yeah, but you won't, will you? Your first instinct is rarely self-preservation.

I didn't bother denying it, because it was nothing but the truth. Although there *was* a repelling spell buzzing around my left hand, so my subconscious was certainly looking after me.

I reached the back step. After another cautious scan of the area, I leaned forward, slid my fingers past the coat hood and the thick scarf underneath, and felt for a pulse.

Nothing. Or, at least, nothing *detectable*.

"I believe you'll find life no longer exists."

I jumped and swung around, my heart racing and the repelling spell half released before I called it back.

The figure now standing a few meters away was decidedly familiar—and the last person I'd really expected to see right now.

"Fuck it, Roger, I almost blasted you to the other side of the parking area."

He was sharply dressed in crisply ironed cream pants and a short-sleeved shirt as pale as his skin. His arms were crossed, his expression amused, and he seemed totally unfussed by the cloying heat in the air.

"It would appear that I have more faith in your control than you do."

Maybe I *should* have blasted him, even if only to make him a little more cautious next time. "Why are you here? Do you know this person? I'm presuming it *is* a vampire."

"I was sent to investigate the reason behind your café's protections firing up, given how unusual it is." His pale gaze drifted to the clothed figure near my feet. "I have not examined the body as yet, so I could not tell you who it is. But given how heavily protected they are, I would presume *your* presumption is correct."

"So it's not one of Maelle's people?"

"She has no fledglings here, or indeed anyone remotely capable of breaking into your café, nor has she any need to hire someone. If she wished to enter this place, she could, as you have previously invited her in. And I have never intended you harm, so can enter unimpeded."

Never intended me harm up to the current point of time, anyway. That could certainly change in the future.

I glanced down at the figure again. "I take it, then, that this is one of Marie's people?"

"Undoubtedly." He walked over and stopped beside me. "It would not be a true adept, however. She wouldn't waste someone so vital when she most likely intended to do nothing more than test the strength of your defenses."

And now she knew them. Which meant I had better weave more spells around the place, just to counter future attacks. I might also add one revoking Maelle's access. Of course, if Maelle did intend me harm, it was unlikely she'd attack me in what was basically my seat of power.

But if there's one thing I'd learned over the last year or so, it was to never *over*estimate someone's intelligence. When it came to revenge, emotions often overtook common sense.

I rubbed my arms, doing my best to ignore the whispered warning of trouble ahead. It was a warning I'd had before when it came to Maelle, and one that was becoming ever more likely. "Is there any way to reveal his or her features without exposing them to the sun?"

"None whatsoever." He quirked a pale eyebrow. "Do you actually care?"

"No." I paused. "If it *is* one of Marie's people, will she feel the death?"

"She'll have severed the connection the minute she felt her creature's pain, thus ensuring it did not echo down the line between them."

I raised an eyebrow. "Does that apply to the connection you share with Maelle?"

"Our connection is somewhat different."

"Yes, because you've fed on her flesh and share her life force. That doesn't answer the question, though."

"My mistress has a higher-than-average pain threshold, even for a vampire. One could say it enriches her, even if it could never sustain her."

Which no doubt explained her penchant for swimming in the bloody remains of her victims.

I motioned toward the body. "Could you check?"

He stepped forward without comment, gripped the

figure's shoulder, and pulled them onto their back. They were wearing a thick leather face mask with no mouth or nose holes. There *were* eye holes, but they were covered by a thick black mesh of some kind. Roger slipped his fingers between the mask and the thick scarf, then roughly, brutally, ripped it off the vampire's face.

It was a man with pale skin, golden hair, and a thick long beard that was artfully plaited. Given vampires stopped growing hair after they'd turned, he'd obviously had it beforehand.

As soon as his features were revealed, his skin began to redden. Roger sniffed and said somewhat disdainfully, "We are not familiar with this person, but we know the lineage. They all have a hankering for ornamental facial hair."

The man's skin began to blacken and burn. I stepped back and used Roger as a shield. I didn't need to see the flames crawling over his skin, erasing his features even as they consumed his flesh and bones.

There was nothing I could do about the stench, however, and it grew ever sharper on the air. My stomach was *not* appreciating it.

"I take it he's one of Marie's fledglings?"

"No, he was one of my mistress's."

I blinked. "I thought you said she had no fledglings?"

"None here," Roger replied, his tone subtly changing. It was Maelle who was now talking. "I dabbled in their creation while I was with the coven, but decided it took too much time and effort. I am not the most patient of souls, and children—because in many respects, that is what the newly turned are, no matter what their physical age might be—are not something I ever wished."

Something that might well explain her somewhat

distant attitude to her own flesh and blood. "Does that mean this man survived the cleansing alongside your daughter?"

"He survived because he was not within the coven at the time and had the sense—and the control—to hide from my wrath."

The stench of burning flesh was getting stronger. I stepped farther away, but the scent seemed to follow me. My stomach stirred more vigorously, and I swallowed heavily. "So, Marie sent your fledgling here, knowing he'd most likely die."

"Undoubtedly." There was no emotion in Maelle's—Roger's—voice. No care. "It is the second warning. With the third will come war."

"You can't start a war, Maelle."

Roger glanced at me, pale eyes burning with Maelle's contempt. "While I have no intention of starting a war, I *will* finish it, as I have said."

I rubbed my arms again, but the chill was internal now, and I doubted it would leave until this whole mess was over. "Your daughter spoke to me via a projection spell this afternoon."

"And did she say anything of interest? Or did she merely warn you not to interfere, as I have done."

"The latter."

"And you will no doubt ignore the advice."

"Like it or not, Maelle, I am what amounts to the wellspring's flesh-and-blood protector. Remember that before you unleash hell on your enemies."

"Then stop my enemies before I am forced to."

"Does that statement encompass your daughter?"

"I have always been a distant parent, but I could not stand by and let you kill her."

"And if she tries to kill me?"

"Restrain her."

"And if I can't?"

Roger didn't reply, but he didn't need to. Kill the child, deal with the mother. I took another step back, as much to get away from the overwhelming sense of danger as the stench of death, but the bitter taste of bile now burned the back of my throat. I gulped in air in a vague attempt to control the rise but failed.

I spun, ran for the bushes lining the edge of the parking area, and lost everything I'd eaten over the day. When I finally turned around, Roger had gone.

Nothing remained of the vampire. Nothing except a vague scorch mark on the concrete and a few scraps of material drifting skyward on the strengthening breeze.

My stomach rolled again, but thankfully remained put this time. I sucked in another deep breath, then walked back to the SUV to grab some water and rinse out my mouth. Then I jumped in and parked it properly. After grabbing my backpack, I headed into the café, making sure not to step on the ashy outline perhaps forever burned into the concrete.

It was tempting—very tempting—to ring Aiden. Not because I felt unsafe or alone, but simply because I wanted his arms around me. Wanted him to hold me and tell me it would be all right, even though nothing could be until our vampires had either worked out a truce or killed each other.

But he'd already said he'd be here as soon as he could. I didn't need to be hassling him when he already had too many deaths to deal with.

Once I'd placed my pack into storage, I headed into the kitchen to make myself dinner. I might have lost my lunch a few minutes ago, but that apparently hadn't blunted my appetite any.

I threw on some steak and chips, and once both were ready, grabbed a bottle of sparkling water, then headed upstairs to eat my meal, watch some TV, and do a bit of research on the basilisk. Monty was right when he said there just wasn't much information out there—not even Belle's grandmother had collected much on them, which was a little surprising given how detailed her listings of other, lesser-known demons were.

It was close to ten by the time I climbed into bed, and to say sleep hit hard would be an understatement. I had a vague memory of the warmth of another body wrapping around mine, of arms holding me gently, possessively, but it wasn't enough to draw me from slumber.

When I did finally wake, I was alone in bed. But the pillow beside mine was dented and the musky, enticing scent of man filled the air. I hadn't been dreaming. Aiden had been here.

So why hadn't he woken me up? Or at least kissed me before he'd left?

The questions had barely crossed my mind when the bedroom door opened and he came in, carrying a tray and wearing nothing but black boxer shorts. It was a decided toss-up as to whether I was more excited by the heat in his gaze or the delicious smell of bacon.

"Your breakfast, ma'am."

His voice was low and sexy, and my hormones did their usual delighted dance. I sat up, well aware his gaze was all but devouring me. He placed the tray over my thighs then kissed me, long and slow. He tasted of toast, honey, and desire, and I sighed regretfully when he finally pulled away.

He chuckled softly, sexily. "Never fear, I plan to spend the entire morning in bed with you."

"So this"—I waved a hand toward the tray—"is a means

of ensuring I have plenty of strength for the planned activities?"

"It is indeed."

"I approve of this plan, then, though it has to be said, I would have been equally pleased to have woken up with your body already wrapped around mine."

"Tomorrow, perhaps."

"There will be no 'perhaps' about it."

He laughed again and moved around to the other side of the bed, stripping off his boxer shorts before climbing in beside me. His shoulder pressed gently to mine, a light touch that burned through my entire body even as his warm, musky scent filled every breath. It felt like heaven. Felt like home. All I wanted to do was lose the tray and make up for lost time.

But my stomach had other ideas, letting its dissatisfaction about being empty be known quite loudly.

I grinned, picked up a sandwich half, and bit into it. The toast was hot and buttery, the bacon cooked perfectly. I made a rumbly sound of contentment, and he laughed. "I take it that means you've changed your mind and now approve of my decision not to wake you."

"Sadly, yes. But you can use the time wisely and update me on what happened yesterday."

He grimaced. "Nothing all that much. It was a domestic rather than a murder, but the victim was bad enough to be taken to hospital. We spent the day tracking her partner down."

"The whole day?" I raised my eyebrows. "Did he flee in a car?"

"No, on foot."

"Then how did he manage to avoid you for so long?"

"Used a lot of trail tricks—walking in creeks and whatnot." Aiden shrugged. "He's currently locked up."

And would remain there until the court case, by the sound of it. While it was unfortunately common for domestic violence perpetrators to be released on bail, reservations were self-regulating and could set their own rules, as long as they worked within the general framework of State and Federal law.

"And what about the meeting you had with the council? Did you get to that?"

"No. It was rescheduled to one this afternoon, which is why I can't spend the entire day loving you senseless, as I'd planned."

I grinned. "Three quarters of the day will do just fine."

He laughed and dropped a kiss lightly on my shoulder. "I like this plan."

I unhurriedly finished my breakfast, and once I was done, he lifted the tray from my lap and placed it on the floor. Then, with a quick grin, he grabbed my ankles and slid me down the bed. The pillow behind me fell across my face, and with a quick laugh, he grabbed it and tossed it across the room. Then he stretched out beside me and pulled me so close that the heat of his erection pressed against my stomach and the rapid pounding of his heart echoed through my entire body. It was a beat my own matched.

He raised a hand and brushed wispy strands of hair from my cheek. "You have no idea how much I missed you."

I laughed softly and trailed a finger down his hip, feeling his flesh jump as I got close to his erection but didn't touch. "Oh, I think I do."

The smile tugging his lips was beyond sexy, and desire surged through me. Of course, desire had never needed much prompting where he was concerned.

His touch moved from my cheek and down my neck, a featherlight caress that nevertheless felt hot enough to brand. When he trailed his fingers across my breasts, delight shivered through me. He chuckled softly, then leaned forward and claimed my lips, kissing me slowly at first and then with more intent, until my heart raced, my head buzzed, and all I could think about, all I wanted, was him. On me, in me.

When he finally pulled away, I groaned.

"Patience," he murmured, then set about deepening desire—something I hadn't thought possible. For the longest time, we did nothing more than explore each other's bodies with hands and lips and tongues, and it was gloriously sensual and utterly frustrating all at the same time.

It was only when the air burned with need and our bodies were slick with sweat and wanting that he finally nudged my legs apart and slid over the top of me.

But he didn't slide inside. Instead, he held my gaze with his, those deep blue depths echoing the emotions that tumbled through his aura.

"I love you, Elizabeth Grace," he said softly. "I have since that first moment in the forest, when I saw you leaning over Karen's body."

Amusement bubbled through me. "You mean when you called me a witch in a most derogatory way and basically shoved a gun in my face?"

"Yeah, then." He laughed softly, a sound I felt through every inch of my body. "But that anger came more from my intense and totally unexpected reaction to your presence than the belief you had anything to do with Karen's death. I wanted you then as fiercely as I want you now. And I will always love you. Never, ever doubt that."

"I never did, Aiden. I just wasn't sure love would ever

be enough for you."

"Love will *always* be enough." His sudden smile was endearingly lopsided. "Of course, it did take me entirely too long to reach that realization."

"Just as you're taking entirely too long to get down to business."

He laughed again, then caught my lips once more and kissed me soundly as he slipped slowly, *agonizingly* slowly, inside. I groaned softly, then slid my hands down his back to his hips, gripping him lightly as he began to move, slowly at first and then with increasing need, until it was all passion, heat, and intensity. Until I was drowning in the storm of it but loving every minute. The rich ache grew, flaring across my body, becoming a kaleidoscope of sensations that washed through every corner of my mind. Once again, I couldn't breathe, couldn't think. I could only feel. Then the shuddering started, and I gasped, wrapping my legs around his hips to push him deeper still. Pleasure exploded between us, and my orgasm hit, ripping through my body, shuddering through my heart, my soul.

When I finally remembered how to breathe again, I opened my eyes and stared into his. "As entrées go, that was pretty damn fine."

He grinned and slid to one side, propping up on one arm before kissing me softly. "Give me a minute or two, and we can start the main course."

"As long as it's only a minute or two."

He raised his eyebrows, delight dancing through his expression. "My wife-to-be has become insatiable."

"A sexual drought will do that to you."

He laughed, pulled me closer, and began another long, slow seduction of senses and body.

It was a glorious way to spend a morning.

Once Aiden had left for his meeting with the council, I headed into the kitchen to do a little of the prep work needed for tomorrow. It was close to three when my phone rang. The tone told me it was actually the café's number being called—we'd started diverting to either mine or Belle's out of hours—so it was tempting to just ignore it, given we were closed. But instinct twitched.

I sometimes hated when it did that.

I hit the answer button, then said, rather warily, "Lizzie Grace speaking. How may I help you?"

There was no immediate answer, then a small voice said, "Are you the witch Nanny says helps her talk to Poppy and finds lost things?"

My heart did an odd flip-flop. It was a kid, and he couldn't have been any older than five or six. He also sounded scared. "Yes, I am. Who are you?"

"Brandon."

"And what have you lost, Brandon?"

"Nanny. I can't find my nanny."

Fuck. I briefly closed my eyes and prayed like hell she wasn't the latest victim of either the basilisk or our vampires. "Are you at your nanny's place right now?"

"Yes."

I reached out to Belle. *You busy? I've got a kid on the phone whose nan is missing. Can you get hold of Tala or Jaz for me?* To Brandon, I added, "Was your nanny home this morning?"

"Yes."

"And your mom?"

"She works in the city."

"Have you tried calling her?"

"I don't know her number." He paused, and I heard footsteps and then voices. After a moment, I realized it was the TV—old episodes of *Playschool*, from the sound of it. He must have moved from where the phone was into another room. "Nanny had written your number down, so I called you. Do you know my nanny?"

"I might—what's your nanny's name?"

"Joselyn."

Joselyn Hankins, has to be, Belle said. *She's a member of the gossip brigade and does indeed come in weekly for chats with her dearly departed husband.*

I nodded, remembering her. She was a tall, neatly dressed woman with long silver hair that was always neatly pinned into a bun. Her being a regular customer explained why she had the café's number, but not why she'd write it down for Brandon rather than that of his parents or even the rangers. "Do you know your nanny's address?"

"It's a big white house," he said.

In a place filled with them. "Do you know the street's name?"

"No."

It's okay, Belle said, *Tala knows her address and has just texted it to me. She'll meet us there.*

Meaning Monty isn't about to miss out on this adventure.

Indeedy, Belle said dryly. *Pick you up in five.*

"It's okay, Brandon, I know where your nan lives. Me and some friends will be there in a few minutes, and we'll help you find your nanny. Okay?"

"Okay."

I hesitated. "Is the front or back door open, Brandon?"

"The back door is. Nanny even left the wire door open. She tells me off if I do that because it lets all the flies in."

Did that mean she'd left in a hurry? Or was she in the thrall of a vampire and simply had no control of her own actions? "Don't worry about the flies, Brandon, we'll deal with them when we get there."

"Okay," he repeated.

"Stay on the phone, Brandon, just in case you need to tell me something."

"I'm thirsty."

"We'll get you a drink and treat when we get there, okay?"

"Okay."

I smiled, shoved my phone through a bra strap to keep it close in case he said something, then headed upstairs to grab my keys. Once I'd collected the backpack—which I hoped we wouldn't need—I locked up, then headed out the front to wait. Belle and Monty turned up a few minutes later.

I jumped into the back seat and, as Monty took off, asked, "Did Joselyn come into the café yesterday with the rest of the group?"

"Yes, though she didn't stay all that long. Said she had to get back home to mind her grandson, as her daughter was staying overnight in Melbourne for work."

"You didn't detect any problems or concerns during the spirit talking?"

While Belle didn't make a habit of telepathically reading her clients, sometimes their concerns or emotions were so strong they were almost impossible to ignore. It was one of the reasons I was rarely present during spirit talking sessions, as my ability to sense emotions through touch had both sharpened and broadened with all the DNA changes the wild magic was making. On the few occasions Belle *did* need to pull on my strength or psi senses for whatever reason, she usually gave me a heads-up so I could get comfortable somewhere.

"No." She hesitated. "But I do think she has a latent skill for clairvoyance. It's one of the reasons her spirit talking sessions go so well."

"Is it possible, then, that she sensed something was wrong and went out to investigate?"

"Possible, but I can't imagine her leaving her grandson unattended like that. She doted on the boy."

I grimaced. "I take it the rangers are trying to contact the mother?"

Belle nodded. "Apparently, Levi knows Brandon's mom."

Levi being Jaz's husband. "She's a werewolf?"

"No, human, but she and Levi had a bit of a fling before Jaz came on to the scene."

Werewolves tended to do that. Hell, I was meant to be nothing more than a "fling" for Aiden. Thankfully, that changed quickly enough, and while we still had a lot of things to sort out, our relationship was at least heading down the right track.

Unless, of course, it all derailed yet again—a thought totally derived from my pessimistic streak than any real fear that it actually *would*.

It didn't take us long to get over to Joselyn's place. She lived in a leafy, well-to-do street in a gorgeous old Victorian-era home with a willow tree out the front and agapanthus lining the front of the porch.

Tala, Aiden's second-in-command, walked toward us as we pulled up behind her SUV. I tugged the phone out of my bra, told Brandon that we were out the front and about to come in, then hung up, dropping the phone into my pack as I got out of the car.

"Liz, given the kid rang you, do you and Belle want to head into the house to check things out there? Monty and I will go around to the back and see if we can pick up a trail."

She turned without waiting for an answer and strode toward the driveway to the right of the property, forcing Monty to run after her. I slung my pack over my shoulder and led the way in. The front door was locked, as Brandon had said, but a quick spell soon fixed that.

I didn't immediately open the door however, glancing at Belle instead. "You sensing anything telepathically?"

"Nothing other than one hungry little boy." She hesitated. "He was fed lunch but hasn't had his afternoon snack, which usually happens around three."

"Which at least gives us a time frame for her disappearance." I opened the door and said, in a voice loud enough to be heard over the TV, "Brandon? It's Lizzie, the lady who finds things."

Footsteps echoed on the lovely old polished floors, and a second later, a cute kid with messy brown hair and the biggest blue eyes appeared. He stopped a few meters away, his expression a mix of uncertainty and relief. "Are you going to find my nanny now?"

I nodded. "I've got two friends out the back doing that right now. Can we come in?"

He nodded. "I need a drink."

"My friend Belle will do that for you while I look for something that can help us find your nanny. Which bedroom is hers?"

He pointed to the room on the left, then pointed right. "Mine is that one. I have trains on the wall."

"Oh, good." Belle brushed past me and held out a hand. "I love trains. You'll have to show me after we get something to drink."

He nodded, took her hand—well, fingertips really, given he wasn't particularly tall, and she was an Amazon—and led her down the hallway. I walked into Joselyn's room, but paused near the door, expanding my senses as I scanned the neat, somewhat flowery room. Nothing immediately pinged, so I held up my hand and did a slow circuit around the room. I was close to the far bedside table when I felt the twitch of life. There was nothing other than a lamp and a glass of water sitting on the top, however, so I opened the first drawer. There, sitting on the top of an intricately carved wooden jewelry case, was a simple silver watch.

The pulse coming from it suggested that, at this point in time, Joselyn was very much alive. More than that, I couldn't gauge, not without picking it up. I swung my pack around, pulled a silk glove out of a side pocket, and tugged it on. I'd taken to carrying both silk and latex gloves around since I'd become Monty's assistant, simply because it was easier for those few times we headed out without a ranger in tow.

I carefully picked up the watch, then opened the psychometry gates. Images immediately surged, but they were little more than a rapid-fire reel of trees, grass, and water that spun around with giddying speed, giving me little information and no chance to understand where she was and what she was doing.

I frowned and tried deepening the connection. The reel slowed, but her emotions remained just as scattered. She was sitting in a small grove of trees, but she had no idea where she was or how she'd gotten there. She couldn't move, but the pain that rolled through her system suggested her immobility wasn't due to any sort of brief contact with the basilisk, but rather because she'd hurt a leg or an ankle.

I swore softly and left the room. Even though the

images gave me little information, I could still use the pulsing in the watch to locate her—though in truth, it might not be necessary. Unless there was magic involved, Tala should be able to track her via scent.

I popped my head around the kitchen door. Belle was in the process of pouring chocolate milk into a cup, and Brandon was happily perched on a stool in front of the kitchen counter, munching on a couple of buttered Teddy Bear sandwiches. My stomach rumbled in appreciation, but I resisted the urge to ask Belle to make me one. We had a nanny to find first.

"Everything okay here?"

Brandon swung around, biscuit crumbs and butter smeared around his mouth. "You found my nanny yet?"

"Just about to head out now to find her. Will you be okay here with Belle?"

He nodded. "She's going to play trains with me."

"Excellent," I said with a grin.

"I'm considering it good practice for when I'm babysitting your kid."

"My kid is a girl."

"Aside from the fact there's no reason why a girl can't play with trains, this is your kid we're talking about. She won't be bound by society's expectations. Not in any way."

I laughed, although it was nothing but the truth. I'd grown up under the heavy weight of both parental and societal expectations, and was absolutely determined that none of my kids, no matter how many I had, would feel that sort of weight.

Rules, respect, and independence of thought were an entirely different matter, of course. Those they *would* be taught.

"Won't be long," I said, more for Brandon than Belle,

169

and then moved on, following my nose—or rather, the slight breeze of warmer, fresher air—to the still-open back door.

I closed the screen door behind me, then paused and looked around. Neither Tala nor Monty were in sight, but the wire gate at the bottom of the garden was open. I walked down, the steady pulse coming from the watch neither easing nor increasing its rhythm.

The gate led out to some sort of nature reserve that followed the creek I could hear but not actually see, thanks to the thick undergrowth between us. Lovely old gums followed the creek line, their crowns thick and lush, dappling the light and easing some of the day's heat. There was no evidence which way Monty and Tala had gone—the breeze, though light, was strong enough to have whisked any scent trail away, but Tala was a wolf and wouldn't be relying on scent alone. Thankfully, neither was I.

I went right. It had obviously rained overnight, and the path was littered with muddy puddles, forcing me to wind my way through them. After a few minutes, the rusty red rooftop of the old train station appeared through the trees on the other side of the creek and directly ahead was the pedestrian overpass that arched over the creek from the parking area. The rhythm in the watch sharpened abruptly, telling me I was very close. No one stood in the shadows of the overpass, but there were familiar voices coming from somewhere beyond it.

I went through the overpass and saw Monty in the trees closer to the creek off to the left.

He glanced around as I approached. "Found her. Dazed, confused, with an ankle sprain, but otherwise okay."

I frowned and stopped beside him. Joselyn was sitting at the base of a tree, her bare feet in the water, and her right ankle looking bruised and swollen. Her normally neat hair was not only in disarray, but full of twigs and yellowed leaves. She hadn't gotten any of those from the scrub surrounding the creek, as it was mainly gorse. If she'd gone through it, she would have been scratched up a whole lot worse. That stuff was the natural enemy of bare flesh.

"Has she said anything?" I asked.

Monty shook his head, but it was Tala who answered. "She seems to be in a state of shock, but I'm not trusting it. Something else is going on, though I'm not sure what. Monty said there's no evidence of magic."

"No lingering evidence," he corrected. "But she obviously didn't walk here. Not with that ankle."

"Could she had slipped while going down the bank?" I asked, even as I did. I caught my balance easily enough, but Joselyn, being older, might not have been able to.

Tala shook her head. "There's no indication of a slip, either here or on the other side of the bank."

"Huh." I squatted beside the older woman and scanned her face. Pain etched her features and filled her aura, but her gaze was unfocused and somehow jumpy. Which matched the images I'd briefly glimpsed in the watch. For some reason, her memories and her mind were on a loop she couldn't escape.

Is something like that possible? I asked Belle.

For a telepath who knows what they're doing, totally.

Could you check?

Hang on while I get Brandon into his room and rambling on about his trains. There was a long pause. *Okay, this will be a surface-level check only unless Tala wants to get someone else here to take over babysitting duties.*

Surface level is fine. We just need to know what we're dealing with.

Right then, let's go.

As the connection between us deepened, I glanced at Tala and said, "Start recording. Belle's going to do a quick scan of Joselyn's mind and memories to see what is going on."

I raised my hands and gently touched Joselyn's temples. Her emotions briefly stirred across my psi senses—mostly confusion rather than fear, oddly enough—but I slammed my shields all the way up, not waiting to get caught in the loop of them.

Okay, Belle said, *there's definitely been some interference in her mind, but I'm not entirely sure it's due to another telepath.*

I repeated it for Tala's sake. *Monty said there was no evidence of magic.*

None here, but I don't think whatever happened to her happened here. The trees in her mind look different from those here.

They're all gums.

Amusement flowed through the line between us. *But not all gums are built the same.*

I smiled. *Are you able to get any sort of indication of where those trees are?*

Hang on, and I'll try to slow and deepen the loop. There was a long pause. *She was pulling washing out of the machine when she saw a small group of strangely dressed people walking past the back gate. She went to investigate and saw them walk under the bridge and disappear.*

An illusion or reality? Either was possible given we were dealing with mage who also happened to be a vampire.

Did she follow them?

Another pause. *Her memories are too confused to get much of an answer. There is a vague impression of an old*

house in the woods, but to get more, I'll basically have to tele-
pathically unscramble what they've done.

Will that work if her memories have been magically
altered rather than telepathically?

I don't know. What I can do right now is unloop her
thoughts and ease her pain. That'll return her to normality,
though she still won't be able to tell us much until we can
sort out her memories.

Normality without the pain is a good start.

Belle's presence in my mind sharpened abruptly as she
worked on Joselyn. I was little more than a bystander, but it
was nevertheless fascinating to watch Belle work quickly
and efficiently in another's mind. It certainly wasn't something I was privy to all that often.

As she withdrew from our minds and I dropped my
hands from Joselyn's temples, the older woman blinked and
glanced around in surprise.

"Where am I? What's happened?" She paused, her gaze
widening. "Where's my grandson? Is he safe?"

I placed a hand on her arm, and her gaze jumped to
mine. Panic surged in her expression, and I hastily said,
"He's safe at your place, Joselyn. Belle's with him."

"But why am I here, and why are you and Belle here?"
She paused and looked around in confusion. "A ranger and
Monty. What on earth has happened?"

"You saw something odd and went to investigate," Tala
said. "Brandon couldn't find you, so he rang Liz here."

"He's such a sensible, clever little boy." She sniffed and
glanced down at her ankle. "I have no memory of what
happened or how I did that. Why am I feeling no pain—it
looks bad."

"We gave you something to numb sensation," I said.

"And with your permission, Belle can help restore your memories, but only after you've been checked by doctors."

"I can't go to hospital. I have Brandon to look after."

"Let's see what the paramedics say," Tala said. "We've called them—"

"Direct them to my home. I need to see Brandon."

She made moves to rise, but Monty stepped past me and lightly touched her shoulder. "Hold on there, Mrs. H. Let me and Tala help you up and shoulder your weight."

She hesitated and then nodded. Tala shifted to the other side of the older woman and, between the two of them, they got Joselyn to her feet and all but carried her back to her home.

Brandon came running out as we walked through the gate and flung his arms around her. "Nanny! You're safe."

She moved her arm from Tala's shoulder and mussed his hair. "I am. I just fell over and hurt my ankle. Let's all get inside and have a nice cup of tea."

Monty helped her the rest of the way, but Tala caught my arm and stopped me from following. "Did Belle glean anything else in her mind that might help us understand how she actually hurt herself or where that house was?"

I shook my head. "She'll try to do a deeper reading once Joselyn has recovered, but I wouldn't advise sending *anyone* out to find that old house. It just might be the base of operations for our vampires."

She raised an eyebrow. "I would have thought you'd be wanting to find that base ASAP."

"We do—meaning us witches, not you werewolves."

She snorted. "A werewolf is more than capable of dealing—"

"*All* of these vampires are magic capable, and at least one of them has mage powers." I eyed her severely. "They could freeze you in place with a flick of a hand and dine from you at their leisure, and there wouldn't be one goddamn thing you could do about it."

"Well, fuck." She scraped a hand through her short, dark hair. "Is there anything we can do to protect ourselves? Can you fashion up some charms that'll ward off the bastards?"

"I can, but there's no guarantee they'll work against a mage."

"If it'll hold off a vamp long enough for us to run in the opposite direction, I'll consider that a win."

I couldn't imagine Tala or any of the other rangers actually doing a runner if they did come across a vampire, simply because it wasn't in their nature, but I simply nodded and said I'd get straight on to it.

You can head home now, if you want, Belle said. *Monty and I can handle this from here. Monty said you can take the beast, as we're not that far from home.*

I'll catch an Uber. It's too hot for any of us to be walking.

There was a slight pause, then Belle said, her laughter running down the mental lines, *Monty said the beast will be getting a complex about nobody loving her at this rate.*

That's because no one does.

My voice was dry, and her laughter bubbled through me again. *See you tomorrow.*

I told Tala I was heading home, tugged out my phone to order the Uber, and headed around the side of the house and through the front gate to wait.

A few minutes later, I was back home.

And discovered that once again someone waited for me.

This time, it wasn't a dead body.

It was Karleen Jayne O'Connor.

Aiden's mom.

CHAPTER NINE

O f the many—*many*—emotions that flooded me, surprise wasn't one of them. She'd always arranged these little confrontations well away from prying ears or her son's presence. What *did* surprise me was the fact that she was here rather than at the council meeting ratifying her son as pack alpha.

Unless, of course, that meeting was over and done with, and she'd scuttled here as soon as possible to warn me off yet again. She might not know that he and I had gotten engaged, but she wasn't stupid. She'd be well aware Aiden intended to use his position as alpha to enforce a vote on the two of us setting up a home within the compound.

But hey, if she was here to fight, then I was fucking willing to give her one.

I directed the Uber into the rear parking area and gave her a wave as we pulled into the laneway, knowing full well it would piss her off to no end. I didn't see her scowl, but the force of her displeasure vibrated through the air, something I could sense despite all the metal surrounding me.

The Uber came to a halt near the rear door. I thanked

the driver, then grabbed the pack and climbed out. By the time I reached the step and opened the door, she was beside me.

"Karleen," I said evenly, "what a pleasure to see your lovely self again."

She snorted. "I'm not here to be pleasant."

"You never are. Come in, or stand on the step and shout at me, your choice. I don't care either way."

I opened the door and walked inside, my back itching with the force of her glare. She couldn't hurt me, not in here, but tiny flickers of energy nevertheless danced across my fingers. I placed the pack in the reading room, then walked behind the counter to flick on the kettle. She might not be here to be pleasant, but I certainly needed a pleasant cup of tea. Whiskey would have been better, of course, but that was sadly out of bounds.

She stopped on the other side of the counter and crossed her arms, her expression giving little away, but her aura practically screaming. Furious did not even begin to describe the current state of her mind.

"You will never be his mate," she growled. "Even if he *is* confirmed, you will never be allowed a permanent place within the compound's grounds."

"*If* he's confirmed?" I countered. "You mean you don't know? Why not, given you're currently pack alpha and the meeting to approve his rise in rank was held this afternoon?"

"That is pack business, not yours."

"Pack business might well be my business one day, sweetie."

In truth, riling her probably wasn't a good idea—and I had the scars to prove that—but there was something inside me that just couldn't help it. Besides, both Katie and Jaz had told me that standing up to her might be the only way to win pack approval, especially given I would never—no matter what I did or said—win *her* approval. She remained too mired in past hurts and memories to ever see future hope.

"Listen here, witch—"

"What the *fuck* is going on here?" a familiar and very angry voice said. "Mother, what the hell are you doing?"

She swung around, surprise flickering across her expression. She'd been so intent on me that she hadn't heard him come in.

But then, neither had I.

He strode into the room and stopped midway between the two of us. "This has to stop, Mother."

Her gaze swept him somewhat contemptuously. "No matter what else you are or what you become, you are my child, and you will not—"

"What I will *not* do is stand by and let you berate and harass the woman I love." His voice held a note I'd not heard before—a whip of censure and command. The alpha had fully emerged. "I've tiptoed around your feelings and memories for too fucking long, and it almost cost me any chance of happiness. But no longer. I *am* pack alpha now, and any decision I make regarding who I choose as a mate is mine and mine alone. Understood?"

She bared her teeth, a low sound of warning rumbling up her throat. I doubted she'd actually attack him, but her hands were clenched, and her control seemed decidedly knife's edge.

"She will *never* be a part of our pack, Aiden. They will never accept her. You know this."

"*That* is a pack decision and one I will abide by when it comes to where we live. I've already called a pack meeting for tomorrow morning, and both Liz and I will be there to present our case for living within the reservation to the wider pack. You will, of course, have the right to state your case against us, but be warned—if you make any attempt beforehand to sway the vote, I will ask the council to rescind your position as co-alpha."

She stared at him. "You can't do that. *They* can't do that."

"You forget, Mother, that with Father dead and my accession officially approved, you only hold the position by default until I'm married. Which, I must point out, I soon will be."

We hadn't actually discussed a date, but I was totally on board with it being sooner rather than later. It wasn't like I wanted a big, fancy wedding. My found family and my mom were all I needed as witnesses when I walked up that aisle and married my werewolf.

Hell, I didn't even really want a church wedding. I was perfectly happy getting hitched in a forest or a garden. In fact, Ashworth's rear garden, with its pretty autumn trees and lovely roses, would make the perfect setting.

She stared at Aiden for a long minute, her expression unreadable but skin decidedly paler. "You can't be serious."

"I have never been so serious about anything—or anyone—in my entire life." He glanced at me then, and all the emotion, all the love, was right there in his gaze for all to see. "I love Liz, and I'm going to marry her, and not you, not the pack, not even the fucking council or a goddamn vampire war is going to stop me."

She blinked. "What vampire war?"

"The one that has already killed at least two people and is threatening to erupt into all-out violence at any moment. Do you not listen to *anything* I say at council meetings?"

"I wasn't at the last one—"

"I noticed."

"I had my reasons—"

"I know, just as I know how hard the last few weeks have been. I'm grieving for my father and uncle too, remember. But it's no excuse for your actions here today or for skipping council meetings and sending a proxy in your place. It will stop. *You* will stop." He paused. "Or I will follow through with my threat."

"Fine," she snapped, then glared at me. "I will see *you* tomorrow morning."

With that, she walked around her son and stormed out of the café.

"Well," I said lightly. "That went better than expected."

He laughed, swept me into his arms, and kissed me so damn thoroughly that by the time he stepped back my head was spinning. "Many would say *that* was well overdue."

I raised an eyebrow, amusement twitching my lips. "That being the kiss?"

He laughed again and lightly ran his fingers down to my kiss-swollen lips. "If I'd confronted my mother the moment our relationship became serious, I might have saved us both a whole lot of heartache."

I doubted it, given her prejudices were too well ingrained now to change. "What you should have done at that point is explain to me you were playing the long game. *Not* explaining it has proven to be something of an emotional minefield."

Of course, I was playing the long game myself right now when it came to my pregnancy, but instinct remained insistent that I keep the secret for a while yet. Maybe instinct was just another word for cowardice—not so much an inner fear of how *he* would react, but rather his family and, to a lesser extent, his pack. Him declaring he intended to marry me would be upheaval enough—I didn't need to be adding to it right now.

"I do have to ask, though," I continued, "was it chance that you happened to walk in at exactly the right time? Or did Belle contact you?"

"She didn't, but even if she had, I was already on my way here." He grimaced. "I figured that, given her previous actions, the first thing she'd do on hearing the news was not congratulate me but come here in an attempt to confront you. She has, apparently, learned nothing about your stubbornness or willingness to fight, even after that last bloody meeting."

"That may change eventually." When hell froze over, most likely.

"We both know that's a statement based in hope rather than reality. But enough of her. I came here to pick you up. We're going to look for engagement rings, and then we're going to dinner."

I glanced at my watch. "It's four in the afternoon on a Monday. The few shops that are open won't be for all that long."

"Who said anything about going to a shop?"

I raised my eyebrows. "Where are we going to buy an engagement ring if not a shop of some kind?"

"I've a friend who's a designer. I commissioned him a week ago to design and make both your engagement ring and our wedding rings."

I raised my eyebrows, amusement and delight dancing through me. "That's a bit presumptuous, given I hadn't even said yes at that point."

"Yes, and your refusal to even take my calls did set back our appointment date several times."

I laughed, rose on to my toes, and kissed him lightly. "I need a shower first—"

"May I offer my services as a back scrubber?"

"I thought you hated my shower—too small to do anything practical in, I believe your comment was."

"A comment I'm fully willing to test the veracity of."

I laughed, grabbed his hand, and tugged him upstairs.

The shower was very definitely on the small side, and very definitely did require a bit of careful maneuvering, but it definitely did *not* hamper a suitable and very satisfactory result.

―――――

Aiden's friend—Maitland—was a tall, well-built man in his early thirties, with thick red hair and merry green eyes. His workshop was a shed out the back of his house in Argyle, and while the building's exterior didn't look all that inviting, it only took one step inside to enter a wonderland. There were metals, stones, jewels, and all manner of other shiny bits and pieces arrayed on shelves, benches, or hanging in bags from the ceiling. It was the sort of place thieves could have had a field day in, so it wasn't surprising that the magic surrounding and protecting the building was almost as strong as that protecting the café. Sans the wild magic, of course.

"So tell me," he said, his voice as pleasant as his looks, "you got a specific design in mind?"

I laughed. "No, although silver is out of the question, and I'm not into big stones or anything too fancy."

"A woman after my own heart." He walked over to what looked to be an old wooden map drawer, pulled out several sketch books, and dumped them on the table in the middle of the room. "These are some designs I've done over the years. You can pick out the ones you like, and we can work on something unique from there."

"This could take forever," I said, with another laugh.

"In my experience, it rarely does. Most women have some idea of what they want, even if they can't verbalize it."

I glanced at Aiden. "It could be dangerous, letting me loose to choose what I want. I have expensive tastes when it comes to jewelry."

"Says the woman who actually wears very little jewelry."

"That's because I can't afford the stuff I love." Although I certainly would be able to once the settlement from my ex's estate came through.

Aiden gently caught my face between his hands and kissed me. "My love, you can have any ring, any stone, any design that you fancy."

I grinned. "You could regret that statement."

"I may well regret many things, but never that."

I laughed, kissed him again, and flipped open the first design book. As it turned out, I was one of those women who knew almost instantly what she wanted when she saw it, and that was a simple jade ring with an inlaid design of leaves done in gold. Our wedding rings would use the same design in reverse. After checking our finger sizes, Maitland promised to start work on them immediately, ushered us out the door, and slammed it closed loudly.

As we made our way back to his truck, I cast a rather bemused look at Aiden. "He seemed in a hurry to get started—how soon did you tell him we needed the rings?"

Aiden laughed and ushered me into the truck. "He's always like that. Before he started taking commissions, he'd often bemoan the fact that not enough people wanted something that's truly different or unique."

"That's because not enough people can actually afford his particular brand of uniqueness."

"Also true, although his physical store is profitable. He just doesn't go too far off center when it comes to his rings there these days." Aiden started up the truck, checked the rearview mirror, and did a U-turn. "Now, to dinner—where would you like to go?"

"How about fish and chips at your place?"

The look he cast me was disappointed, though it was muted by the amusement dancing in his bright eyes. "That's hardly what I'd call an appropriate dinner for such an auspicious occasion as our engagement."

"Perhaps not, but I have a hankering for them. Besides, if passion rises, we don't have to drive all the way home to satisfy it."

"I like your thinking," he said, smiling.

It didn't take us all that long to reach our favorite fish and chip shop in Argyle. Thankfully, they weren't all that busy—no doubt due to the fact that it was a Monday rather than a Friday or the weekend—which meant we didn't have to wait the usual twenty or so minutes to get our order.

Twilight was casting ruby fingers across the storm-clad sky by the time we reached his home away from home. It was situated at the far end of a six-unit complex built close to the sandy shoreline of the vast Argyle Lake and surrounded by trees. The building itself was a two-story A-frame design and cedar-clad, with the lake-side wall consisting completely of double-glazed glass that gave amazing views over the water.

I followed him across to the front door, the strengthening wind tugging at the hem of my dress and revealing a rather indecent amount of thigh. Appreciation gleamed in Aiden's eyes as he waved me through the door. Though I hadn't shared this space with him all that long, it nevertheless felt like coming home. If the pack *did* reject the notion of us living within the compound, I wouldn't object to making this our permanent base.

The lower floor was basically one long room divided by the open wooden staircase. At the far end was a modern kitchen-diner, complete with a bench long enough for six people to sit around and, on this side, an open fireplace, around which was a C-shaped, hugely comfortable leather sofa. The TV—a monster of a thing—was tucked into the corner between the fireplace and the outside glass wall. The stairs led up to two bedrooms, each with their own en suite bathroom. Aiden's was the front one—the one with the balcony and the long views over the lake. Our daughter would take the second. Any more kids than that, and extensions would have to be added.

I dumped the fish and chips on the coffee table, then walked down to the kitchen end to grab tomato sauce, chicken salt—because I loved the stuff, and they sometimes didn't put enough on the chips—and a couple of glasses.

"Bubbles, red, or white?" he asked.

"Just sparkling water, if you've got any."

He raised his eyebrows. "Sparkling water is hardly—"

"It is when instinct is warning we both need to remain sober."

Which it actually wasn't—not majorly, anyway.

He groaned. "Seriously, why can't darkside just control their murderous impulses for a few days? Is that too much to ask of them and the universe in general?"

"Hey, be thankful our vamps didn't just charge into the reservation and immediately start an all-out bloody war."

I put the sauce, salt, and the glasses down, then tugged the cardboard trays free of their white paper bags and snagged a chip as I sat on the floor behind the coffee table. The chicken salt, I was pleased to note, was not lacking.

"Aside from the body count factor, I'm actually not sure releasing a basilisk and randomly sucking people dry is that much better." He sat beside me, poured our drinks, and then grabbed a potato cake. "Rocco sent me a text, by the way. Suzanne's regained consciousness, though she remains somewhat confused."

"Confusion sure beats being frozen and dead," I said. "It also supports the current theory that unless you meet the basilisk's gaze full on, it is survivable."

"The problem being the bastard appears out of nowhere and most people generally look up at the first scent or sign of movement."

"Which is why at least everyone on your team needs to start wearing mirrored sunglasses whenever they're out patrolling, whether on foot or in the car."

He raised his eyebrows. "Seriously?"

I grinned, poured sauce onto a section of the paper tray, and swirled a chunk of battered fish through it. "Belle said that exact same thing."

"It wasn't Monty's idea, then? Because they remain in the loved-up glow of the newly engaged, don't they? She hasn't been her usual snarky self around him."

"Oh, yes she has. You just haven't been in their company much of late." I pointed a chip at him. "And I will have you know that the newly engaged glow won't stop *me* from disagreeing with you or even challenging a statement I think is utterly stupid or wrong."

"I would be disappointed if it did. Your forthrightness is

one of the things I love about you, even if it is also one of your most frustrating traits."

I laughed, picked up my glass, and lightly tapped it against his. "To us annoying the shit out of each other for decades to come."

He laughed and took a drink. "Seriously, though, have you discovered an easy means of tracking and stopping the basilisk?"

I grimaced. "Nothing more than we've already discovered. But I've got Katie tracking the basilisk's movements. If there's a visible pattern, we've a better chance of trapping the bastard."

He nodded. "Tala mentioned in the report she made that Joselyn Hankins managed to get a glimpse of some of our vampires."

I raised my eyebrows. "Was she able to give a description? Because her memories were pretty scrambled at the scene."

"No, though Tala did mention that Belle was going into the hospital tomorrow morning to see what she could do."

"Just don't expect miracles. Belle might be an extremely strong telepath, but if magic or another telepath has interfered with Joselyn's memories, there might be nothing to retrieve."

"Exactly what I said to Tala. I think she was hoping to give Joselyn and her family reassurance that it wasn't another memory-loss episode."

I raised my eyebrows. "Why would they think that?"

"She's a diabetic—"

"Really? Wouldn't have thought so, with all the cakes she eats."

He lightly nudged me. "Being diabetic doesn't mean

you can't eat cake. It just means you have to be more careful to test and manage it."

"And you know this how?"

"A previous short-term girlfriend who had diabetes and loved cake."

"Ha." I grabbed another bit of fish and then motioned for him to continue.

"Apparently Joselyn did suffer memory losses a few years ago, though it was before she was diagnosed."

"The doctors would surely have tested for that and confirmed, one way or another."

"Blood tests results aren't immediate."

No, but the first thing they'd have done is prick her finger and tested her sugar levels. Not that it really mattered right now. "The little Belle could immediately pull from Joselyn's mind suggests they're using some sort of transport spell to get around, as nothing in her memories matches where she was found."

He nodded. "Unfortunately, there are a ton of abandoned houses within the reservation, many of them long-forgotten and barely habitable."

"A mage or even a capable witch can make a place habitable with little more than a spell or two."

He raised his eyebrows. "Spells can't create water or power."

"No, but vampires don't really need either to exist." And while I couldn't imagine the woman who'd given "birth" to Maelle living in drafty squalor, if they were capable of transport spells then they were capable of getting whatever furniture and other supplies they needed. "Has there been a spate of strange or unusual robberies reported recently?"

"If you're talking furniture and the like, yes." He frowned. "But they're not confined to one area."

"They wouldn't be. Our vampiress has been around a very long time, and she isn't likely to make such an obvious mistake." I picked up another chip. "But that's enough shop talk for one night, I think."

"Agreed." He draped his left arm around my shoulder, lazily brushing his fingertips across the top of my breast while he ate a fried Dim sim with the other. "Shall we discuss our upcoming nuptials instead?"

"I like that you informed your mother they'd be happening very soon before we'd actually discussed the matter." My voice was dry, and he smiled.

"That was a statement designed to annoy my mother rather than you."

"I know, but—"

"Do you disagree with sooner being better than later?"

"I'm wholeheartedly behind the idea." And for more reasons than he was currently aware. Not that I needed to be married before I had our child. I just wanted it to happen before fate decided to throw another spanner in the works. "That doesn't negate the fact you need to stop making these announcements without discussing them first with me."

He laughed and hugged me. "Consider it a work in progress."

I rolled my eyes, but before I could say anything my phone rang.

"Ignore it," he said. "Unless you've changed dial tones recently, it's not anyone important."

"Yeah, because you'd totally ignore your phone if it happened to ring right now."

As if to emphasize this point, his phone rang. I raised my hands. "I promise, no magic involved."

He laughed again, rolled to his feet, and walked over to the counter where he'd left his phone. I dragged my purse closer and retrieved mine. It had stopped ringing by the time I got it out and the number wasn't one I knew.

I glanced across at Aiden, saw the consternation in his expression, and knew something bad had happened. I glanced down at my phone again and, after a slight hesitation, copied the number and did a "who is" search.

The number belonged to Émigré.

My stomach dropped. Something must have happened for her to be ringing me. Usually, she just sent Roger along with whatever message she wished to impart. Me being here rather than at the café generally wouldn't have made much of a difference, as she was no doubt fully aware of where Aiden lived when not at the compound.

I let my finger hover over the return call button for several seconds before finally hitting it. The phone at the other end rang out then flicked over to a "leave a message" message.

I did so, then hung up and glanced at Aiden. "Problem?"

"Yeah, another missing person, this time near Shepherd's Flat." He answered without looking up, his attention still on his phone.

I wrinkled my nose. "Where's that?"

"Ten or so minutes outside Argyle. Why?"

"Just wondering if it's connected to the basilisk or not, given it was last seen in the Maldoon area."

"If the bastard *is* ringing the reservation, then Shepherd's Flat could be considered a midpoint between Rocco's compound and the area where he was called into being." He shoved his phone into his back pocket. "I'll have to go. Jaz is on call tonight, but I can't leave her to handle this situation alone, given what we're likely dealing with."

"You've contacted Monty?"

He nodded. "Sent him a text. Mac will pick him up on the way through."

"And you mentioned that they both need to grab mirrored sunglasses?"

"Jaz hasn't any, but she said she'd borrow Levi's."

Meaning she was home, not at the station. I snagged a potato cake and rose. "I might grab an Uber back to Castle Rock. That call I missed was from Maelle, but she's not picking up. I've a gut feeling something might be wrong."

He hesitated. "Keep me updated."

I nodded and followed him out the door. Night had set in, but despite the ominous clouds, the air remained warm. I waited until Aiden had left, booked an Uber, and then walked up to the main gate to wait. It took just over thirty minutes to get to Castle Rock, but by the time we arrived, my tension had ramped up so much that tiny sparks were dancing across my fingertips.

I ran into the café to grab my backpack, then jumped into the SUV and sped around to Émigré. There were no lights on around the exterior, nor any sign of the magic that had been so evident earlier. While even someone as powerful as Maelle could not continue to cast and support multiple spells at the one time without taking some sort of break, it nevertheless felt... wrong.

The fact there were no guards stationed out front only emphasized the feeling of wrongness. Every time I'd come here previously, they'd been present. Granted, unless they were thralls like Roger—and I had no evidence that they were—they'd have to take time off at some point. But Maelle would have rostered on others. She wouldn't have left her building unprotected—especially now, when she knew her maker was in town intent on revenge.

I climbed out of the car and slung my pack over my shoulder, but didn't immediately cross over to the club area. I scanned the building's façade and roof, searching for something, anything, to hint at the trouble I sensed waiting.

There was no foreign magic, no blood scent, no sound, and no sign of building damage.

Trepidation nevertheless swept me. After a slight hesitation, I grabbed my silver knife and a small bottle of holy water from the backpack, tucking the latter into my dress's pocket. Neither were exactly welcome inside Maelle's lair, but I wasn't about to walk in without some form of physical protection. I had plenty of the other kind, of course, though whether they'd be enough if this *was* some kind of a trap set by Marie, I couldn't say.

Although if Marie *had* set a trap in the very heart of Maelle's powerbase, something must have gone seriously wrong for our resident vamp.

Like, Roger was dead, and she was captive somewhere. Although I couldn't imagine Maelle allowing herself to be taken without one hell of a fight, even if Roger was the price she paid.

I ignored the whisper that suggested intuition rather than reason was right on the money—if not now, then not too far ahead in the future—and, with wisps of inner wild magic buzzing all around me, walked across the road. The sheer weight of silence that surrounded the building felt deeply, darkly menacing.

Trepidation increased, although my psychic senses weren't yet picking up anything untoward. The outer doors were closed but not, I soon discovered, locked. I opened one warily and peered inside, all my senses, physical and magical, alert.

And caught the faintest metallic scent.

Blood.

Fuck.

I pressed back against the half-open door and slowly, carefully, eased inside. Nothing had changed in the brief time since I'd last been here. The foyer area remained empty, and plastic still covered the entry into the main bar.

The farther I stepped inside, the stronger that metallic scent became. I still wasn't hearing any movement, and there was no hint of magic. There wasn't even the lingering remnants of darker magic, and there should have been if there'd been an attack on Maelle's base. She definitely wouldn't have gone down without a fight. Hell, if her earlier comments were anything to go by, she'd have welcomed it, simply because such an attack would counter the restrictions the turning ceremony had placed on her.

When I reached the plastic covering the door, I pushed one edge aside with the knife and peered inside. The place was darker than hell itself and just as fucking hot.

Not that I'd personally been to hell, but hey, I'd read the stories.

I created a light sphere and cast it forward. If there was someone or something waiting deeper within the building, it would give warning that I was here. But if that something waiting was vampires, it wouldn't actually matter. They'd have sensed my erratic heartbeat as soon as I'd entered.

The sphere's light cast warmth across the area directly ahead of the door, but long shadows continued to haunt the vast spaces beyond the sphere's reach.

At first glance, it appeared nothing had changed since I was last here, and to me that was just more evidence to the fact that something had happened. Maelle had been pulling out all the stops—magical and physical—to get the building up and running ASAP. I couldn't imagine her just letting everyone down tools and take a break.

I frowned and cast the light toward the ceiling. The front face of the control unit the electrician had been working on was back in place, and there wasn't a dark stain underneath it to suggest Maelle had forgotten about the man and let him drop. Which was a relief, though it was somewhat tempered by the fact that I couldn't see anything else close by to explain the scent.

I eased inside the main room then stopped to the right of the plastic and moved the sphere's position. Its light caressed the various bits of building equipment and tools piled on the floor near the base of the steps, but the bar remained in shadows. I flicked the light in that direction. The blood scent wasn't coming from that area, but I wasn't about to take one step farther until I was sure the shadows there hid nothing unusual.

They didn't, as it turned out.

I nevertheless ran the sphere down the bar's full length. The marble's purple veins gleamed in the soft light despite the faint coating of grit and sawdust on its surface. I warily inspected the long walkway between it and the currently empty alcohol fridges lining the wall. Still nothing. The danger—and the blood—I sensed definitely wasn't coming from this area.

Which only confirmed what I already knew.

I swept the light across the building's rear wall and then around to the staircase leading up to Maelle's lair. It was open, which didn't really mean anything, as it had been the first time I'd come back here.

I moved the light on toward the booths and discovered

two more had been completed since I'd last been here. Which wasn't all that much progress in the scheme of things.

I flicked the sphere back to the entrance into Maelle's lair. As much as I didn't want to, I had to go up there and check. I flexed my fingers against the hilt of my dagger, then headed down the steps, my footsteps echoing softly on the bare concrete.

The closer I got to the staircase, the stronger the blood scent became. I pushed the sphere into the stairwell and spotted a bloody handprint that was little more than a red smear across the marble's purple veins. I swore softly and scanned the walls and steps above me, searching for bloody puddles or, God help me, bits of flesh and gore. But that lone print was the extent of it.

Instinct was pretty damn certain I'd find a while lot more than bloody prints in Maelle's lair, but she refused to say whose.

Which meant there was only one way to find out.

I edged up the steps, my back against the wall opposite the bloody print and the knife held in front of me. The silence was oppressive, as was the heat, though the sweat trickling down my spine had very little to do with the latter.

I reached the top step, then paused. There was another bloody print on the wall beside the door into Maelle's office. Someone had obviously pressed one hand against it while they opened the door with the other.

Did the fact the door no longer remained open mean whoever had might yet wait inside?

I still wasn't sensing any sort of presence—magical or not—but that didn't mean squat when we were dealing with vamps capable of transport spells.

I didn't want to go inside. I really didn't.

But we all know you will, which is why I'm here and ready to help if you get into trouble, Belle said. *And by here, I mean in Monty's car, parked outside the building. Don't you dare say that could be dangerous, because we both know it's far less so than opening that goddamn door right now.*

A comment that had amusement stirring, despite the situation. *It might be nothing more than my imagination being overly dramatic.*

Though the bloody handprints very much suggested it wasn't.

Exactly the point I was about to make.

I smiled, though it quickly faded as I stepped onto the landing and edged toward the door. There was a thick streak of blood on the ornate handle. Our bleeder must have been seriously injured to be leaving streaks like that, but if that were the case, why weren't there any blood spots on the floor?

If there're vamps waiting inside, maybe they've already licked them all up.

A delightful image I could have done without. Besides, surely even the newest vampire wouldn't be that desperate.

Hey, after discovering Maelle loves to bathe in the remains of her victims, nothing would surprise me.

I swung my pack around and tugged a glove from the side pocket. My psi senses had in the past pulled images from blood spots, and I really didn't want that happening in a vampire's lair.

After tugging on the glove, I reached out and gripped the door handle. The smear still warmed against my palm, and vague images of pain flickered across the outer reaches of my psi sense. I had no sense of death, but would I if the bleeder was a vamp? Technically, they *were* actually dead.

I warily pressed gloved fingers against the door to open it, then sent my light sphere in.

I didn't get a chance to see anything more than the black glass opposite, because the blood scent hit like a hammer, overwhelming my olfactory senses and sending me reeling back toward the stairs. I regained my balance before I fell down them, but remained at the top of the landing, desperately sucking in the "cleaner" stairwell air to clear the stench from my nose and throat. Otherwise, I was going to puke all over what might yet be a major crime scene.

Though in truth, Aiden was going to be unhappy regardless, given I hadn't called them in the minute I knew something was wrong.

He's resigned to you doing shit like this, Belle said. *Besides, you're better than you used to be, and you're hardly alone right now.*

A statement I'm not sure he'll agree with. I pushed fully upright and returned to the door, resolutely pushing it all the way open.

And discovered our bleeder.

He lay in a pool of blood facedown on the floor in the center of the room, but I didn't have to see his face to know who it was.

Roger.

It was fucking Roger.

CHAPTER TEN

Is he alive? Belle asked.

I don't know. He wasn't breathing, but then, he was a thrall and maybe didn't need to.

He does breathe. I've seen him breathe.

Doesn't mean he actually has to.

I scanned the rest of the room warily. There was no sign of magic, no sign of Maelle. The latter didn't really surprise me, because I knew she had escape routes in both this room and the stairwell. She'd have known the minute Roger was attacked and been ready for anything that came at her. The question was, why had she not retaliated *through* him? Surely an attack on her creature would be considered an assault on her, thereby shattering the restrictions.

Maybe it doesn't work like that, Belle said.

Maybe. I sent the sphere skimming through the room, just to ensure there was absolutely nothing here that shouldn't be, then warily approached Roger, breathing through my mouth rather than my nose in an effort to prevent my olfactory senses being overwhelmed again. My stomach did *not* need another dose of bloody foulness.

There was a thick gash across the back of his head, but the wound no longer bled, and the blood in his hair was already stiffening, suggesting he'd been attacked not long after he—or perhaps Maelle—had called me.

I hesitated, then bent down and pressed two fingers against his neck.

The bastard let loose an inhuman scream and somehow leapt to his feet from the prone position. I screeched and pushed back, landing heavily on my butt several feet away. Wild magic automatically surged, forming a protective net around me even as it danced across the blessed knife. The blade shimmered with a deadly blue fire that reflected brightly in his pale eyes.

"Roger, Maelle, or whoever the fuck is currently in there, it's me, Lizzie Grace." Thankfully, the slight tremble in my hand was not reflected in my voice.

He didn't respond, and even though standing still, his body was making odd, almost jerky, movements. It was almost as if he was having trouble controlling... fuck, someone was in his mind.

Someone who *wasn't* Maelle.

Belle, can you— I broke the rest off as he lunged for me, his fingers sharp claws ready to rend and tear. He hit the barrier hard, briefly bending it inward and sending a concussion-like wave through the rest of it. He was so close that I could not only smell the blood on him but also see the desperation in eyes that bulged in his now emaciated features. An outside force might be in control of his mind, but somewhere in the background, Roger not only existed but was aware.

Then the wild magic responded and sent him flying across the room. I quickly created a containment net, using more wild magic to strengthen it, and cast it after him. I had no idea if the person wielding control over Roger was a telepath or one of our witchy vampires, but at least with wild magic woven through my spell, it couldn't easily be dismissed.

He smashed against the black glass with enough force to crack it. It would have knocked out—or at least severely hampered—anyone else. But Roger slid down to the floor and almost immediately scrambled upright.

Before he could take a step, my net hit him, flowing over his body like a wave, surrounding him in a globe of glowing threads. He screamed—a raw, furious sound—and clenched his fingers so tightly blood oozed between them and dripped slowly to the floor.

Then his eyes rolled back in his head, and he collapsed.

Belle, was that you?

"No, it was not." She stepped into the room and offered me a hand up. My barrier made no move to stop her—in fact, it expanded to include her within its protection. Which was a new development and one that I welcomed, even if it was also rather scary that these things seemed to be happening without any direction from me.

"Maybe not on a conscious level," Belle said, "but given all the other changes it's making, it's obviously working at a subconscious one."

I flicked my knife over to my gloved hand, then gripped hers and let her pull me upright. "Yes, but this is the first time it's included you in the response."

"Maybe it's got a checklist of tasks it's slowly working through, and I've finally reached the top."

I snorted and glanced at Roger. If he was breathing, I still couldn't see it. "I'm guessing his mind is as messed up as Joselyn's?"

She narrowed her gaze and studied him for several seconds. "Yes, which surprises me given Maelle's deep connection to the man."

"Could she have been caught in whatever snared his mind?"

"It's notionally possible, but I've never heard of a telepath capable of imprinting and controlling two minds at the one time."

"I can't imagine there'd be many telepaths who'd have come across a thrall and their master, though."

"True." She wrinkled her nose. "I'm not sensing an ongoing connection to either the telepath or Maelle, though."

"Would you sense his connection to Maelle, given it works on a deeper level than mere telepathy?"

"Yes, because in many ways it resembles our link."

Even though I hadn't actually thought about it until now, I guess our ability to share energy and allow our souls to partially step into each other's body *was* very similar to that of a thrall and his master. We just didn't have to eat each other's flesh to make it happen.

"Thank God for that," Belle muttered, and waved a hand toward Roger. "Whoever was controlling him has definitely retreated."

"Can you block a return?"

"Possibly, though it might be a good idea to also cast a protection spell of some kind around him in the event they try a magical takeover next."

"Surely they wouldn't, given Maelle is more than capable of defusing any such attempt."

"I would have said the same thing about their telepathic connection, but here we are."

I studied the sack-like figure for a moment. "I'm not sure any spell we cast is going to stand up against the might of an old vampiress who's also a mage."

"Except you have control over the one thing she does not," came the softly accented, deeply furious reply behind us.

My heart just about leapt out of my chest, and both Belle and I spun around, repelling spells buzzing around our clenched fists.

Maelle stood at the far "corner" of the room and was surrounded by shadows that concealed her form to the point only her eyes were visible.

They were little more than silver slits that promised death.

I immediately released my repelling spell and lowered my knife. Best not to antagonize her given she seemed on a knife's edge temper wise. "Maelle, you're alive."

"Of course I am. I would never be caught by such a cheap trick as this." Her fingers briefly shredded the shadows as she waved a hand toward the inert figure on the floor. "We had presumed he'd be a target, but we did not expect it to happen so soon in the game."

"It's hardly a game when lives are at risk," Belle commented.

The silver slits briefly looked her way. "Revenge is the biggest game of them all, my dear witch. And this?" Her fingers briefly appeared again. "This is merely a first play."

I'd have thought sucking the life out of a woman who resembled her daughter the first play, but maybe she meant on a personal level. "Is it a first play that allows you to retaliate?"

"Against her? No. Not unless she kills him—and she

won't, not until she's ready. Against any of her creatures—and she would have more than me, as her taste for the elixir of life goes far beyond mine—yes."

"But if she does kill him, it'll negate your oath to her?"

She hesitated. "It is something of a gray area. He was created long after I left the coven, but there is little information on whether he would fall under the scope of my oath or not."

And she understandably had no desire to test those boundaries.

I hesitated, but couldn't help asking, "And was it her 'tastes' that led to you decimating the coven in the first place?"

Just for an instant, her fury surged again, and I had to resist the urge to step back. The wild magic continued to pulse around both me and Belle, so there was no logical way she could hurt us.

Logic, however, wasn't in any way quelling fear.

"No, it was not," she growled after a second.

"Then what was? Honestly, Maelle, we need to know what lies at the base of this if we're to have any hope of stopping her."

"You will *not* stop her. *I* will."

Not if we got to her first. And I hoped we did, and soon, because the reservation really couldn't deal with the wave of bloody deaths that was coming.

Was coming, not might be.

Fuck.

Let's hope this is the one time your intuition is incorrect, Belle commented grimly.

You and I both know it fucking won't be. To Maelle, I added, "If you want our help—and you obviously do given one of you rang us before all this went down—then you need to answer the goddamn question."

Her fury flared yet again, and it made me wonder if Roger was in some way her calming influence. Without him, she seemed far more... temperamental? Volatile?

Was that why she'd disappeared for so long after she'd killed Clayton? Because Roger was in repair, and she didn't trust her own bloody nature?

"I do not *wish* your help," she said, her tone still barely above a growl, "but I cannot stand idly by and let her take out my people one by one. Roger might be the biggest blow to my support system, but he will not be the last."

"You could run," Belle said.

The silvery slits burned toward her again. "I could. I won't. This ends here. *She* ends here."

"Why?" I asked again. "What did she do that made you destroy your entire coven?"

There was another long pause. Though I couldn't see the flex of her fingers, I saw the movement through the shadows. Felt the burn of her barely contained anger and frustration. She really, *really* didn't like being questioned.

Let's hope us forcing the issue doesn't come back and bite us in the ass. Belle paused, then a wash of amusement came down the line. *Or wherever else Maelle likes to bite.*

I resisted the urge to physically whack her and gave her a mental one instead. Her mental laughter increased, bright and light in the dangerous gloom still surrounding us.

"She turned a great-grandson of mine into a thrall and did not even have the courtesy to tell me or ask permission," Maelle said eventually. "He was the first person I killed. He did not wish that life. He was miserable."

Well, fuck, Belle said. *I guess that explains why Roger was attacked. It's nothing more than a bit of tit for tat.*

I think you're missing the bigger problem in that state-ment, I replied. *It implies becoming a thrall is not always a choice.*

She swore. Vehemently. *How the fuck do we protect ourselves against something like that?*

We use wild magic to ramp up the vamp protection spells in our charms and make sure everyone we love has one.

I'll send Monty a message. He can grab Ashworth and Eli on the way home. We need to do this tonight, because your response here with Roger will have alerted Marie to your use of the wild magic.

She was already aware of it—she had one of her people attempt to break into the café, remember.

Yes, but tonight would confirm that you can apply it to spells at will.

And there was absolutely nothing we could do about that now. Nothing except hope like hell she didn't come after me before either Maelle killed her, or she killed Maelle.

"Can you restore and protect Roger?" Maelle said into the silence. "My magic—and our connection—cannot."

"Because Marie is stronger?"

The contempt that rolled off her was almost as fierce as the fury. "Marie is my *equal* when it comes to magic and would therefore be able to dismantle anything I construct. However, it is a simple case of ignorance. Neither of us had any reason to use or indeed be taught such a simple spell."

Because they used blood magic and ritual for protec-tions? Or because there were actually few mages alive who could magically best them?

I rather suspected the answer lay in a combination of both.

"I can try to protect him, Maelle," Belle said. "But restoring his mind will depend on what has been done and how strong the opposing telepath is."

"All I ask is that you try."

"Whether or not Belle can restore him to some semblance of normality," I said, "it might be worth acquiring some telepathic protection devices for your people. They're not perfect—a telepath as strong as Belle will break through them with a bit of time—but they will at least add an extra layer of difficulty and give you some warning. I'm not sure where'd you get them legally, but I dare say they'd be available on the black market."

Monty could probably let her know, given he was wearing one when he first came here, Belle said.

Yes, but let's not make things too easy for the bitch, because she's certainly not returning the favor. Besides, I have no doubt she'll know more than one black marketeer.

"I will make inquiries through my contacts," Maelle said, basically confirming my suspicions. "In the meantime, do what you can for Roger. I shall be nearby should you need anything."

And with that, the shadows rolled over the gleam of her eyes and all sense of her presence melted away. She'd no doubt simply retreated into her escape room, but it was nevertheless an unnerving sensation.

In fact, her remaining in the shadows the entire time was utterly out of character. It wasn't due to fear—not of us, at any rate. Did that mean the takeover of Roger had affected her in some way? He certainly looked far more emaciated than when I'd last seen him, so had Maelle for some reason drained his energy?

Or had it been *Marie* who'd done so?

Was it possible she'd used Roger's connection to Maelle to siphon *her* energy in an attempt to weaken her?

Possible.

More than possible, I suspected.

"Right," Belle said, after a deep calming breath. "Let's get down to business. I'll need you to dismantle the net around him, because as much as I don't want to, touching him will make it easier to sort out the damage done to him."

I quickly dismissed the containment net and also let the protection shield go. I could raise it again easily enough if needed, but it tended to pull on my strength after a while. Given Roger's repair might take a while, I didn't need it draining me when Belle might yet need to tap into my energy.

"How bad is it?" I asked.

"Imagine someone flattening a car's accelerator and ramming it straight through a crowd—that's basically what's happened here. If it was done with purpose, I'm not currently seeing it."

"Can you fix it?"

"Broad stroke destruction is actually easier to fix than fine-tuned intentional, but it's still going to take time, and there's no guarantee he'll regain all his memories."

"Maelle will be able to fill in the gaps, surely." I paused. "Do you think it's the finer details they wanted to pull from him and the broad stroke destruction is simply a cover? He not only knows every little detail about everyone she employs—whether as feeders or workers—but all her security and financial details."

"That's a definite possibility, though surely it's one Maelle would already be aware of."

I'd have thought so, but who really knew, given she remained intent on telling us as little as possible.

Belle knelt in front of the collapsed Roger, carefully rolled him onto his back, then pressed her fingers against his temples. After a deep, calming breath, she slowly—carefully —entered his mind. Though our connection was only light, I got enough of a glimpse to see the broad stroke brunt of the attack had happened through the section controlling bodily function such as balance and breathing. In fact, to me, it looked as if a ragged strip of black had been painted through that part of his brain.

That's a telepathic block preventing functional movements, Belle said. *The only reason he's alive is the fact he's no longer truly human. I can dismantle it, but it'll take time.*

And his memories?

Her telepathic eye briefly turned that way. *Mostly repairable, but the area that stores procedural memories appears to have been erased. I'm not sure recovery is even possible. It's not something I was ever trained for.*

Because she'd left Canberra with me long before her training was complete.

Don't you start with the whole guilt thing again, she warned.

I smiled. *Wouldn't dare.*

She harrumphed and got down to business. When she'd said it would take some time to undo the damage, she hadn't been kidding. It was close to an hour later by the time she'd released his temples, and her exhaustion rode our link even though she was resisting my efforts to push some strength her way.

"Right," she said, sweeping a hand across her forehead to brush away the beads of sweat. "I've done as much as I can, and I'm about to wake him. Be prepared for anything."

I nodded and raised another protection shield. She reached out mentally and removed the last vestiges of that black block. His eyes immediately snapped open, but for several seconds he didn't move, didn't respond, did even look truly aware.

Then from behind us, Maelle said, "You can rise, Roger. All is well."

My heart rate jumped, but I did at least manage to resist the urge to cast something nasty her way. I half turned. Though she remained in the shadows, this time, her whole face was visible. It was definitely more drawn than it had been the last time we'd met. "I do wish you'd stop sneaking up on us like that."

She chuckled softly. "Why? I rather enjoy the enticing leap of your heart rate."

It appears her temper and humor have improved now that Roger is back online, Belle commented.

And thank the fuck for that. "One of these days you might just get a blessed blade in your flesh or a face full of holy water rather than a simple enticing leap."

She chuckled again. "I have great faith in your control, my dear witch. Roger, rise."

He did so, though it was with some effort, and then bowed. "I fear I am currently incomplete."

"That we can fix. Belle, thank you for restoring my thrall. I am in your debt."

Belle nodded but didn't reply. Roger stepped around us and walked across to Maelle. The shadows enveloped him, and all sense of his presence disappeared. I couldn't help but wonder if restoring him meant him dining on some of her flesh again...

I shivered and hastily thrust the resulting images away. "Do you want us to lock up when we leave, Maelle? I noticed the guards weren't there—"

"They have already been replaced," she cut in. "You

may leave unhindered."

A rather ominous statement if ever I'd heard one. I nodded and caught Belle's arm to ensure she didn't stumble or fall as we left the room. The door closed behind us, the soft sound following us down the stairwell.

We retreated across the dance floor, the light sphere bobbing along above our heads, but the shadows seemed closer, thicker, and definitely more threatening now than they had earlier. The plastic covering the exit was pushed aside as we neared it, and a big man in black silently motioned us through. Another big man in black held the external door open. Neither were familiar. Neither spoke. Both smelled of death and ash.

They're not human, Belle said. *Or not entirely, anyway.*

Thralls? Maelle had implied she didn't have any others, but that didn't mean she was telling the truth.

No.

Then what are they? Demons? It would at least explain their scent.

If I had to guess, I'd say a combination.

Is that even possible?

A question for Ashworth or Eli, I'm thinking. But she obviously had them on hand, because surely the creation of such creatures would take time.

And effort. Though it could explain the gauntness in both her and Roger.

"You want me to drive?" I added. "It's not like you're in a fit state right now."

"What about the SUV?"

I shrugged. "We can pick it up later. I mean, it's full of bullet holes, so who'd steal it?"

She laughed, winced, then handed me the keys. I

helped her into the passenger seat, then jumped into the driver's side and spun the car around.

"Do you want to go straight home?"

She shook her head. "I told Monty to meet us at the café. We need to add the additional protections, because I don't trust Maelle's maker not to come after one of us in an effort to snare you."

"She might know about you, but surely she hasn't been here long enough to uncover all the minutiae about our friends and families."

"Except Roger did know all that, and it was part of the information they stole." She thrust a hand wearily through her hair. "They didn't erase as fully as they thought, and I was able to pick up echoes of what they went after."

"Well, fuck."

"To put it bluntly. But there is one good thing to come out of it—thanks to that echo, I have a feel for the other telepath and should be able to find him."

"How? By some sort of telepathic probe? Would that warn him you're looking for him?"

I swung into the laneway and slowed as I approached the rear parking area.

"Yes, it would," Belle replied, "which is why I'm not using a probe. I've got my spirit guides on the hunt for us."

"Your spirit guides?" My eyebrows rose. "The same guides who insist their purpose in life is to do nothing more than impart information and advice?"

"They have apparently decided this situation is dangerous enough that they can break their usual rules." She paused, her eyes narrowing a little. "I stand corrected. The rules have apparently been adjusted since events up in Canberra."

I hadn't thought my eyebrows could rise any higher, but

I was wrong. "Does that mean there's some sort of spirit guide council making rules and adjusting them as necessary?"

She laughed. "No, but many spirit guides were once witches, remember, and they do get together to discuss events and share pertinent information. It's how they're able to continue providing relevant guidance to those of us gifted with their presence."

I switched off the car and climbed out. "And what about feline and other non-human familiars? Do they get to participate in such gatherings?"

"Of course." She glanced at me. "Why?"

I grinned. "I was just wondering if your spirit guides could pass on a bit of tolerance advice to Monty's wretched familiar."

She laughed. "Eamon is okay once he gets to know you."

"And how many decades will that take? Because the bastard meets me with claws every time I go over there."

"Because he's well aware it'll get a rise from you. He *is* a feline, remember, even if his spirit once held human form. He won't ever draw blood. Not much, anyway."

I remained unconvinced, but kept my doubts to myself. We made our way inside and, after flicking the kettle on, I made us both a strength potion, adding honey to make them taste a little more palatable. Belle usually made bare-bones ones that tasted like swamp water, because she insisted sweetening the potions diluted their potency. I was willing to risk that in favor of palatability.

Monty, Ashworth, and Eli arrived about twenty minutes later. I made another round of coffee and tea and served up the last slices of the banana bread cheesecake.

"Did you find the missing person?" I poured my tea and then slid a cheesecake slice toward me.

Monty nodded. "It was the basilisk."

"Did the victim survive?"

"No. Aiden was heading over to inform the kid's parents." He grimaced. "We need to find a way to stop this bastard, stat. You had any luck with the wild magic?"

"Not yet, but it might be too early to get a full idea of his movements." I glanced at Ashworth. "Any luck with RWA?"

He nodded. "We've a wrangler coming in tomorrow afternoon. If we could pin down the basilisk's movements by then, it would be handy."

I nodded and made a mental note to contact Katie before I climbed into bed. I took a sip of my tea. "I don't suppose you've had time to do some more reading?"

"Actually," Eli replied, "I did, and I came across what amounts to an interesting sidenote."

"Interesting how?"

"It appeared at the end of the chapter explaining why conception within the source well was absolutely necessary—"

"Because it connected the wild magic and the embryo," I cut in, "allowing the latter to use and control the power of the spring without consequences."

Which was something we'd actually guessed before the book had confirmed it. It didn't explain what was happening here now, however. The wellspring that had infused *my* DNA wasn't the reservation's, and while a connection had definitely formed, there was also something *else* going on.

He nodded. "The sidenote briefly mentioned the offspring of a Fenna must either be conceived within the spring or bathed in its power within a set period afterward, so that the guardianship can move on smoothly from one

213

generation to the next, but also so that the spring could continue to evolve."

"We're talking about a force of nature here," Monty said. "It's literally the energy of the earth itself. How on earth could it evolve?"

Eli grimaced. "It doesn't say. I suspect, given the sheer amount of missing information, that the author either didn't know or simply thought it was such common knowledge it wasn't necessary to add."

"They'd surely be talking about the gain of sentience, though, given what's been happening to the wellspring here," Ashworth said. "Perhaps, in linking generations, they hoped the wellsprings would eventually become self-protecting."

"If that were the aim, wouldn't they have mentioned it in the chapter dealing with the origins of the Fenna?"

"Maybe other tomes *did* go into greater depth," he replied. "Just because this is the only book in *our* archives doesn't mean there can't be other tomes held in the UK or Europe that hold greater details."

"I guess." I scooped up the last of my cake. "Did the sidenote say how long the introductory grace period was?"

"Not in that particular note, though it might well do so later in the book. It also didn't go into the specifics of what would happen if the Fenna's offspring *wasn't* introduced, though it did say to heed the warning of Llan Cewydd."

"I take it you've googled the name?" Belle asked.

Ashworth nodded. "It's an old village in Gloucestershire, England, though little of the place remains. It was reclaimed by the forest, apparently."

"Do we know if there's a wellspring in that area?"

"Not according to current records, but that doesn't

preclude the possibility there once was. They do occasionally dry up."

And once again, we had no real idea why. "So, if the warning is to be believed, a wellspring was responsible for the destruction of that village because the Fenna's child was not introduced within the set timeline," I said. "But that doesn't explain what's happening here. I wasn't exposed to *this* wellspring as an embryo, so there shouldn't be any need for a child of mine to be bathed within her power."

And to be honest, I didn't really want to risk her existence by doing that. Just because I'd survived immersion didn't mean she would. Just because the text implied that survival was a given didn't mean it was. Not with what the earlier chapters had said about the survival rate of the conception ritual.

"The wild magic all comes from the same source," Monty commented. "Given this wellspring has apparently accepted your presence as its protector, it's possible the ceremony might be necessary for *any* child of yours."

Obviously sensing my doubts, Eli reached out and gripped my hand. "I've plenty of the book yet to read, so maybe the answers will be found. It still might be worth asking Aiden to get you into the O'Connor compound so you can check the wellspring."

"I'm heading there for a meeting tomorrow morning, so I'll be able to check."

Speculation suddenly glimmered in Ashworth's eyes. "I'd heard that Aiden had been cleared by the council to assume his father's mantle as alpha and had called a pack meeting, but why are they calling you there?"

I grinned. "Because he intends to push a vote on the matter as to whether we live in the compound or not once we're married."

"I can just imagine how his mother will react to that." Ashworth's voice was dry. "Oh, to be a fly on the wall to watch events unfold."

"To say it will be interesting could well be the under-statement of the year, in a year that's had plenty of them," I said, with a grin.

He laughed, and we finally got down to the business of altering our protection charms, laying not only wild magic through the vampire and demon repellent spells but also additional layers via spells created by Ashworth and Eli. Then we repeated the process, creating new charms for the two of them and also Aiden.

To say we were all exhausted by the time we'd finished would be an understatement.

After they'd all left, I revoked Maelle's access to the café, hoped like hell it worked, then walked upstairs and out onto the balcony, quickly snaring a thread of Katie's wild magic. I was too tired to converse very long with her, but she promised she'd update me on the basilisk's movement by lunch tomorrow.

With that done, I fell into bed and dropped into an exhausted sleep—one so deep not even dreams plagued me.

I once again woke to the delicious and rather erotic sensation of a muscular body snuggled against mine. I smiled and gently turned, watching the lovely planes of his face shift from sleep to awareness.

Then his eyes opened, and he smiled. "Morning, gorgeous."

I kissed him, soft and lingering. "What time did you get in last night?"

"Around one. Informing a parent about the death of their child is never a pleasant task, and I tend to stay until relatives or friends can come around and look after them."

"I don't know how you do it. It would break me."

He grimaced. "It is, thankfully, a relatively minor part of the job. And one that's not fair to pass on to the team."

I nodded and lightly touched the charm around his neck. "Before we leave the café this morning, we need to change this over for the new one we made last night."

"Why? What's wrong with this one?"

"It won't be strong enough."

I quickly updated him on last night's events, and he frowned. "From the sound of that, we better start preparing ourselves for an influx of bodies utterly drained of blood."

"I'm thinking if Maelle and Marie do go after each other's people, there's not going to be much in the way of remains left to identify them as human." Not given Maelle's bathing taste—one I suspected her maker might share. "What time do we have to be at the meeting this morning?"

"Nine."

I ran a finger lightly down his hip and smelled the delicious leap of desire. "What time is it now?"

"Just after six."

"Then we probably have twenty minutes or so before Belle arrives for the day." I slid a leg over his hip and pressed him closer. "Would you like bacon and eggs for breakfast? Or something else?"

Being the wise man that he was, he voted for the "something else," making me a very happy woman.

Aiden stopped the truck just beyond the compound's main entrance, and we both climbed out. The air was sweet and warm, and the sky clear of clouds, despite the weather bureau's prediction of storms later this afternoon.

What I couldn't see was any evidence of the wild magic, though I could feel the thrum of the wellspring's power clearly enough through the soles of my feet, despite the fact I was wearing shoes.

Tension wound through my limbs, but I did my best to ignore it and walked around the rear of the truck. Aiden caught my hand and led me forward, though I remembered the way clearly enough.

The trees quickly closed in, allowing shadows to cluster in this lower forest area. But the farther up the mountain we walked, the sparser the greenery became and the brighter it grew, until the wide canyon that led into the main living areas was bathed in sunshine. The canyon's walls were almost sheer, and thick with reefs of quartz that appeared jewel-like and precious in the bright morning light. Given much of the gold discovered in the area surrounding the compound had been found in quartz reefs, the latter might not be all that far from the truth.

As we moved through the canyon, people appeared, silently watching us pass before continuing with whatever they'd been doing. Aiden's confirmation as alpha would be old news now, but me appearing with him on the morning he'd called his first pack meeting would naturally stir some gossip and questions. At least the overwhelming emotion seemed to be curiosity rather than animosity, and that was a hopeful sign Karleen hadn't yet persuaded the pack I was bad news. Now we just needed to convince them it would be beneficial for *everyone* if Aiden and I lived—and raised our children—within the compound.

As the canyon widened even further, buildings of varying sizes appeared, most resembling longhouses of old. Much of the stone used in their construction was quartz, which meant they shone as brightly as the canyon's walls. All of them had earthen rooftops on which different grasses and wildflowers grew, presenting pretty mats of color even in the heat of summer. There was a proliferation of green technologies here as well, with every house having a combination of solar panels, wind turbines, and battery storage.

The closer we got to the compound's heart—which lay in the remnants of an old crater and held not only the main residences of the various alphas within the pack, but also the civic and industrial center—the larger and grander the longhouses became.

The grand hall—which was not only the pack's main meeting place but the building in which I'd confronted his mother and bested the demon trying to kill her—remained partially hidden by the trees that lined the end of the path, but it was circular in design with an angular earthen roof that pitched up to the stone chimney dominating the center of the structure.

The massive, double-width wooden doors were obviously open, as the soft babble of voices coming from within the hall rode the air. The pack leaders awaited to pass their judgment on us.

Aiden squeezed my fingers as we passed the final row of trees. "You ready for this?"

"As ready as I ever—"

I stopped abruptly, my gaze widening. The wild magic was here. It was *all* here. The whole building literally shone with it. Tiny threads of glowing moonlight crawled across the stone and through every fiber of every piece of wood within the frame. It was almost as if it were intent on imprinting its presence on every part of the building...

Realization hit, and horror surged.

The wild magic wasn't intent on imprinting its presence on the building.

It was intent on *reclaiming* it.

CHAPTER ELEVEN

T his was what had happened to that little village in Gloucestershire. This was *exactly* what had happened. I had absolutely no doubt of it.

And if we didn't stop it—if *I* didn't stop it—then a good portion of Aiden's pack would die.

Because that building was on the verge of collapse, and it wouldn't be the last to fall. The energy building under my feet very much suggested this whole area was about to be obliterated, just as that little village had been.

"Aiden," I said urgently, "the hall is about to collapse. You have to get everyone out. *Now.*"

He didn't question the statement. He simply turned and ran for the hall, his form flowing from human to wolf, his howl filling the air.

People began to file out of the hall, but they were moving too slowly, the wild magic too fast, and the building was beginning to shimmer and shift.

It would collapse before everyone got out.

I swore and ran after Aiden, the wild magic buzzing

around my fingers a stark contrast to the power and fury consuming the building ahead.

I didn't understand the fury.

Didn't understand how mere energy could even *be* furious or why it seemed intent on taking it out on the O'Connors rather than me, especially if what Eli had said was true and this was all connected to the child I now carried.

Aiden disappeared into the hall's cool darkness. A second later, he was yelling at them to leave, to hurry, that they were in danger, and they needed to get out.

Then a hand grabbed me, spun me, and I found myself staring into eyes as blue as Aiden's. His sister, Ciara, not his mother. *She'd* still be inside.

"What the fuck is going on, Liz? Why is Aiden ordering everyone out of the hall? He's the one that called—"

"I haven't the time to explain, but please, you need to evacuate the area. The wild magic is about to bring the hall down and maybe everything else in this damn area."

Her gaze jumped past me. "I know it's caused a few minor problems, but—"

She cut the rest off as a low rumble filled the air. It wasn't the building; it was the earth, beginning its rise to reclaim.

The hall would fall first, and people remained inside.

Aiden remained inside.

I peeled Ciara's fingers off my arm and said urgently, "We're about to be hit by a quake. Evacuate the entire area —*now!*"

This time she didn't argue. She just began shouting orders.

I turned and ran for the hall. People were now streaming out the doors, a fast-moving wave that parted around me without impeding my speed. *My* wild magic, gently creating a pathway.

The buzzing of the wellspring's power was strengthening, the earth's rumble growing louder, and the sense of doom deepening.

I tried to reach out, tried to connect to the power that burned all around me, but the old wellspring wasn't listening. She wasn't even acknowledging my presence.

I ran through the hall's entrance, then paused, my gaze scanning the tiered seating areas that ringed the currently covered firepit in the center.

Aiden, his mother, and several others I didn't know were standing on the far side of the room arguing.

"What the fuck are you doing?" I shouted. "The whole place is about to come down. You need to get out of here, now!"

"I should have known you were behind this," Karleen growled. "What is this? A little demonstration of just how powerful you are? How much of an asset you could be?"

"Mother, don't be fucking ridic—"

He stopped, his gaze snapping upward as a huge wooden support beam cracked. The sound echoed, as sharp as any gunshot. Then the earth began to undulate, the ground cracking, opening.

The earth was ready to reclaim.

Fuck, fuck, *fuck*.

"Get them out, Aiden. Get them out *now*."

I didn't wait to see if they left. I couldn't afford to. As chunks of wood and stone began to rain around us, I did the only thing I could think of. I dropped to my knees and, with every ounce of power I had, punched my right fist through the ground and connected, physically and psychically, to the pulsing heart of fury intent on destruction.

Power exploded through me, a wave of white-hot heat that crawled through every inch of me, stretching the very fibers of my being as it had stretched the fibers of the building. I felt insubstantial and ghostly, at one with the power and yet not. Its scent—earth and fire, wood and stone, rot and life—filled my nostrils even as she whispered of places no human soul could or should ever see.

Places she would take me if I didn't pull back and control the force of the energy.

As that realization surged, my inner wild magic rose, forming a protective barrier even as it deepened the connection.

We hear, I screamed into the fury. *We will come. I promise we will come to you. Do not destroy this place.*

For an instant, nothing happened.

Then the earth stopped shaking, the building stopped shimmering, and only dust fell from the roof. The glowing threads of wild magic crawled from the structure into the earth, healing the wounds it had caused as it left.

I pulled up my hand—scraped and bloody thanks to the force of my punch into the dry ground—then dropped my head and sucked in great gulps of air. My whole body shook, and I stank of sweat and fear, though the latter wasn't entirely due to what had happened, but rather the promise I now had to fulfill.

But if my child could survive the energy that had crawled across every fiber of my being, surely she could survive whatever complete immersion in the wellspring entailed.

I guess I'd know one way or another in the next few hours.

The air stirred as someone approached. I didn't have to look up to know it was Aiden. His scent filled my nostrils, making me feel safe. Making me feel like I was home.

He dropped beside me, wrapped his arms around me, and held me. He didn't say anything. He didn't need to.

"Well," Karleen said, her voice sharp in the silence. "While that was a lovely demonstration of your skills, all you've really done is prove that it's too fucking dangerous to have you living amongst us."

Aiden's anger rose so sharply I could practically taste it. I touched his arm lightly and then lifted my head and looked past him. Karleen and two other people—a man and a woman—stood near the firepit platform. The remnants of destruction were scattered around them, and the woman bore a bloody scratch down her arm that obviously wasn't as bad as it looked, given she hadn't bothered to shift shape and heal it.

"That wasn't a demonstration of my power, Karleen. It was a demonstration of the wellspring's."

She snorted. "The wellspring may well be a source of the earth's energy, but it is one only witches have the capacity to use and direct."

"I did *not* instruct the wild magic to destroy anything—"

"And we only have your word for that."

I smiled. There was absolutely nothing friendly or warm about it. "True, but I'm quite happy to call in an outside independent source to verify my claim. That would of course necessitate contacting the high council and would likely result in not only the council declaring your wellspring an area of national scientific interest, but also annexing a good portion of your lands."

Her gaze narrowed. "Is that a threat?"

"No, a reality. What is happening here, with your wellspring, is something that has *not* happened for centuries." I took a deep breath and then went to the one place I really didn't want to. Not yet, anyway. "But in the interest of complete transparency, Eli discovered some information last night that suggests I could, in part—and very unknowingly—be responsible for the wellspring's current course of action."

"Oh, color me so surprised." Karleen's tone was sarcastic. "Get her out of here, Aiden. We do not need her kind—"

Aiden surged to his feet so suddenly, I briefly unbalanced. "Enough with your hatred, Mother. Enough with your inability to see beyond the past. Liz isn't responsible for your sister's rape and subsequent death. Neither she nor Gabe is responsible for Katie's death. Liz has put her life on the line countless times to keep this reservation safe. She even saved your goddamn life right here in this building, and yet all you can do is live in the past rather than see the future. I intend to marry this woman—"

"You cannot—"

"You can't fucking stop me. I'm *head* alpha of this pack now and its representative on the council. I have a duty to this pack that I will never ignore, but I *will* choose the mate of my heart. The only decision to be made here today is where we live once we marry. And that, I assure you, will be happening very soon."

A soft murmur rose behind us. I glanced around. The other pack alphas had returned. Aiden motioned them inside.

As they filed in, I drew another deep breath and then said, "Before we get around to discussing our living arrangements, it's probably best I explain my statement about why these quakes are happening, and what needs to be done to stop it."

Karleen's expression was contemptuous. "The pack

doesn't need any more of your lies—"

"What the pack doesn't need," Aiden cut in, "is the whispers you've been spreading about our witches, who even now are working their butts off to stop a goddamn vampire war while trying to catch the basilisk that just turned Jenny Sinclair's son into goddamn stone."

Karleen's face paled. "Jenny's son? Vander?"

"Yes, Vander. And if you stopped swimming in the pool of your own misery for two seconds and actually concentrated on reservation and pack business, you'd realize that the problem here isn't the witches, it's the decision the council made over a year ago *not* to immediately replace Gabe or protect the wellspring. Almost every single murder that has happened since then is a result of that decision. If you'd had your way six months ago and convinced the council to run Liz and Belle out of town, this reservation would be *dead*. Or, perhaps even worse, under the control of the goddamn High Witch Council."

He was so damn angry his fists were clenched. This was the alpha fully unleashed, and I wanted to stand up and cheer.

Karleen definitely *hadn't* been expecting it, despite their confrontation yesterday. He'd played the waiting game so damn well she'd obviously believed it was a one-off, that with the backing of the pack she could still rule even if he'd now assumed his father's place.

Her expression suggested she was now very aware of how badly she'd misjudged her eldest son.

She didn't say anything, however. She simply turned and walked across to an empty section of seating. Ciara, I noted, was already there, along with a number of other wolves I didn't recognize, but who were obviously part of Aiden's extended family.

Aiden glanced down at me. "You want a hand up?"

I nodded and raised my good hand. He effortlessly pulled me upright, then wrapped a hand around my waist and helped me over to the covered firepit.

"Do you need a medic for that hand? You're dripping blood all over the place."

I glanced down and saw that one of the cuts was deeper than I'd initially presumed. The price of connection, perhaps?

I doubt any sort of blood price would be needed when it comes to wild magic, Belle said. *Especially when that's the one thing witches have been told to avoid when it comes to wellsprings.*

I'd agree, except for the fact we still don't have a full understanding of Fenna beyond how—and possibly why—they were created.

Which is why I've just contacted Eli and told him we need more information about "bathing" a Fenna's offspring in the wellspring STAT.

Here's hoping it's there to find. But even if it wasn't, I had no choice except to fulfill my promise and walk into the wellspring. Maybe not right now, but sometime soon. The wellspring's patience would not hold for all that long.

Perhaps, Belle said, *you need to wrap a sliver of it around your wrist so that the old wellspring is aware of your intent and actions.*

Good idea. I silently put out a call and a solitary thread drifted in and wrapped around my wrist. It felt like I was being branded by fire. The wellspring's dangerous fury might have retreated from the area, but it very definitely hadn't abated.

"Liz?" Aiden said softly, making me jump.

"Sorry, I was talking to Belle." I glanced down at my

hand. "The bleeding will stop quickly enough. I might not be a werewolf, but I've gained a werewolf-like healing ability, remember."

It was said for the benefit of those listening, and the glimmer in his eyes suggested he was well aware of that fact. "And not just healing, but the ability to *physically* hold your own against a werewolf, as Mother can attest."

Another soft murmur ran around the room at that. Karleen neither elaborated nor denied the statement, but her gaze burned holes in my spine.

A wolf sitting in the section opposite us rose. "It's been implied by Monty and now yourself that the destruction happening within this compound is due to our wellspring—a wellspring that has never, in all the time it has been a part of this reservation, proven dangerous in any way. What has changed?"

"Two things," I said calmly. "The first is, as Aiden said, your council's refusal to call in a replacement for Gabe after he disappeared. The second is my arrival."

"How is your arrival connected?" another voice asked.

Sparks began to dance around my fingertips, though the ones around my right hand had a reddish glow thanks to the wound—which, thankfully, was already beginning to heal. "To explain that, I have to give you a little bit of history about witches, werewolves, and wellsprings."

I did a quick rundown of everything we'd discovered about the Fenna and their connection to wellsprings, and then added, "My mother—who is, for those who don't know, Eleanor Marlowe, one of the most powerful witches in Canberra and a leading member of the High Witch Council—"

Another murmur rose. Obviously, Karleen hadn't bothered mentioning that tidbit, either.

I waited for it to die down, then continued. "Mom was unknowingly a few weeks pregnant with me when she was sent to protect a newly emerged wellspring. It resulted in both her and me being fully exposed to the unbridled power of the spring. It should have killed us. It didn't, and we now believe it's because there's Fenna in our bloodline."

"Which would explain," Ciara said, "why you've got werewolf-like healing and fast reactions. There *is* actually werewolf blood in your veins."

It was a leap of logic I wasn't about to gainsay—not if it made it easier for the pack to accept me. "We can't confirm any of this, of course, not only because no records remain from that period of time, but also because if the High Council ever got wind of the fact it was possible to connect a witch to the wild magic, half of Canberra would descend on this reservation."

"Which is why both Ashworth and Monty have been falsifying their reports to Canberra since their arrival," Aiden said.

A sliver of surprise came from the group behind us. Though it was hard to tell who it had originated from without looking, I suspected it was Karleen, given Ciara was already well aware of this fact. Maybe Karleen was finally understanding not only how badly she'd misread the whole wellspring situation, but also the precarious position her interference had placed the reservation in.

"Why have we not been told any of this?" The woman who asked had a face full of freckles and appeared only a few years older than me, though given how well werewolves aged, she could have been in her forties. "Why have we been left in the dark in regard to all the murders and their connection to the wellspring?"

"The council placed an embargo on the news because

they did not want to cause reservation-wide panic," Karleen said evenly. "None of us were sure how long the problem would last."

It was tempting to say that was a lie, that we witches had known it would be years, not months, before the siren call of an unprotected wellspring stopped echoing across the shores of darkness.

But if I wanted any chance of living within the compound then I couldn't keep adding fuel to her fires... although me being alive and present seemed to be all the fuel she needed.

"If you're now connected to our wellspring," the man seated beside the freckled woman said, "then its continued attacks on us very much suggest it is—even if on some weirdly subconscious level—acting out your anger against Karleen and her objections to your relationship with Aiden."

"If that were true, then these events would have started months ago, when she began her campaign to split us," I said. "But in fact, the first rumblings only started after I left to testify at my father's trial."

Another murmur ringed the room. These people obviously didn't watch the news, because despite the embargo the High Council had placed on the trial, there'd still been mention of it online and in the various gossip mags.

"Then what is the cause and how do we stop it?" Ciara asked.

I drew in a deeper breath and released it slowly. This really wasn't where I'd wanted us to be when I informed Aiden of his impending fatherhood, but I guessed, in some respects, it was also absolutely perfect. His reaction, for good or for bad, would be there for everyone to see. Unfaked, unforced.

"As I mentioned earlier, Eli uncovered some new information that mentioned the need for the offspring of any Fenna to be bathed in the wellspring's power." The man beside me stiffened at that, but I ploughed on. "And it gave the name of a small village in Gloucestershire as an example of what would happen if they weren't. That town was basically erased. The earth rose up and consumed it, just as the earth here tried to consume this hall and everyone within it."

"Does that mean...?" Aiden asked softly.

I glanced at him. His eyes shone, and his expression held an endearing mix of hope, excitement, and disbelief. "I'm afraid it does."

He let out a whoop that damn near deafened me, then pulled me into his arms and kissed me very, *very* thoroughly, utterly uncaring about the fact we had an audience.

But then, he was a werewolf, and they did all run naked through the forest—and do a whole lot more, if the whispers were to be believed—in full view of everyone every full moon. A kiss, however intense, wasn't ever likely to faze the pack.

"When?" he asked eventually. His eyes shone with happiness, and his grip on my fingers was fierce. Like he didn't want to let me go just in case it somehow all went away. "And how? Weren't you protected the entire time?"

"Yes, but it appears that the changes the wild magic was making to my DNA blunted the effectiveness of the contraception I was on. As for when—I've yet to go to a doctor, but she's likely to appear in eight or so months."

"Why haven't you said anything?" He paused, understanding dawning. "You didn't because of everything Mom has said about crossbreeds."

"I'm sorry, but if she happened to be right, and I lost our

child..."

He hugged me, whispering, "That's not something you should have contemplated going through alone."

Footsteps approached, and we glanced around a heartbeat before Ciara swept her arms around us both and hugged us fiercely. "Congrats, big brother. You are going to be a most excellent dad. And Liz? Welcome to the family."

Tears stung my eyes, and I blinked them back rapidly. "Thanks."

A throat was cleared to our right, then a big man with graying hair rose. He wasn't a typical-looking O'Connor—his coloring was darker, his features swarthier. Aiden's pack was a little smaller, numbers-wise, than the norm, even if there were five distinct family lines within it, which made the national/international exchange programs vital to prevent interbreeding. This man had obviously married in from elsewhere.

"I appreciate the desire to celebrate such news," he said, his tone gravelly but pleasant, "but this compound was almost destroyed, and we really need to understand how an embryo could possibility be responsible for it."

"In truth, we don't understand it either," I replied. "But it's pretty evident from the wellspring's actions over the last few weeks that, even if it makes no damn logical sense to any of us, the child I carry has to be bathed in the wellspring's power, otherwise these attacks will continue until the compound is destroyed." I hesitated. "In fact, it was only my promise to do so that stopped the attack today."

"How is walking into the wellspring not going to kill you both?" Ciara asked bluntly, voicing the question—and the fear—I could see in Aiden's eyes.

"Mom survived immersion. I should be able to."

"'Should' is not a very comforting word," Aiden

muttered. "When do you plan to visit the wellspring?"

"I don't want to do anything without Belle, Monty, Ashworth, and Eli here, because we have no idea what will happen when I enter the spring or how it'll react. They can protect the compound—or at least its people—if necessary. As to when—there's stuff we need to do to prepare, so this evening would be best. I have no idea how long the wellspring will wait before it attacks again."

Aiden glanced at the wolves gathered in front of him. "Is everyone in agreement to allowing the witches entry?"

A round of mostly "ayes" swept the room.

Karleen rose and cleared her throat to gain attention. I hadn't heard her voice in the "ayes" but she hadn't given a no, either. "Given what now has to be done, can I suggest the vote relating to where our new alpha and his mate will reside be deferred until this matter is over."

Until it was clear whether I lived or died was what she meant.

Another round of "ayes" swept the room. It did make sense to delay, but I could feel the annoyance radiating from the man still holding my hand.

Another man rose. Though I didn't know him, his features were similar to the big man with graying hair. A son, perhaps? There wasn't a woman sitting in the area next to the older man, so perhaps their son had taken her place. "Are we able to witness the event?"

I hesitated. "The wellspring is ringed by magical protections that will prevent you from getting too close. And to be honest, I'm not really sure there will be much to see, given wolves are incapable of seeing magic."

"If you are to be a part of this pack, then this pack needs to understand your relationship with our wellspring," he said.

"I agree," Aiden said, surprising me. "Does everyone agree to the attempt being made at dusk?"

I glanced at him, eyebrows raised, but didn't question his statement. Not here, not in front of his pack.

A murmur of assent ran around the room. Aiden dismissed the meeting, then tugged me from the room. We walked silently through the main compound and were halfway through the canyon—and well out of earshot of those who'd been watching us—before I asked, "What's the point of agreeing to the pack being there when you know they won't see anything?"

"Because of what happened in the hall, when you punched your hand into the ground."

"When the wellspring's power swept through me?"

He nodded. "For the briefest of seconds, you were incandescent and amorphous. It was fucking scary, let me tell you. They need to see that. They need to understand the risks you—and the others—take for us."

I squeezed his fingers lightly. "Sorry to worry you."

"It's not like you had a choice in the matter. And it's not like it's the first time you've done something dangerous." He paused for what seemed ages. "But it is the first time that it's not just you I'll lose. It's our daughter, too."

I swallowed the lump in my throat and tried for light-ness. "You never know, my dreams could be wrong, and 'she' might well be a 'he.'"

"Your dreams are never wrong." It was wryly said. "But I guess I should take heart in the fact that those dreams mean she *will* survive this immersion. Which, thankfully, means you will as well."

"The book did say bathing was necessary to ensure guardianship could move smoothly from one generation to

235

the next. It wouldn't do so if there was little chance of survival."

"I shall cling to that belief and try not to worry." He opened the truck, ushered me inside, then ran around to the driver side. "What's the likelihood of our unwanted vampires sensing what we're doing at the wellspring and using the opportunity to attack us?"

"There's always that chance, but I think the reality is pretty low. It's more likely they'll use the opportunity of our absence to create havoc elsewhere."

"I hope you're right."

So did I. Because I'd put the assertion out there now, and that was always pretty damn dangerous.

The weather finally broke near dusk, just as we were heading for the wellspring. Aiden, Ashworth, Eli, and I were in Aiden's truck, with Belle and Monty following in our SUV. The rain pelted against the windshield so hard it sounded like ice rather than water, and I very definitely did *not* look forward to going out in it. I'd grabbed my waterproof gear, just in case, but despite the storm, it remained unbearably sticky, and the waterproofs didn't really breathe. I'd be a puddle of sweat before the evening was out, of that I was sure.

We didn't enter the compound via the main entrance but rather a side road that was closer to the wellspring and barely wider than a goat track. Aiden's truck chugged up the long, steep incline and, once we reached the top, he turned off the road, then switched off the engine and the headlights.

Ghostly figures emerged from the nearby trees. The

pack—or at least some of it—had indeed come to watch the show. I really, *really* hoped they left disappointed, because I did not want to go through that whole amorphous thing again.

Even if I suspected being amorphous might be the least of my problems going into the wellspring.

I pulled on my waterproofs and then climbed out of the truck.

The gray-haired gentleman—whose name was Larkin, and who'd been a close friend of his father, Aiden had informed me—stepped forward and gave me a friendly enough nod. "Is there anything we need to be wary of? Will the magic—or whatever it is you need to do—present a threat to any of us?"

If they're worried about a threat then they shouldn't be here, Belle said, mental tone cross.

You can't blame them for being curious, given werewolves can't see magic and very few of them have any working knowledge of spells or indeed witches. Besides, if we want them to get over their natural prejudices, then we need to get over our reluctance to share.

She snorted. *It's not like we don't share. Besides, we've been in the reservation for a year now; if they were so damn curious, they could have just popped into the café and asked.*

You forget who has been running the show up until now.

She harrumphed, but didn't argue the point.

I smiled and tugged the coat's drawstrings tighter to prevent the wind blowing off my hood. "We don't actually know what will happen when I step into the wellspring. That's why I requested permission to bring Belle, Monty, Ashworth, and Eli into the compound—if something does go wrong, they'll be able to either magically nullify it or throw a protection spell over everyone to keep you safe.

"But if I say run," Aiden added, "then don't think, just go."

A murmur ran through the forest; we had a bigger crowd than was initially obvious.

Aiden glanced at me. "You ready?"

"No, but there's no avoiding it."

Not if we wanted to save the pack.

He lightly touched my arm, though I wasn't sure if he was reassuring me or himself, then turned and led us through the trees—though in truth, the caress of the well-spring's power was strong enough that I didn't really need a guide. I could have found it with my eyes closed.

Dusk was closing in fast, and the shadows haunting the trees deepened into darkness. Monty and Eli created a couple of light orbs that bobbed along above our heads, their muted glow lighting the path while not affecting our night sight.

The closer we got to the wellspring, the stronger its heartbeat became, until all I could feel was the pulse of its energy. It was bright, fierce, and powerful, a force as ageless and as endless as the earth under our feet.

That force wanted me.

Wanted to embrace me.

Trepidation skittered across my skin, but I did my best to ignore it. There was nothing else I could do, because I had no real choice. We knew well enough what would happen to the compound if I refused to do this, but there was also the growing question of what would happen to our child if I didn't. The book hadn't said there would be any consequences other than destruction, but I couldn't escape the notion that perhaps that destruction would extend to the new life growing within me.

We finally reached the hill's crest and began to descend.

Magic pulsed through the air, a signal to those who were sensitive to its presence that a number of protective spells were active up ahead. But it was overrun—at least for me— by the earth's power. It crawled across my skin, stinging and biting, filled with the anger I'd sensed earlier. Had I not come here this evening, it might have lashed out again.

Eli hadn't been able to find anything in the book to explain why the wild magic would destroy the very people it needed to protect it, nor had there been anything further to explain the bathing and what we might expect. We really *were* going into this blind.

I flexed my fingers, and once again tried to calm the surge of fear and worry. Naturally, it didn't help, but my inner wild magic nevertheless responded, creating a gentle net of energy around my body that lessened the impact of the wild. Which was a really interesting response, given my inner wild magic ultimately came from the same source, and had only truly emerged on connection with *this* wellspring.

We finally came out of the trees. Ahead of us lay the wellspring and, despite it being wrapped in multiple layers of protecting magic, it burned as fiercely as the sun. This wellspring, unlike Katie's, had been here for a very long time, perhaps even longer than the werewolves. If a wellspring could be said to be in its prime, then this one was.

Aiden stopped a few feet away from the barrier. Though he couldn't see the magic that burned the air, we'd ringed the entire area with white quartz stones to ensure no wolf stumbled unknowingly into our protective barriers. While none of the spells would hurt them, they *would* repel them. The last thing any of us had wanted was an accidental injury giving Karleen additional ammunition against us.

I stopped beside Aiden, then briefly turned and

scanned the trees. There were at least two dozen wolves that I could see and plenty more that I could smell. I wasn't very good at sorting through the various scents to pick out one particular person, but I had no doubt Karleen would be in there somewhere. If things went wrong, she'd want to witness it firsthand.

After all, it was much harder to gloat or to use information against someone if you were relying on secondhand reports.

Not necessarily, Belle said, *but if things do go wrong and she seizes the moment to use it against us, she'll find herself at the wrong end of a telepath's fury. She won't even know what hit her.*

I smiled. *As tempting as that thought is, screwing with her mind will only cause greater problems for us in the long run.*

If you get dead and she starts in on us or Aiden, I don't fucking care. She paused. *Just make damn sure you don't get dead.*

I'll definitely try not to. I glanced at Ashworth as he and Eli stopped beside us. "How long will it take to weave the exceptions through the various layers of magic?"

I already knew the answer, but said it for the benefit of our watchers. There wouldn't be many who had any real idea about what would happen or what we intended, and that needed to change if we were to live in this reservation without having the possibility of being evicted constantly hanging over our heads. Karleen might have failed to convince the council last time, but there was no guarantee that wouldn't change in the future. Especially if her opposition to my very existence continued.

"Only a few minutes each," Ashworth replied, then glanced at Monty. "You're up first, lad."

He immediately stepped forward and, after studying his spell for a moment, found and disconnected the completion line. He quickly wove in the exception, saying the spell out loud for the benefit of our watchers. Once it was done, he closed and reactivated the spell, then motioned Eli to proceed. He, and then Ashworth, repeated the entire process with their spells, but I didn't need to. While a witch could generally pass through their own protective magic without an exception thread being added, I'd nevertheless fallen on the side of caution when I'd first woven my spell around the spring.

I took another of those deep breaths in a vague attempt to calm my nerves. As per usual, it didn't help. Tiny sparks of energy continued to dance all around me, a starry light show none of those behind us would see.

"Ready?" Aiden said softly.

"No, but hey, when has that ever mattered." I flicked off my shoes, then bent and picked them up. "Keep them safe for me."

He snorted. "I think your ratty old sandals would be safe from thieves even if you dumped them in the middle of the street with a 'take me' sign attached."

"They're not ratty," I retorted, in mock offense, "they're just perfectly worn in."

"If you say so." The amusement dancing in his eyes faded as he leaned closer and kissed me softly, tenderly. "Come back to me."

"Always." I lightly touched his face then, before fear got the better of me, turned and walked toward the barriers. Magic briefly resisted my presence, each layer gently examining me before allowing me through. As I stepped through my spell, my wild magic surged, as if in response to a threat I couldn't yet see.

In truth, I couldn't even see the wellspring, simply because its glare was so damn bright it was nigh on blinding. I closed my eyes and used the heartbeat under my feet to guide me forward. I didn't trip, didn't fall.

Though instinct was very much suggesting that would change when I reached the wellspring's source. I kept all things crossed intuition was just messing with my head.

Though I kept my eyes tightly closed, I could clearly see the wellspring in my mind's eye. Rather than being an actual spring, as Katie's was, this was a deep pit in the ground, with a mound of tailings on one side, and an old, rather degraded-looking wooden ladder on the other.

It was a mine. The wellspring's source was a goddamn mine.

I guess, if nothing else, that explained my tendency to discover these things the hard way. Thanks to the wild magic, I had an unwelcome bond with them.

I stopped on the very edge of the shaft and glanced down. All I could see was the brightness. It was a heated river of power that flowed over me, through me, running through my veins like fire and making my whole body vibrate.

I had to step in. Had to become part of it.

For the longest of moments, I just couldn't force my feet forward.

The heartbeat under my feet increased, and wisps of gathering fury ran around me. I had to do this. I had no choice.

I clenched my fists and stepped into the hole.

And fell.

But this wasn't like the other times I'd fallen into shafts. This descent wasn't rapid, wasn't uncontrolled. My magic burned around me, meshing with the wilder power, and acting as some kind of a brake.

But the deeper I got, the stronger the pull of that power, the more it infused me. It crawled through muscle, veins, and bone, seeming intent on drilling down to the very atoms of my anatomy and tearing it apart, until I was nothing but a consciousness swimming in a sea of white.

Nothing but a voice that cried out in pain and confusion and hope of acceptance.

But I was not alone in this place.

There were other voices here. Voices that rejoiced in my presence, offering me comfort and a deep sense of presence. I couldn't see them, couldn't feel them, but they surrounded me nonetheless, ushering me forward, ushering me deeper, into the deeply resonating heart of the power.

In that core, we were considered.

Not me so much as the child I carried.

The little girl who would one day master this energy in a way I couldn't even begin to imagine.

A little girl whose very existence now hung on the judgment of the amorphous power that surrounded us and the voices that sang to us.

Voices that were even older than this wellspring; voices that belonged to all those who had traveled this path before us.

The Fenna.

Singing to my child. Explaining to me.

Then the tenor of their song changed. Rejoiced.

The earth had accepted my child.

But it rejected me.

A heartbeat later, it sent me careening out of the mine, back into the real world.

CHAPTER TWELVE

I stumbled forward several meters and then fell, landing heavily on my hands and knees. Stones tore into my palms, but that was nothing compared to the pain that burned through my entire being. Absolutely everything hurt—even my goddamn hair. Even worse was the fact I just couldn't drag in enough air to ease the fire in my lungs or the racing of my heart.

I stayed there for what seemed like ages, shaking and sweating, but gradually the pain eased enough for some semblance of awareness to return. The earth's fury had also eased, and while the wellspring's light continued to burn as bright as any sun, there was no anger in her now.

The spring had accepted her guardian. My daughter would become one with her when she was old enough. In the meantime, I remained the temporary protector, able to call on her power while never fully integrating.

I didn't know whether to laugh or cry.

Didn't know how I felt about the life I'd committed our daughter to. She was now forever linked to this wellspring and those voices. In very many ways, I'd doomed her to an existence and a way of life she might never have willingly chosen.

And there was nothing, absolutely nothing, I could do about it.

Because thanks to those voices, I also knew that had she been considered unworthy, her existence would have ended.

As the pain abated even further, sensory input returned. It was no longer raining, but the air remained sharp with the threat of it. Overhead, thunder rumbled, a sound that echoed through the earth itself. Only it wasn't thunder but an odd sense of movement and chaos. It wasn't the wellspring; it was something else.

Then the scent of blood and fury hit my nostrils, even as howls of anger and confusion rent the air.

We were under attack...

Belle? What's happening?

For several seconds there was no response, and my fear surged. I pushed upright and staggered forward, but my legs didn't want to support my weight and I fell again.

Here, Belle said. *Sorry.*

What's happening?

The basilisk attacked. It's fucking chaos.

Where are you?

Eli and I are protecting everyone who'd been watching the show. Monty and Ashworth are chasing the basilisk.

And Aiden?

Organizing ambulances and trying to keep everyone calm.

I'd half expected him to be chasing the basilisk with Monty and Ashworth, but he was the new alpha, and his duty did now lie with the pack. *Were many hurt?*

Two frozen. A dozen or so mown down and partially crushed.

Which was bad but, in many respects, it could have been far worse.

Yeah, came Belle's response, *the vamp mages could have used the basilisk as a distraction.*

She'd barely even finished that statement when magic burned the air. Dark magic, not clean.

The vamps *had* used the basilisk as a distraction.

Eli's and Belle's magic flared in response. I pushed upright once again and stumbled forward, zigzagging through the layers of protection spells before falling again. My hands hit the ground so hard they wedged into the soil, and in that moment, I felt the vampires. Felt their movement. Each step they took was a heavy weight that stained the ground with darkness.

There were three of them here, which in itself was rather odd if Marie *had* intended serious destruction. But perhaps this was nothing more than a magical test, a means of discovering the strengths and weakness of the witches who lived within the reservation. Aside from the fact the vamps cast spells that were gradually ramping up in power rather than hitting Eli and Belle with everything they had first up, all three moved with unnatural speed. Vampires were fast, I knew *that* from experience, but this was next level, and very much suggested they were using spells to enhance their physical capabilities.

Which meant that this secondary attack could also be nothing more than yet another distraction.

After all, Marie would have felt the flare of power as I'd entered the wellspring. Perhaps she'd sent her troops in to uncover what was happening.

Or perhaps she intended something more nefarious, like

kidnapping me while everyone else was otherwise occupied.

I suspected the latter was probably true, but right now I couldn't feel the presence of anyone else other than those three vamps. I had to concentrate on the problem that *had* presented itself, rather than the one that might.

I gathered the shredded remains of my strength and reached for the wild magic—the wellspring's rather than mine, simply because mine couldn't do what I needed it to do. Just for an instant, the Fenna's chorus ran through my mind, sitting in judgement of my need. Then the connection formed, and the wellspring's magic answered my call. I gathered it around my fingertips, then narrowed my gaze and concentrated on the trails of darkness. After a few, very long seconds, I found the pattern in their movements and sent the wild magic after all three.

Not to kill but to capture.

These vamps might be capable of dark magic, but even they couldn't break or bend the threads of this wellspring. Not now that the Fenna had acknowledged and accepted both its protector and its temporary guardian.

As the wild magic leapt away to do my bidding, the inner pain exploded. A groan escaped, and I fell forward, my forehead hitting the ground hard enough to bruise. I barely felt it. I just huddled in on myself, hugging my body tightly and rocking back and forth in an effort to keep awake, keep aware.

There had to be more behind this attack.

Had to be.

It didn't make sense otherwise.

Movement echoed once again through the earth, heavy with the weight of dark intent. A vampire, coming straight at me. I tried to raise my head but couldn't. Tried to reach for Belle, but the pain locking my mind was somehow inter-fering with the signal. I could feel her, but I couldn't hear her.

The darkness was growing stronger, closer.

Magic flared around me, a protective net that wasn't as fierce, wasn't as strong, as the power coming at me.

More footsteps vibrated across the soil. Light, fast, and from the left.

Not a vampire. Not a mage. Aiden.

"No," I somehow croaked, "don't—"

Too late.

As a spell began to stain the air, a blur of silver leapt over my body. A heartbeat later came the ragged tearing of flesh, followed by a sharp scream that was fury and pain combined. A woman's scream, not a man's. The dark spell faltered, but another took its place, and my wolf was punched away. The woman retreated rather than attacked, the scent of her blood strong on the air and no doubt the ground, leaving a trail for the wolves to follow.

More movement, again from the right. Knees hit the ground, then familiar arms wrapped around me. Belle, not Aiden. "He's okay, you're okay."

I actually wasn't, and she knew it. Our connection might not be firing on all cylinders, but she'd nevertheless be aware of the agony that currently locked my body and mind.

"Yes," she said softly, "and I'm about to do something about it. Hold still for a few seconds."

She pressed her fingers lightly to my temples, and the connection between us sharpened, abruptly unhampered by waves of pain that seemed to be shorting things out. She dove deep and hard into my mind, mentally shoving bits aside as she reached for the sensory and pain center of my brain. Within seconds, the agony had receded enough for me to think, breathe, and move with some semblance of normality. It remained a background beat, however, and would undoubtedly need confronting with strong painkillers and a few hours of sleep at some point in my near future.

Belle dropped her hands, then sat back on her heels. "Better?"

"Yes. Thank you." I pushed into a sitting position and took a cautious, somewhat quivery breath. "We need to go chat to the vamps I snared."

"I'd rather chat about what the fuck happened in the wellspring, but I get that's not practical right now." She placed her hand under my elbow, steadying me as I rose. "But just to let you know, those white streaks in your hair? They've spread."

I automatically reached up and tugged sweaty strands of fringe down to check it out. Still red. "One or two more isn't going to bother me."

And it wasn't like I could do much about it unless I wanted to dye them out, and the crimson red of a royal witch was notoriously hard to replicate.

Belle's amusement bubbled through me. "That bit of fringe you're holding? It's the *only* bit of crimson remaining in your hair."

I blinked. "Seriously?"

"Yes. It shines moon bright, too, I might add."

Movement echoed through the ground again and, a second later, Aiden appeared. Relief hit so hard that my knees wobbled. Belle once again caught my arm to ensure I didn't fall.

I didn't say anything. I just drank in the sight of him as he strode through the last of the trees. His jeans were torn and bloody, and there was a fresh scar across his cheek, evidence to the fact that he *had* been hurt when the witch had flung him away.

Better injured than killed, though.

God, wouldn't it be the mother of all ironies for us to finally start planning a future together only to have him snatched permanently from my life? From our daughter's life?

The mere thought had tears stinging my eyes. I blinked them away furiously and tried to get a grip.

His nostrils flared as he got closer, no doubt smelling the deeper edges of pain and weariness. Then he was in front of me, wrapping his arms around me, his relief and love flowing over me, burning my senses with their fierceness.

"I'm okay," I said softly.

He didn't answer, but an unspoken "this time" seemed to hover between us.

After a few more seconds, he lightly kissed my bruised forehead, then stepped back, his gaze on my hair rather than my face. "*That* is quite a change."

"A good one or a bad?"

"Good. And, streak aside, it gives you the coloring of an O'Connor wolf."

"Shame it won't make the pack accepting me any easier."

"No," he said lightly, "but at least you won't stand out like a sore thumb when we're living here."

If we were allowed to live here. That wasn't a given at this stage. "I guess that's one benefit of going gray at such a young age."

"Silver, not gray." He swung round and hooked his arm through mine. "Shall we head back to deal with your captives?"

As we made our way through the trees, Belle's phone dinged, the sound echoing lightly above the gentle babble of conversation coming from up ahead. She tugged the phone from her pocket and glanced at the screen. "Monty and Ashworth are on their way back. They lost the basilisk and weren't able to place a spell tracker on it."

"Does he say why?"

"No, but I daresay he will when they get here. They're about twenty minutes away."

"Which means they're currently outside of the reservation," Aiden said. "That's quite a distance for the two of them to have run."

"They might have used a spell to enhance their speed," Belle said. "The vampires certainly were."

"Which explains why none of us could catch the bastards."

His voice was grim, and I glanced at him. "You got the one running at me—I heard her scream and smelled the blood."

He nodded. "It wasn't any old vampire, either, but Maelle's daughter. Looked the spitting image of her."

Meaning it was a good thing Aiden *hadn't* killed her.

"How badly was she injured?" Belle asked. "Because if we collect her blood and can keep it viable long enough, Liz might be able to track her."

"One step ahead of you."

He pulled out a glove that contained wet, dark-looking soil. Though the blood was no longer fresh, dark energy still echoed from it.

I glanced at Belle. "Could you wrap a containment spell around the glove? I need to deal with our captured vamps before I can try and run a trace on Jaqueline."

"No, you need to rest and regain your strength before

you tackle it." Belle accepted the glove with a nod of thanks. "You will also drink several strength and revitalization potions. I'll even make them palatable for a change."

"Gee, thanks."

It was wryly said, and her cheeks dimpled. "Don't ever say I don't look after my witch."

I snorted, and we continued on, the soft caress of the containment spell Belle was creating a sharp contrast to the deeper pulsing of the protection circle that shimmered through the trees up ahead. It appeared to have been secured onto spell stones to enhance its stability, though how the hell Eli and Belle had managed that at such short notice—

Not me, Belle cut in silently. *Eli. I was too busy batting away spell arrows.*

That she could only strengthened the belief that both attacks had been nothing more than a distraction. Belle might be classed as an extraordinarily strong Sarr witch these days, but that still placed her just below mid-range on the witchy power scale. She should never have been able to combat the dedicated attacks of a dark witch. Not if they'd truly intended harm.

That surely meant I'd been the target all along.

Was that why Marie had sent Jaqueline after me, rather than any of her other vampires? While I had no doubt she wanted to taste the power in my blood, she'd also know that, had I managed to kill Jaqueline, Maelle's wrath would hit me. Hard. The aftermath of such a battle would weaken us both and leave Marie in a sweet position to take the survivor out.

And her plan might have succeeded if not for Aiden.

Eli stepped through the barrier and walked toward us. His face was drawn, and weariness rode every movement.

"Aiden, your mother wants to know if it's safe for everyone to return home."

Meaning, if I was reading the annoyance in his expression correctly, that she was *demanding* rather than asking.

"I'll go deal with her." He glanced at me. "You still intending to question the vamps?"

I nodded. "I've this vague feeling Marie will prevent them from talking once she realizes we've captured them."

How she did that all depended on whether these vamps were her fledglings or simply solo vampires drawn into her coven or whatever the hell else she might be calling it these days. I doubted she could long-range kill the latter, but given how intimately linked a maker was to their fledgling, it was more than possible that she could erase them.

"I'll send Jaz over to record the interview, then," Aiden said. "Just... be careful."

"Always."

It was my standard answer to such a request. He smiled and brushed a finger down my cheek—a caress that spoke to my heart—then turned and followed Eli back through the shield.

Belle and I continued on. Our first captured vampire was ten or so meters ahead, though we couldn't immediately see him thanks to the thick cluster of trees between him and us. As we moved around them, the wind stirred, the smell hit, and, oh lord, it was *vile*. I clamped a hand over my nose, but the scent clung to my throat, and my stomach stirred in warning.

"Fucking hell," Belle muttered. "He smells like rotting meat."

He certainly did. And there was a part of me—a big part of me—that thought it might be better to walk away now rather than discover why.

I ignored that bit of wisdom and kept on going.

And almost immediately wished I hadn't.

The vampire wasn't only dead, but fast-time rotting. His skin and muscles sloughed away from his bones in oozing, meaty chunks that splashed wetly around his feet...

My stomach rose, and I lurched away, losing everything I'd eaten during the day in the nearby bushes. When the heaving stopped, Belle handed me a small bottle of water but continued to study the disintegrating figure.

"How is something like this even possible?" Her voice held a weird mix of horror and fascination. "Vampires might *technically* be dead, but surely if meltdowns like this were frequent occurrences when *truly* killed, it'd be common knowledge."

"I doubt this has anything to do with them being dead, and more to do with who they're connected to." I wiped my mouth with the back of my hand, then opened the bottle and rinsed out my mouth. Then, warily, I turned around. Nothing remained of the vampire now except a small mound of clothes that oozed bloody liquid... my stomach started to churn again, but at least this time it stayed put. "We'd better get to the others, before it's too late."

I spun and ran, as fast as I was physically able, through the trees. By the time we reached the second vampire—a woman, if the shoes were anything to go by—she too was little more than an oozing pile of human remnants. I continued on, mentally crossing all things that we found the third vampire alive.

We didn't.

I swore and thrust a hand through my matted hair. "Marie really doesn't give a shit about her people, does she?"

"Which is at least one thing that can't be said about

Maelle." Belle stopped beside me. Though the night wasn't cold, goose bumps prickled across her skin. "I just don't get why she went to this extreme. Why not just take their lives rather than melting them?"

"Perhaps because she could. Or perhaps she simply wanted to freak us out."

"Or perhaps it's a warning of what she intends for us."

"We're not connected to her magically or mentally," I said. "It's doubtful she could. Unless, of course, dark magic is involved, and I wasn't sensing any sort of dark spell around those vamps."

"Would you, if Marie spelled from a distance and it hit these vamps through whatever connection they have with her, be it a blood oath or something else?"

"I don't know."

Belle rubbed her arms, her expression uneasy. "At least you have the wild magic to protect you. I don't."

"It automatically protected you at Maelle's, remember, so that may no longer be true." I hesitated, then added, "Besides, my ability to call on the wild magic might now be... curtailed."

She glanced at me sharply. "Meaning what? What happened in that wellspring?"

"I met the Fenna, Belle. My daughter was accepted. I was not."

She blinked. "Why the hell not?"

"Because while Mom's line *did* descend from the Fenna, there's no direct werewolf link."

"So why is your own wild magic giving you wolf-like characteristics?"

"It's enhancing the DNA 'leftovers' I've inherited via our distant Fenna heritage. The changes won't continue—

I'll never be any more than I already am. But our daughter—she'll not only be Fenna, but a full wolf."

"Meaning she will be able to shift shape?"

When I nodded, Belle smiled and touched my arm. "That's brilliant news."

It certainly was, because it meant, unlike me, she would not be considered an outcast or an oddity within the pack. She'd be one of them—could run with them—from the very start, while having all the power of the wellspring at her disposal. Not to mention the wisdom of the Fenna to tap into.

"Her own private spirit guide army," Belle murmured. "But does your rejection mean you no longer have any access to the wellspring's power?"

"No, it means the Fenna will sit in judgement of my needs. I suspect the only time I'll bypass that is when my life is on the line."

Because if I died, my daughter—the first true Fenna to be born in centuries—would also die.

"Which suggests," Belle said, "they won't ever let you call more power than you can handle, and that's not a bad thing."

It certainly wasn't, especially when I'd already come far too close to doing just that. I knelt, pressed my fingers into the ground, and released the wild magic that still caged the vampire remnants. Thankfully, none of the bright threads had been in contact with the vamps when they'd died, so there was no risk of them being stained by their deaths.

I pushed upright and brushed the dirt from my fingers. "Maybe I should try—"

"No," Belle cut in before I could finish, "*not* before you get some rest."

"But—"

"No. You can't keep pushing yourself to exhaustion, especially now that you're pregnant."

"I'll be—"

"Fine, yes, I know," Belle said. "But only *after* you've had a few potions and gotten some rest."

I rolled my eyes, but didn't argue any further. She was right, and we both knew it. I just couldn't escape the notion that by not acting straight away, we might be losing our one opportunity to capture Jaqueline without battling either Marie or a horde of other vampires.

The soft sound of movement had me looking around. A heartbeat later, Jaz appeared out of the trees, her nose twitching in distaste.

"I take it you two aren't responsible for that steaming pile of goop?" she said.

"Nope," Belle said. "Nor did we manage to get answers before he became goop."

"Well, you won't find me grieving for answers lost, even if it does mean it takes us longer to wrap things up. Those bastards caused plenty of chaos in the few minutes they were here, and got what they deserved." She glanced at me. "Aiden said that once we were done here, I was to take you home while he and the other witches deal with the aftermath. He also said I'm to ignore all arguments to the contrary and pick you up and toss you over my shoulder if necessary."

I laughed. "Not necessary, although I'd like to see you try and carry both of us."

"I don't need to carry Belle, because she's the sensible one in your outfit."

Belle grinned. "Have Monty and Ashworth returned yet?"

"No, but I believe Aiden *has* contacted them and let

KERI ARTHUR

them know what's happening." She handed me my sandals and then added, "This way."

I hastily shoved my shoes on, then hurried after her as she strode off through the trees. Belle caught my elbow and kept close. Her support was only light at the beginning, but I leaned into it more and more. To say I was shaking with exhaustion by the time we reached Jaz's SUV would be an understatement.

I don't remember much about the journey home, and only had vague memories of drinking Belle's potions and being helped into bed. When awareness finally *did* resurface, it was obvious many hours had passed. Not only was it daylight, but the wave of noise coming from downstairs suggested the café had hit peak period.

I reached for my phone to check the time—it was just after one—and saw a message from Aiden that had come in late.

Staying here the night to sort out the mess and answer the pack's questions about what happened, he said. *Get some sleep and I'll see you tomorrow.*

He added a few hearts, making my heart happy.

I sent a text to let him know I was awake and rested, then threw off the sheet and staggered into the bathroom for a quick shower. Once dressed, I shoved on a newer pair of sandals and headed downstairs. Belle greeted me with a chicken, avocado, and cheese toastie and a mug of hot chocolate.

"You're an angel." I leaned a hip against the counter and picked up a toastie half, the delicious smell making my stomach rumble in appreciation. "What happened after I collapsed? Anything?"

She shook her head. "Just the usual, from what Monty said when he finally got home. But Ashworth's tracker arrives tonight, so hopefully our basilisk will soon be one less problem we have to deal with."

"I'd better contact Katie, then, and see if the snake's movements form a pattern or are simply random."

She nodded. "There's also the blood Aiden collected. I sealed it in the vacuum box but I'm not sure if it or my spell is strong enough to have kept it viable this long."

"Damn, I'd forgotten about that. You should have woken me earlier."

She gave me the look. The one that said "not a snowball's chance in hell." "You needed sleep more than we need to track that bitch."

"I'm thinking Monty might not agree with that statement."

"Monty is insane. We all know this."

"You're marrying him, so what does that make you?"

"A sucker for a man with a hot bod and a heart of gold who adores me as much as I adore him." She glanced around as the bell above the door chimed and the man in question strolled in. "Of course, I'm not sure the café or I can afford his appetite for cake."

She said it loud enough for him to hear, and he grinned. "Too late to retreat, my dear witch. You're stuck with me and my appetite now."

The devilish twinkle in his eyes suggested he was *not* talking about cake. She laughed, caught his face between her hands, and kissed him. "What are you doing here so early? Afternoon tea is another hour away."

"I figured I'd come and see how Liz was feeling—"

"And whether I was up to tracking Jaqueline," I finished dryly.

"You wound me to the core, but yes, there is also that."

259

I grabbed my mug of hot chocolate and pushed away from the bench. "I guess there's only one way to find out."

He followed me into the reading room. I placed my mug on the table, then moved across to the bookcase and opened the hidden compartment that held the specially designed vacuum-sealed box. We generally used it to keep the various leafy herbs we sometimes needed for spells fresh, but it was also useful in situations like this, where air could have a detrimental effect on an item.

I pushed the portable sealing pump to one side, tugged the box out, and returned to the table. The glove and its dark contents sat in the middle of the glass container, looking deceptively innocuous. I released the sealing plug, then opened the lid.

"Anything?" Monty immediately asked.

"Not yet."

I carefully touched the glove. No pulse of power. No warmth. Nothing to indicate there was anything within the glove other than soil. I untied the top of the glove then shoved one finger into the dirt... and found the faintest pulse of darkness. My psi senses immediately flared to life and leapt away, following the link until it found the woman who'd shed the blood. The connection was tenuous and faint, but information flowed down the line regardless. Through her eyes, I saw cracks of light peeking past the edges of a torn and dirty-looking curtain. The room in which she sat was dark but not empty. There were several worn chairs scattered about, and a couple of cobweb-hung bunk beds, all of them occupied. They were little more than shadows, but the anticipation that pulsed from them ran high. Higher than the seething river of pain and anger emanating from the woman I was connected to.

From beyond the dark confines of the building came the

whisper of rustling leaves and the distant trickle of water. A heartbeat later, three sharp, controlled cracks echoed. The shadows stirred, and their voices rose in brief conversation that I couldn't catch, though they seemed unconcerned. Then the last vestiges of power bled from the blood and the connection died.

I swore softly and tossed the glove into the nearby rubbish bin. "They're in a cabin that's surrounded by trees and close to what sounds like a creek."

"Which isn't really helpful given there would be tons of places matching that description in this reservation."

"I know. Sorry." I picked up my hot chocolate and took a drink. "Does Castle Rock have a shooting range?"

"Hang on and I'll check."

He got out his phone and put Google to good use. "We do. It's over Walmer Forest way, right on the edge of town. Why?"

I had no idea where Walmer Forest was, but that was beside the point. "Because I heard what vaguely sounded like rifle or gunshots, and given only the rangers are allowed to carry—"

"Farmers are allowed to own guns," Monty cut in.

"I know but—" I shrugged. "The shots were too controlled, if that makes sense. If a farmer was shooting at a fox or some other sort of vermin, wouldn't the shots be more rapid fire?"

"Depends on the farmer and weapon, I would think." He motioned to my mug. "Finish that, and we'll head out and check the area."

I raised an eyebrow. "You're not going out demon hunting with Ashworth and Eli?"

"Of course I am." His expression implied he was offended by my suggesting he wouldn't, though amusement creased the corners of his eyes. "But there's a good four hours to fill in before then, so we might as well do something useful."

"Meaning you're voluntarily missing afternoon tea?" I reached forward and pressed the back of my hand against his forehead. "I'm not feeling a temperature…"

He laughed and knocked my hand away. "There *is* such a thing as takeaway, you know."

"And while you arrange that, I'll go upstairs and don more appropriate shoes."

He nodded and headed out. I finished my hot chocolate, then grabbed the last toastie triangle and munched on it as I headed upstairs.

I shoved on sturdier boots—walking around the bush in anything less was basically an open invitation to be bitten by any snake nearby—then grabbed my phone and sent Aiden another text, letting him know what we were up to.

Meet you at the front of the gun club came his reply. *Don't proceed without me.*

Maybe it was my overly active imagination, but his reply seemed a little terse, making me wonder if his mother had been causing trouble again.

I'd find out soon enough.

I grabbed a sun hat, then went back downstairs for the backpack. There was no way in hell I was about to go vampire hunting without a *physical* means of protecting myself. Jaqueline might or might not be capable of overwhelming us magically, but no dark mage, be she vampire or not, was immune to the effects of holy water or a blessed silver knife.

Monty, I noted with a smile, was already eating his cake —our version of a Boston bun, which, after taste-testing our first batch, he'd declared was quite passable.

By the time we made it across to the rifle range, Aiden was there and waiting. Monty pulled up beside his truck, then stopped and reached past to open the glove compartment. Inside were a couple of dark-framed, dark-glassed sunglasses onto which elastic had been tied.

"To keep them in place in the event of an attack," he said, handing me one before tucking the other into his shirt pocket and climbing out of his car.

I shoved the glasses on, looped the elastic around my ponytail to keep them in place, then grabbed my pack and hat and got out. Aiden caught my free hand and pulled me into his arms. He looked and smelled tired.

"Hell of a night, hey?" I said softly, my gaze searching his and seeing the deeper flickers of frustration. His mom had definitely done or said something annoying.

"Always is when you're dealing with the aftermath of a tragedy, whether it be big or small." He dropped a quick kiss on my lips, then released me. It was then I saw he'd tucked sunglasses into his shirt, though his were fancier-looking than the ones Monty had purchased. "What are we searching for?"

"An old hut surrounded by trees with some sort of creek nearby."

He frowned. "There's only a couple of huts around here that are abandoned, and none of them are near creeks."

"Could it have been a water channel? There's enough of them scattered about the place," Monty said. "Maybe what Liz heard was a farmer pumping water from one paddock to another."

"There *is* an open gravity channel not far from here," Aiden said, "and the old man who owns the nearby farm has been known to use it from time to time to move water down from his top dam."

"Is the old man still alive?" Monty asked. "Has anyone checked on him lately?"

"We only tend to do welfare checks when someone reports that they've not been seen for a few days." He pushed away from his truck. "This way."

He headed past the newish-looking brick building. There were at least three cars parked on the other side of it, but no one visible on the range. Perhaps they'd retreated into the building's no doubt cooler confines.

The trees beyond were sparse and offered little in the way of protection from the sun, making me doubly glad I'd worn a hat. The scrub itself was dry and patchy, but we followed what looked to be a roo path so avoided most of the weeds. After ten minutes or so, we found the water channel. It wasn't as wide as the others we'd seen, but it was full of weeds and bone dry.

"Jason's sluice lies that way," Aiden said, pointing to the left. "I can hear water running so he's obviously opened the gate."

"If he's opened the gate, that surely suggests he's alive." Monty stopped and swiped at the sweat dotting his forehead. "Unless, of course, it's open because they've used him as a snack and there's no one left to shut the thing down again. Is his place near the channel?"

"No, but the old shed and bunkhouse the shearers used to use isn't far from here."

"Is it a large bunkhouse?" I asked. "Because I only saw a couple of bunks and a few chairs."

"That sounds about right. Jason never had a huge herd of sheep." Aiden glanced at me. "Any idea how many vamps we could be dealing with?"

"Six or seven, max."

"Which implies it's probably not our main group," Monty said. "Not if Maelle's estimates were right."

And they would be, even if she made it seem more of a guess.

"If the vampires *are* there," Aiden said. "Will either of you be able to sense their presence before they sense ours?"

"That depends on a number of factors," Monty said, "like whether they're asleep or awake, and whether they've ringed the place with protections."

"They weren't asleep," I said. "In fact, they were wide awake and in an anticipatory state."

"Maybe they were waiting for the farmer to cruise by so they could dine in rather than take away," Monty said.

"Or they expected us to track Jaqueline, and this is a trap."

His amusement died. "That's a rather unsettling thought."

"And there's only one way to confirm it," Aiden said. "We need to check the bunkhouse and see what awaits. This way."

We walked along the channel's bank until we reached the rickety old wooden flume funneling water into the old channel, scrambling under it before continuing on. The tree line gradually crept closer to the channel but remained sparse and continued to offer little shade from the sun. As the channel swept around to the left, Aiden moved away from the bank and headed deeper into the trees.

"The shearing shed and stockyards are a couple of hundred meters ahead," he said. "The bunkhouse lies on the far side of them."

"Are we dealing with open ground around all three?" Monty asked.

Aiden nodded. "The bunkhouse did have a few shade

trees situated close by last I saw, but nothing that'll conceal our presence. The channel loops around the back of it but there's open ground between the two."

"Which will make approaching that building very difficult, given they'll likely sense any concealment spell we attempt."

"Yes, but we do have one thing in our favor—the sun."

"Then maybe," Monty said, "our best option is to just rip the roof off the fucking building and let them all fry."

I glanced at him. "Thereby killing Jaqueline in the process. Not a good move, trust me."

"We might not have any other choice," Monty said grimly. "Especially if it comes down to a 'them or us' situation."

And it would. Maybe not here, but the longer this "game" went on, the more likely it became.

"You're also forgetting there's more of them than us. They can counter any magic we raise longer than we can attack."

"Yes, but not all of them will be as powerful as Maelle and Marie. Maelle has already said that Jaqueline isn't."

"By *her* standards, and her standards aren't the norm. From what I sensed of Jaqueline when she attempted to snatch me, she's still up there on the power scale." I swiped at the sweat trickling down my cheek. "We need to find a way to keep Jaqueline safe while we deal with the others."

"Maybe *we* don't have to," Monty said slowly. "Maybe our best option is to let Maelle deal with her daughter. She might not be able to walk about in sunlight, but Roger can."

"*That* is a brilliant idea," I said.

"And it comes with the bonus of her not being able to blame us if things go to hell and Jaqueline ends up dead."

Amusement stirred. "Hate to tell you this, but I'm sure Maelle *will* find a way to blame us if her daughter dies."

Especially given her emotions when I'd been questioning her about Marie and Jaqueline hadn't exactly been on an even keel.

Though, in truth, that wasn't really surprising. While there was no doubt she loved her daughter, there was also no escaping the fact that not only had she killed her daughter's lover but then left her in Marie's care rather than taking her away from such a volatile situation. To worsen matters, it sounded like they'd had little contact in the intervening centuries.

In some respects, their relationship reminded me a little of my relationship with my father, though at least my father had only forced me into an unwanted marriage, not eons of eternal darkness and bloodlust.

I dragged my phone out and made the call.

"Elizabeth, what an unexpected pleasure to hear from you again." Maelle's tone was soft and decidedly husky, which made me suspect I'd interrupted a feeding or perhaps something more intimate. Or both, given she preferred to combine them. "I take it this call is not a social one?"

She was definitely doing *something*. She was in too good a mood.

Shame I was about to spoil it.

"We've tracked Jaqueline down and were wondering—"

"Do not confront her," she cut in, all trace of sultriness gone. "Not alone. I'll send Roger out to assist you."

"That's what I was hoping." I gave her the directions and then added, "She's not alone. I think there are six or seven others with her."

"Is Marie one of them?"

"Not as far as we're aware."

"My priority will naturally be Jaqueline's capture," she said, "but once Roger is there, we will assess the situation and perhaps offer a safe means for you to deal with the others. He'll be there in ten."

Meaning he was capable of moving *extremely* fast. It had taken us close to ten minutes just to drive to the rifle range, and a good fifteen to walk from there to here.

I shoved my phone away. "Roger's on his way."

Aiden nodded. "There's a small rise off to the right that'll give us a view over the paddocks with minimal risk of being seen. We might as well head there and get the lay of the land while we wait."

"Should one of us go back and wait for Roger?" Monty asked.

"He'll find us," I said. "He may not be a vampire, but he'll hear—or Maelle will through him—the beating of our hearts."

"Which is another reason why I suggest we move to the rise," Aiden said. "It's downwind of the bunkhouse, so there's less likelihood of the vamps in there sensing us."

I motioned him to lead the way. We left the path and cut through the trees, the grass dry and crackly under our feet. The ground soon sloped sharply upwards; by the time we reached the top, I was sweating profusely.

I tugged a bottle of water free from my backpack and took a long drink before offering it to Aiden. He shook his head, but Monty accepted it gratefully.

I squatted next to Aiden and studied the paddocks below us. The sweeping arc of the canal was evident by the line of greenery that clustered its banks. The stockyards were in a state of disrepair and the shearing shed was missing half its roof, which was probably why the vamps weren't using it. It was mighty hard to keep the sun out when a good percentage of the metal sheeting was missing. The bunkhouse wasn't particularly large and looked more like a longish wooden shed than a cottage. There was an entrance and three simple wooden steps at the right end of the building and five windows lining the side. Three had been boarded up, while the other two were covered by the grimy curtains I'd seen when briefly linked to Jaqueline. Between us and that building lay a long stretch of dry grass.

"There's been a van here recently," Aiden said, pointing. "It looks like they drew up as close as possible to the door."

I scanned the end of the building he was motioning to, but couldn't see anything as obvious as tire tracks. And I wouldn't from this distance, if I was at all honest. My eyesight was almost werewolf sharp these days, but that "almost" obviously made a big difference. "How can you tell?"

He glanced at me, a smile tugging the corners of his lips. "If you look past the line of trees to the right, you'll see, in what little grass remains, faint tire tracks. It was a van of some sort, by the look of them."

A van being the perfect escape vehicle for a vampire if there was a bulkhead in place between the cabin and the rear, and no windows along the side. It meant the only true danger to any of the vamps inside came in the form of whatever gap there'd been between the van and the building—and that was something easily countered by an overlay of heavy clothing, just like the vamp who'd tested the café's protections had been wearing. The only reason he'd ended up ashes was because Roger had ripped off his face mask.

"What I'm not seeing are any sort of protection spells," Monty said. "Nor can I see any obvious sign of guards. It has to be a setup."

"Even if it wasn't," I said, "we're going to have a hell of a time getting anywhere near that building before they see us or hear our heartbeats."

"I could act as bait," Aiden said.

"So could I," I retorted. "And we all know what your reaction to that would be."

He cast me a wry glance. "They know and want you. I'm just the local ranger checking out properties."

"Do you remember Monty's comment about them 'dining in?' That does also apply to you, you know."

"I have no intention of becoming a vampire's last meal, Liz, but if I can draw their attention, it gives you two the chance to hit them from behind."

"A sentiment with which I agree," came a cool, calm voice behind us.

My head snapped around. Roger strolled casually toward us. His pale cheeks were untouched by the heat, and there wasn't a drop of sweat on the man, despite the fact he must have run most of the way here. More interestingly, it appeared not even Aiden had heard his approach. Granted, Roger was downwind of our position, but a werewolf's senses were far sharper than a human's, and he should have picked up Roger's movements before he'd gotten this close.

That he *hadn't* was rather scary—and made me wonder if we needed to add some sort of proximity alert to the protection charms we were all wearing. If Maelle's thrall could creep up unheard, then it was a fair bet she and the other vamps could as well.

"I take it," Monty said, "that you arrive with a plan?"

"I arrive with an intention more than a plan," he replied evenly. "As my mistress has already said, I will capture Jaqueline. You will deal with the others."

"And how do you propose we do that?" I asked. "In case

you've forgotten, there's at least six mages in there aside from Jaqueline, and there's only three of us."

His gaze met mine. Maelle lurked in the deep recesses, but it was the energy radiating from him that had my skin crawling. It was somehow malevolent and corrupt, power-ful, and yet putrid, and it spoke of intentions that were ungodly at best. This was Maelle at her basest. Her true self, a face she rarely showed to the world, unleashed and uncontrolled. *This* Maelle was more dangerous, more deadly, than any demon we'd ever come across. If she ever lost control, if her base self ever gained the upper hand, heaven help us all.

A chill seeped through my soul.

Wheels within wheels, I thought suddenly.

I might have been right in thinking the initial attack was a distraction to snatch me, but Marie's machinations went way beyond that. That's why Jaqueline had fled here, to a place that obviously wasn't their main bolt-hole, into a building with no real protections or comforts other than the few dusty bits of furniture that had obviously been there for some time.

It *was* a trap.

Not one set for me, but rather for the man who was the key to Maelle's sanity.

"You can't go in there, Roger," I added abruptly. "This is a trap that has been set for *you*."

He raised a pale eyebrow, amusement evident. "Perhaps it is, but I am not so easily caught."

"They don't want to trap you, Roger. They want to kill you."

"That's a task many of our enemies have set themselves over the centuries." It was Maelle speaking now, not Roger. "As you can see, none of them have been successful. Those within that building will also fail, as only Marie has the power to erase what I have created."

"Even if this trap fails, Maelle, Roger will remain a target."

"As has ever been the case." He paused. "We will not ignore your intuition, of course, but we refuse to allow such a threat alter the course of our actions. Jaqueline will be saved, and the others dealt with appropriately."

Appropriately meaning by us. "How?"

"The ranger provides the distraction out front. I will enter from the far side of the building and snare Jaqueline. You and Monty will approach from the side and raise the roof once I give the signal. The sun will take care of those who remain within."

"I'm thinking the vamps won't let us approach without some kickback," Monty said, voice dry.

"Perhaps not, but you, young witchling, are almost certainly capable of dealing with whatever those inside throw at you."

A statement that was all Maelle, and somewhat damning in its faint praise. Monty raised an eyebrow but didn't reply.

"It'll take you and Elizabeth ten minutes to get around to the side of the building," Roger continued. "It'll take me a second or two from there to get into position. Ranger, in exactly twelve minutes, you will walk down toward the bunkhouse and snare their attention."

Aiden's gaze flickered to mine, his expression a mix of amusement and annoyance. I totally understood both. It might have been Monty's idea to call in Maelle and Roger, but there was a part of me—a big part of me—that suspected it wasn't such a good idea to let them completely run the show.

But it was too late to do anything about it now.

Roger stepped back and motioned us to precede him. I opened my backpack and tugged out my knife and several bottles of holy water, handing the latter to Aiden. "Use these if any of those bastards manage to get close to you."

He accepted the bottles with a nod. "You be careful."

"Back at you, Ranger."

He smiled yet again, but his concern chased us as we headed back down the hill.

I was gripping my knife so tightly my knuckles ached. Its weight in my hand was comforting, though in truth it was more a symbol of protection than an actual one. I didn't have a good arm when it came to throwing, and while I had used the wild magic in the past to guide its path, that option might no longer be available to me.

Not that I could use it for a kill shot, anyway. Not without risking the purity of the wellspring.

We moved quickly through the trees, the babbling of water growing the closer we drew to the bunkhouse. The trickle of water coming from the sluice wouldn't have accounted for the rush of water we were hearing, so there were obviously other sources feeding the channel. It was probably loud enough to counter any noise Monty and I were making; I just hoped that we remained physically far enough away from the bunkhouse that they wouldn't hear our heartbeats. Surely if we weren't, Roger would have said something.

Unless, of course, this was all part of his evil plan. Maybe he was using us—using our humanity—to distract the vamps from the real danger coming in from the back of the building.

We finally reached our destination. This end of the

bunkhouse had no windows or door, which at least gave us the advantage of them not physically being able to see us.

Not that they actually needed to.

Roger didn't immediately continue, instead staring at the building for several seconds. Amusement—and perhaps a trace of contempt—crossed his expression. "They've placed a repelling spell across this end of the building."

My gaze shot to the building. If there was a spell, I wasn't seeing it... I narrowed my gaze and, after a second, caught the faintest shimmer—one that I would normally have passed off as heat haze if Roger hadn't said anything.

"Just this end?" Monty was saying, "that makes no sense, given a spell to raise the roof can be cast from any direction."

"I rather suspect there's more to that spell than mere repelling." I glanced at Roger, but if he knew what else it contained, he wasn't about to share.

"In one minute, the ranger will appear," he said. "When he reaches the halfway point, I will enter the building and seize Jaqueline—"

"Is she actually still there?" I asked. "She is capable of transport spells, isn't she?"

"If a transport spell had been used, its backwash would linger. They are not easy spells to develop or use."

I was well aware how unpleasant the things were to use, having stepped into one up in Canberra. But that didn't mute the relevance of my question. The fact that Roger—or rather, Maelle—didn't seem concerned was troubling. The certainty of their own superiority over those within that building might yet be their downfall.

And ours, if we weren't all very careful.

"I'll leave now," he said. "When I hit the building, you attack it."

He spun and left, moving so fast he was little more than a pale blur through the trees.

"Am I the only one disturbed by their lack of concern?" Monty's expression was pensive as he stared after Roger.

"No." I flexed my fingers against the knife, but it didn't really ease the gathering tension. "I've got a really bad feeling about all this."

"Me too." He switched his gaze to the bunkhouse. "I agree with you about that spell—it feels too heavy to be a mere repelling spell."

"I'm not seeing anything to indicate what else it might contain, though."

"Neither am I, and that's what worries me."

"If that's the only thing worrying you, you're getting off lightly."

Movement caught my eye, and I glanced past him. Aiden had moved out of the trees and had begun his descent toward the bunkhouse.

My tension ratcheted up several more notches.

"The game is afoot," I said. "How do you want to play this?"

"Aside from carefully? We stay in the trees and pray for a miracle. The minute we raise our magic, that spell is going —" He stopped, his gaze widening.

My head snapped around in time to see a shimmer of movement. Roger, in the air, in what I would call the "Superman flying" pose as he smashed, arrow-straight, through a boarded window.

A heartbeat later, the screaming began.

Screaming that was abruptly cut off.

CHAPTER THIRTEEN

Monty cursed and began to spell, his magic rising swiftly and filling the air with power. I hastily followed his lead, weaving my inner wild magic around the blasting spell to strengthen it before sending it chasing after his.

The two spheres tumbled through the air, one curving to the right, one to the left. But before either could hit the building, the spell locked around the end of it reacted.

It didn't repel. It simply absorbed.

"Oh, fuck," Monty said, "that's not good. Perhaps if we move around—"

The rest of his sentence was cut off by a huge *whoomph*. Then the whole building exploded, and a wave of power knocked us off our feet and sent us tumbling backward. I hit the ground several yards away and slid into a tree hard enough to elicit a grunt. I rolled onto my back, only to see a thick wave of metal, wood, and God knows what heading my way, and immediately curled up into a ball, my hands over my head in an effort to provide as small a target as possible. The deadly rain fell all around us, and several chunks of wood or metal hit me, cutting deep enough to draw blood on my legs and across my shoulders.

Had we been any closer, had we not been semi-protected by the trees, the wave would have been deadly.

Oh fuck, *Aiden...*

The second the rain eased, I scrambled to my feet. Monty was several yards away and also rising. There was blood on his face and a deep gash on his arm, but he seemed okay otherwise. I tossed him my backpack and said, "Use the first aid kit," then raced back to the tree line.

There was nothing left of the bunkhouse, other than the remains of a few wooden stumps and, rather incongruously, the three steps that had led up to the door. Debris lay scattered all around the place, and dust rose, a thick curtain of brown that made visibility difficult.

There was no immediate sign of Aiden.

I swore and raced around the tree line, avoiding the brown curtain and the lingering threads of magic that still hung in the air.

Saw him, halfway down the hill, struggling to get back onto his feet. As I raced toward him, his form shimmered, switching to wolf, then back to human again. That he'd had to suggested he'd been hurt far worse than either Monty or me.

He glanced around as I approached, his gaze quickly sweeping me, then coming up relieved. I all but threw myself into his arms, hitting him so hard that he grunted.

"I'm okay," he said, traces of amusement and relief riding his voice. "Aside from that wound on your leg, it appears you are, too. How's Monty?"

"He's got a few cuts, but otherwise, he's fine."

"Good." He briefly hugged me tighter, then released me. "What the hell happened?"

"Either Roger triggered an explosive spell, or we did." I shrugged. "Hard to be certain."

"And Roger?"

"No idea."

He slid his hand down my arm and twined his fingers through mine. "Then we'd best get over there and check."

As we headed toward the destruction zone, Monty appeared out of the trees. He was carrying my backpack, and his arm was roughly bandaged. There was also a smear of brown antiseptic across his cheek, though the cut still oozed blood.

He stopped just shy of the few still-lingering threads of magic and glanced around as we approached. "I'm not seeing much in the way of human remains."

"Would you, after such a powerful explosion?" I asked.

"Surely there'd be at least *some* evidence—the odd bone, smears of blood, random bits of body parts. That there's nothing suggests there was no one inside—at least at the time of the explosion."

"I *can* smell blood," Aiden said, "although certainly not enough if there were seven or eight people inside when this thing went up."

"Roger wouldn't have arrowed into the building like he did if he believed the place was empty," I said.

"Which leads to another important question," Monty said. "What the hell happened to Roger? Is it his blood Aiden is smelling?"

"Good question—and one we can get an answer to straight away." I dragged my phone out of my pocket and discovered I'd smashed the screen when I'd landed on my butt and slid into the tree. Luckily, despite the damage, the thing still worked.

Maelle answered my call almost before it had a chance to ring.

"What has happened?" she growled. "I've lost contact with Roger."

That wasn't good. "There was an explosion—is he dead, Maelle?"

"If he was dead, I would not be answering this call."

She would be out, and hunting. "Have you got a way of tracing him?"

"Again, if I could do that, I would not be talking to you." There was a brief, angry pause. Maybe I was reading too much into it, but I very much suspected she was battling to remain calm. To control her bloodlust and need for revenge. "You have not answered the initial question—what happened there?"

"Roger triggered an explosion going into the building." We didn't know that for sure, of course, but there was no way in hell I was about to admit we might have been responsible for it. Especially if Roger wasn't just missing but dead. "The building is destroyed, but there's not enough blood or body bits to suggest there was more than one or two people inside."

"There were seven before he entered. I checked."

"Then they either magicked themselves away or—"

My gaze shot to the ground. Was it possible there was a mine shaft close by? While most of the old mines seemed to be situated on the other side of town, there were several out Muckleford way, and that really wasn't all that far from here. It certainly wasn't an uncommon practice in the gold rush era for miners to randomly dig mines in what would be unlikely areas hoping to find the mother lode.

"Or?" Maelle growled.

"Sorry, but I need to call you back after I check something." I hung up without waiting for her response. "Aiden, are there any known mine shafts or tunnels around this area?"

He frowned. "Not that I know of—why?"

"Maelle said seven people were inside the bunkhouse just before Roger entered. So, either they magicked themselves out—"

"Which could have been what that explosion was covering," Monty said.

"Or," I continued, "there's an unknown mine system near here, and they used one of its tunnels to drop into after they'd grabbed him."

"If he *is* still alive, then he'll be used as bait," Monty said. "He's the closest thing to family—Jaqueline aside—Maelle has."

"And even *I* know Maelle isn't going to take *that* happening too kindly." Aiden scanned the ground for a second. "Is it safe to approach what's left of the building? Magic wise, I mean."

"Yes," Monty said.

Aiden carefully stepped between two of the remaining stumps then grabbed what looked to be a five-foot remnant of stud wall, forcefully prodding the ground before taking a step forward. He was close to the middle when the bit of wood hit something with a soft *thunk*.

"That sound suggests we might have found the answer to your earlier question." He tossed the wood to one side, then knelt and began scooping aside the dirt. In no time at all, several bits of wooden planking that didn't look all that old appeared.

"A trapdoor?" Monty asked.

"Maybe, though I would have expected the explosion to

have dumped building rubble more than dirt on top of it," Aiden said.

I wrinkled my nose. "Maybe one vamp stayed behind to ensure it was covered. He was their sacrificial lamb, so to speak."

"Possible, although there wasn't all that much time between Roger entering the building and the explosion," Monty said. "Certainly not enough for them to capture Roger and then get into a tunnel."

"Unless most of them were already in the tunnel." I squatted beside Aiden. "Can you see a catch or something?"

"Not immediately."

Aiden continued shifting the loose dirt until a square of planking roughly a meter square was completely revealed. There was no latch on this side, but he worked his fingers into a gap between two of the planks and heaved upwards, the lovely definition in his arm muscles briefly increasing. The door moved fractionally, but an obvious metal rattle came from the right edge.

"Locked from underneath, from the feel of it," Aiden said.

"That isn't a problem." Monty squatted on the opposite side, pressed his fingers against the wood, and quickly crafted an unlock spell. Or, as the case was here, a "slide the bolt aside" one. The trapdoor dropped open; below it was a newly cut shaft supported by beams that looked to be the same age as the trapdoor. The sunlight didn't quite get to the bottom of the shaft, so I created a light sphere and cast it down. It revealed a shaft about three or four meters long with hand and footholds cut into the heavy clay soil, then hit the bottom, revealing an old metal track running east to west and what looked to be the disintegrating remnants of a trolley or cart.

"You were right," Monty said. "They've tapped into an old shaft."

"Which means this is a trap they've been planning for a while." And that was not only scary, but made me wonder just how many other traps were out there, waiting to be sprung. They'd obviously gotten to know the lay of the land —and possibly us—very well indeed in the short time they'd been here. "I guess the next question is, do we go down after them?"

I wasn't keen on the idea myself after already having had several unpleasantly close encounters with mines and shafts. This was likely to be a little different, given it was in good enough condition for the vamps to cut a new shaft into it, but that wasn't enough to counter the overall reluctance.

"I think we have to," Monty said. "They wouldn't expect us to find the trapdoor after that explosion, and it's unlikely they would have set any traps."

"I wouldn't be underestimating them in *any* way." Aiden's voice was grim. "But given your obvious intention of not doing the sensible thing, I'll run back to the car and retrieve the ropes and harnesses. Don't go in there before I get back."

I smiled. "Promise."

"I don't," Monty said, then held up his hands when Aiden glared at him. "Joke."

"One I suspect Belle would *not* appreciate." He pushed to his feet. "I'll be fifteen minutes at most."

He raced away without waiting for an answer, his form shifting mid stride, his coat gleaming silver in the late afternoon sun.

When he'd disappeared into the trees, I returned my gaze to the surrounding mess. Though magic still lingered, it was fading fast, and wouldn't be of much use now when it came to tracing, though the fact it still lingered so long *after* the explosion spoke to just how powerful the spell had truly been. In fact, maybe that was why there'd been so many vampires present—they'd needed to craft not only the explosion, but also a trap strong enough to snare Roger.

Had Jaqueline had a hand in either of those? None of the threads here had the same feel as the magic I'd sensed near the wellspring, but in truth, most were too far gone to be certain.

"You'd better call Maelle back," Monty said. "The last thing we need right now is to get her offside."

"If Roger gets dead, then it won't matter which side of her we're on. Everyone will pay."

"Well, there's a cheerful thought."

"More a reality we might yet have to face." I dragged my phone out again. "What are you going to do?"

"See if I can figure out how they trapped Roger. Might be useful knowledge in the future."

I nodded and once again called Maelle.

"What happened?" she immediately asked, her tone surprisingly even considering I'd unceremoniously hung up on her. But maybe it had simply given her time to control herself.

"We discovered their escape route—it was via a shaft into an old mine tunnel. We're still trying to ascertain how they snared Roger." I paused. "Is it possible he was simply knocked out?"

"No."

She didn't elaborate, and I didn't ask her to. She might well seem calm right now, but I suspected it would disintegrate if we pushed her too much. Besides, the answer would undoubtedly lie in their deep connection.

"We're going to head into the tunnel in an attempt to

find them, but if that fails, I'll need something of Roger's to track—"

"You will not be able to do so. He walks the path between life and death, and that makes him invisible to psi talents such as yours."

Demons weren't invisible, nor were ghouls, so what made Roger so special? Or was it more the fact that, having shared her flesh, he'd read more as her than himself?

"Will Marie kill him? Or use him to draw you out?"

"She will attempt the latter. She will fail."

I raised an eyebrow. "You'd let him die?"

"I would prefer he did not, but..."

I had a vision of her casually shrugging, though there'd be nothing casual in her response if he *was* murdered.

Would Marie really be that stupid? Would she really risk destroying the restraints that currently bound the woman who'd decimated their entire coven?

That, Belle said, *will probably depend on whether she believes she has the upper hand or not.*

Roger's death might well give her that.

It is nevertheless a risk, as none of us—not even Marie, I suspect—know just how much Maelle relies on Roger's presence to keep her baser instincts in line.

If what *my* instincts were saying was correct, the answer was "quite a lot." To Maelle, I added, "I take it you still have no sense of Marie's location?"

"When I severed the ties between us, I severed our ability to 'perceive' each other."

"And yet she must be able to sense you, or she would not be here."

"What remains is a general perception rather than specific."

My ears pricked up. "Meaning you can give me a general location for her?"

"She is to the west of Castle Rock. More than that, I cannot say."

The tunnel appeared to be on an east-west axis, so maybe, if luck was on our side, following it to the right would lead us to the vampires.

Or a trap, Belle commented. *Possibly both.*

Possibly. Probably. "If Marie contacts you—or even makes a move against you—will you let me know?"

"If she makes a move against me, you will know soon enough."

Because the shit would hit the fan. Or rather, the blood and body parts would. "Maelle—"

"Keep me updated," she added brusquely, then hung up.

She's still off-kilter emotionally, Belle said. *I don't think it'll take too much to push her over the edge.*

Which is exactly what Marie intends.

So why isn't Maelle helping us find her? I know she said she can't because of that whole oath thing, but I'm not sure we're getting the whole truth out of her.

And probably never will. I glanced around as Monty returned. "You found anything?"

He held up a glove-wrapped spell stone. "It was buried in one of the stumps—I think the blast must have dislodged it from wherever it had been initially set."

"Is there any magic on it?"

"No, but I figured you might be able to psi track the owner through it."

"Worth a try." Especially if it meant I avoided going into the tunnel. I warily accepted the glove but didn't immediately grip the stone. As Monty had said, no magic lingered on it, but darkness nevertheless emanated from it.

And that darkness was familiar.

I met Monty's gaze, my heart beating faster. "This stone comes from Jaqueline's set, and I think there's enough of a connection to track her."

"Did she go down in the tunnel? Or was she the one in that van?"

I gripped the spell stone tighter through the glove and narrowed my gaze. No images rose—unsurprising given the glove would mute all but the strongest of connections. After a moment, I said, "I have no sense of her having gone underground."

Quite the opposite, in fact.

Which didn't make sense. Roger—and by definition, Maelle—had been certain she'd been inside the bunkhouse when he'd first arrived. She'd obviously been deceived, but how? Was it the presence of her magic that they'd sensed? Or something else?

"Which means," Monty was saying, "we might have to split up."

"And that makes me thankful we now have additional help," came Aiden's comment from behind us.

I jumped and turned. I'd been concentrating so hard on the stone that I hadn't heard his approach. And he wasn't alone. Ashworth and Eli were with him, along with a tall, rather rugged-looking man I didn't recognize. He was wearing dark overalls and was carrying a sack with several hard hats in it, which suggested he was either a caver or an Emergency Services officer.

All four were wearing sunglasses, which made sense given the brightness of the day, but also had the psychic bit of me relaxing just a little.

Although I wasn't sure why, given we'd yet to test the theory they'd offer some protection from the basilisk's glare.

And, personally, I hoped we never did.

"What are you two doing here?" I asked. "I thought you were waiting for the basilisk hunter to arrive?"

"We were," Ashworth replied. "But she called and said the plane had been delayed, and she now won't be getting in until tomorrow. What's this about splitting up?"

I held the glove-wrapped spell stone aloft. "Monty found this in the rubble, and it holds enough resonance to trace."

"So, we try a two-prong assault," he said. "Two witches underground, two above?"

"Seems sensible," Monty said. "I take it our tall friend is a caver?"

"Mine guide," the stranger corrected. "And the name is Joel."

"Are you familiar with this mine?" I asked.

"No, but I'll be able to tell you whether a shaft or a tunnel is safe to traverse." He glanced at Aiden. "How do you want to play this? Me first, or one of the witches? You implied we could encounter supernatural problems down there."

He didn't seem fazed by the prospect, which was interesting.

"Probably safer with you down first," Aiden said, "just to ensure the tunnel is safe to use."

"I'll toss in a protection spell once you're ready to head down," Eli added. "That'll keep you safe until Monty and I get down there."

Leaving me, Ashworth, and Aiden to follow whatever lead I could glean from the spell stone.

If I could glean a lead and it *wasn't* a trap.

Right now, I wasn't putting anything past them.

As Eli crafted his spell, I grabbed my pack from Monty, then stepped away from the destroyed building to find a debris-free area to set up a protection circle. We were dealing with a dark mage, so it was probably best not to take any chances.

Ashworth followed me over and watched my construction through slightly narrowed eyes. When I finished, he nodded, as if in approval, and then said, "Be careful when you search. If that spell stone belongs to either Jaqueline or her mistress, it's possible they'll feel your presence through it."

I frowned. "How?"

It was certainly possible for a witch to cast a spell to prevent a psychic finding them, but I'd never heard of a witch being able to *sense* a psychic search through a stone unless they were a psychic themselves—and that usually only happened when there was human blood within the witch line.

Maelle never said who Jaqueline's father was, Belle commented. *Maybe he was human rather than witch.*

I really can't imagine Maelle getting married to a common old human, can you?

No, but they were very different days back then. Maybe she had no choice. Or maybe she was simply fucking him and got pregnant by mistake.

"Dark mages generally use blood to create and set their spells," Ashworth was saying, "it inevitably leaches into their spell stones, and when an opposing force interacts with them—"

"It sets off a warning that resembles a flash of light going off in the darkness," I finished.

"That's a lot more poetic than what I was about to say,

but yes." He grimaced "You'll be well protected by your circle, so it shouldn't be a problem, but these vampires have shown no inclination to act logically. While they might not be able to stop you physically, it's almost certain they will attempt to stop you magically."

"Meaning if I *am* able to connect to Jaqueline's mind via the blood that lingers on this stone, it would be best to keep contact to a minimum."

Ashworth nodded. "The chances of discovery rise the longer you linger, and that exponentially increases the likelihood of an attack."

"Meaning you, my dear man, had best keep an eagle eye out."

He laughed. "Indeed. I can't have anything happening to my adopted granddaughter, now can I?"

I stepped into my circle, tied off and activated the spell, and then sat cross-legged on the ground. "Speaking of which, how do you feel about said adopted granddaughter holding her wedding in your garden?"

He blinked. "It would be an honor, but there are plenty of lovely places within the reservation that would be more suitable."

"But none that I feel so at home in." I smiled up at him. "I'd also like you to walk me down the aisle."

The blinking increased, and I'd swear I spotted the sheen of tears. "Surely Monty—"

"It's a father's duty to walk his daughter down the aisle, and you are the closest thing to a father—or at least a grandfather—that I now have."

"Ah, lass, it would be my great honor to do so."

"Good." I smiled. "But you should know that the wedding will be held in weeks, not months—"

"More a matter of days, rather than weeks," Aiden

corrected as he approached. "I'm not risking her escaping me again."

Ashworth laughed and clapped Aiden on the shoulder. "Oh, I doubt there's any risk of that. You've been the problem, lad, not our girl. However, I'd advise waiting until we've at least dealt with our current vampire problem."

"That goes without saying."

But the look he cast my way was determined. The alpha had finally set his mind on marriage, and he would not be persuaded to delay very long.

I couldn't say I in any way disagreed with that determination.

"As long as we have time to get my mom and Belle's family down here," I said, "I really don't care when the wedding is held."

"Good. I shall start immediate arrangements."

I laughed. "And off goes the alpha without consulting his wife-to-be about said arrangements."

"The alpha has absolutely no intention of doing *anything* in that regard without preapproval from said future wife. I have learned that lesson the hard way."

"Happy wife, happy life," Ashworth said. "Glad you've learned it early, lad."

"Righto, gentlemen," Joel said. "We're a go here whenever you're ready."

Aiden turned. Joel had secured the ropes to the larger of the remaining stumps, and he, Monty, and Eli were now wearing harnesses and hard hats.

"You'll probably lose phone signal down there," Aiden said. "So make sure you use the two-way to keep me updated."

Joel nodded, then carefully went over the edge, feeding

out the rope as he disappeared down the shaft. Once he'd given the all clear, Monty and then Eli followed him down.

Leaving us and the darkly pulsing spell stone in the bright sunshine.

I took a deep breath and released it slowly. It didn't calm the nerves. Didn't calm the sudden certainty that this would all go horribly wrong. "Okay, let's get this bit over with."

Aiden walked around the protection circle to stand at my back, his closeness sending skitters of awareness down my spine. With the two of them guarding me, I should be safe.

So why did the opposite feel true?

Precognition? Or simple fear?

I did my best to shove it—whatever "it" was—away, and carefully peeled the glove away from the stone, dropping it into my palm.

For several, seemingly long seconds, nothing happened. The darkness continued to pulse from within the stone's black heart, but my psi senses didn't immediately react, as they had with the blood.

But maybe that was because I was currently keeping a very tight leash on them.

I took another of those long breaths that didn't calm the growing sense of danger, then released the leash. My psi senses immediately leapt away, chasing the faint line of the heartbeat at dizzying speed, not giving me any chance to see the lay of the land or where we might be heading.

Only to stop with an abruptness that had my breath catching in my throat.

Once again, nothing else immediately happened. The steady beat continued, but I was surrounded by blackness. Then, gradually, images formed. This time, they weren't coming from the mind of whoever owned this stone, but rather the cold hearts of the *other* spell stones.

Which was not something I'd ever thought possible, although in truth there weren't many witches who made a habit of losing spell stones, either, and therefore little reason for anyone to employ a psychic to find them. Aside from the fact good stones capable of enhancing a witch's magic were rare and expensive, it was often better to buy a new set than try to match the harmonics of a new stone to older ones.

I frowned and tried to sharpen the tenuous, hazy images flickering through my mind. The stones appeared to have been tossed onto a coffee table, and the views I was getting very much depended on where they were situated.

I couldn't see the whole room in which they were sitting from my current angle, but it appeared large and had a very "old-fashioned" feel. The nearby chair was well stuffed but old, the wallpaper—peeling and yellowed—was a flocked, floral design, and the taped-down curtains were ornate. A fire burned brightly somewhere beyond my current line of sight, its warm light flickering across the cobwebbed ceiling. There were newspapers on the table close to the stone, along with several newish-looking books and a hand.

A man's hand.

I had no idea if that hand was attached to a body or some sort of macabre souvenir. The stone's "vision" was weirdly limited and unmoving, but I guessed I was lucky to be seeing anything given it was *actually* a stone.

I deepened the connection and tried to get some sense of an actual location. There was nothing in the way of sound—again, unsurprising—and aside from that hand, I had no sense that anyone else was in the room.

I frowned and tried switching to a different stone.

There was a gut-wrenching step sideways, and suddenly, I had another viewpoint.

There *wasn't* a body attached to that hand.

Thankfully, it wasn't Roger's hand; aside from the fact it was far too masculine, the skin was sun-kissed and freckled.

I jumped to another stone. The room was much larger than I'd initially thought. Not only were there a number of tables and chairs in the center of the room, but an old-fashioned wooden bar at the far end. Five stools lined the bar's front, while on the wall behind it were several shelves holding a variety of spirits, most of them open and, presumably, empty—and had been for a while, I suspected. Vampires could consume liquids of any kind if absolutely necessary, but it tended to play havoc with their altered body functions. Above the shelving was a sign that said, Lola's Place.

The vamps were hiding in an old pub.

Time to retreat.

But as I started to pull back, a woman said, "Well, well, well, what have we got here?"

I couldn't see her, but her voice and intonations held echoes of Maelle.

Jaqueline.

Fuck.

I fled the stones and tried to drop the one in my hand, but it suddenly seemed glued to my skin. Panic surged as her awareness chased me down the still open line between us.

I will have you, little witch.

No, you fucking won't, I replied, and reached for my inner magic.

It rose in a thick wave and repulsed her attack, but not, I suspected, before she was able to confirm we were all here.

The stone dropped from my palm and hit the dirt, sending a soft spray of dust pluming upward.

For several seconds, I couldn't do anything more than gulp down air. That had been close. *Too* damn close.

"Lizzie?" Ashworth's voice broke through the lingering panic. "You're here. You're okay. She can't break through your circle."

Not now, I wanted to say. I lifted my gaze to his. He was squatting in front of me, magic buzzing around his fingertips, ready for the threat he could obviously sense but not see.

"I know. Her reaction just caught me by surprise, that's all." Which seemed to be something of a mantra for me of late.

"What happened?" Aiden walked around the protection circle and squatted next to Ashworth.

"I got sprung." I dismissed the circle, resisted the urge to stomp Jaqueline's stone deeper into the ground with the heel of my boot, and put it back into the glove instead. "But I did get a glimpse of where they were. Do you know of somewhere called Lola's Place?"

He frowned and pulled his phone from the back pocket of his jeans. "Is it a bar, the name of a farm, or even a café?"

"Bar, I think, but I can't say for certain it was in use before the vamps got there, though the number of cobwebs and the empty booze bottles suggests not." I hesitated. "There was also a severed hand on the table next to the spell stones and a blood smear down the wall."

"If the bar was still being used, the locals would have investigated it not being open or contacted us if they'd suspected something wrong."

"Because nothing gets between a local and their beer?" I asked in amusement.

"The local pub is often the only gathering place many smaller communities have." He glanced down at his phone and began to type. It didn't take long to get a result. "Okay, Lola's Place was an old tavern in McKenzie's Hill that also did short-term room lets. It closed down some six years ago when the old couple who ran it both died."

At least that meant the smear of blood wasn't Lola's or her husband's. "Why hasn't it been sold?"

"Because they're still searching for heirs."

Odd that they couldn't find them in the day and age of social media. I handed Ashworth the glove and collected my spell stones, depositing them in their leather pouch before tucking it safely away in my backpack.

"How did Jaqueline spring you?" Ashworth asked, examining the glove-encased spell stone through narrowed eyes. It was still emitting a dark pulse, and though its rhythm hadn't altered in any way, I suddenly had a sharp desire to get the hell away from this area while we still could.

I wasn't about to gainsay it.

I pushed to my feet and slung the pack over my shoulder. "I'm presuming—given what you said earlier about the spell stones—that she must have seen or felt their activation. Thing is, I wasn't actually seeing things through *her*, but rather the rest of the spell stones."

Ashworth rose with me, surprise evident. "I wouldn't have thought that even possible, given they are inert objects."

"I know, right?" I waved a hand. "The problem we now have is, after chasing me down the psi link until my magic stopped her, she now knows we are all here. We need to leave, ASAP."

"We can't," Aiden said. "Not yet. Joel contacted me

while you were doing your thing to say they found the mine's exit. It'd been widened to enable a vehicle to reverse into the mine; the photos Monty sent me suggest it was a van of some kind."

Probably the same one that whisked Jaqueline away. "No sign of Roger anywhere, I take it?"

Aiden shook his head. "And no traps set, according to Monty. For all intents and purposes, it seemed they got out of that tunnel as fast as they could."

"Which is no surprise, given they couldn't be certain the explosion wouldn't damage the tunnels," Ashworth said.

Which made sense. "I take it they're already on their way back here?"

Aiden nodded and glanced at his watch. "Should be another ten minutes or so. Apparently, the tunnel wasn't very long or deep."

I nodded and scanned the immediate area again, not sensing anything, not seeing anything. And yet, that sense of doom was increasing.

I rubbed my arms and fought the urge to pace. Aside from the fact it wouldn't achieve anything, it was too damn hot to move around too much.

"Once the laddie and Eli are back," Ashworth said, "I think we need to head over to Lola's and hit them while the lead is fresh, so to speak."

"Will the five of us be enough?" Aiden asked. "Or will we need to call in additional help?"

"Like who?" Ashworth said. "There're no Regional Witch Association investigators in the area apart from me, and getting someone in from Canberra will take twenty-four hours, at least. Which means, aside from Belle—"

"And I'd really prefer it if she was kept as backup rather than in the middle of the fray," I cut in.

I wouldn't, came her comment, *not when it will take the combined strength of all of us to deal with these people.*

Oh, I agree with you on that bit, but keeping you in reserve means I can call on your help if necessary. Plus, if the shit does hit the fan and we're captured, you can ride to the rescue.

She harrumphed. *Yeah, because one lone, middling-powered witch will be able to overcome all of them after you lot failed.*

My amusement ran down the line between us. *Except it's going to take every bit of their strength to stop us. If you hit them telepathically before they have a chance to recover, you have a fighting chance.*

You're talking through your butt, and you know it.

Which doesn't make the comment any less legitimate.

"The only other person we can call in quickly is Maelle," Ashworth continued, "and she's already said she cannot directly attack her maker."

"She also said we're not to kill Jaqueline," I said, "and I'm not sure that's even achievable now. If she wants her daughter alive, I suspect she is going to have to help us."

"Then she needs to be contacted," Ashworth said. "She'll be confined to protective darkness until tonight, of course, but it might be worth ringing just to check if she is willing to help."

My gaze drifted to the distant trees and the hill on which we'd stood. There was nothing to see and yet... something was definitely coming.

And I had no idea if it was magic or something else.

Something like the basilisk, perhaps?

I licked my lips and glanced over to the trapdoor. "How far away are they? Because we really need to get out of here. I think we're about to be attacked."

"Jaqueline?" Ashworth asked sharply. "Or the snake beastie they conjured?"

"I don't know. It just feels... wrong."

Ashworth scanned the area, but if he sensed anything more than me, then it wasn't obvious.

"I can hear them talking," Aiden said. "They must be close."

He walked over to the trapdoor, Ashworth and me two steps behind him. By the time we got there, the rope was jumping about lightly as someone grabbed it and climbed. I peered past Aiden's shoulder and saw the top of Monty's sweaty head.

He climbed over the shaft's edge, stepped away, then undid the rope from his harness. "Well, that was a wasted effort. Did you have any more luck up here?"

"You could say that," I said. "But in the process, I might just have endangered us all."

"Well, we are dealing with dark mages, so that's not surprising." He bent and offered a hand to Eli, helping him over the edge. "I take it we need to hightail it out of here in order to escape said danger?"

"'Fraid so." I glanced over my shoulder again.

Whatever it was, it was closer.

Tension rolled through me, and I flexed my fingers, sending sparks spiraling through the air.

Monty raised his eyebrows but otherwise didn't comment.

Once Joel was out of the shaft, he wasted precious time undoing the ropes and closing the trapdoor. It was a good few minutes later before we headed off across the paddock, and I couldn't help but think the delay would be costly.

But maybe that was pessimism speaking again, even if instinct said otherwise.

I hated instinct sometimes. I really did.

We quickly made our way past the broken stockyards and silent bunkhouse, hurrying toward the trees I feared would offer as little protection from what was coming as they did the sun.

Movement to our left caught my eye. My heart leapt and I stopped abruptly, but it was threads of wild magic twisting toward us, not a spell.

Not the basilisk.

Aiden stopped beside me, his gaze scanning the area. He couldn't see the wild magic, but his expression was nevertheless concerned. "Something comes."

"Yes, but the question is, what?" I raised a hand, and the threads curled around my wrist, briefly filling my mind with a chaotic mix of images.

"I don't know," Aiden was saying. "The earth trembles underfoot, but I'm not scenting anything."

As the images slowed, Katie's voice rose, *You need to get out of there, now!*

Why? I asked, even as my gaze moved back to the hill ahead of us.

That was the moment the basilisk erupted from the trees.

CHAPTER FOURTEEN

It was *huge*.

Well over the four meters mentioned by John— the dead man Belle had questioned—with black scales that shone a rich purply-green and a head that was at least triple the size of a human's, suggesting this fucking thing had grown since it had been summoned here. Its mouth was open and its fangs—as long as my arms—gleamed darkly in the sunlight.

"Sunglasses," Monty shouted. "Whatever you do, don't look directly into its eyes."

I quickly wrapped the elastic attached to my sunnies tighter around my ponytail, then called to the inner wild magic.

A wave of magic from the men rose with mine. It was fierce, sharp, and powerful, but even so, I feared it wasn't going to be enough. Not against a basilisk that was bigger— more powerful—than any demon we'd dealt with before.

"Get into the forest," Aiden said. "It's too fucking open here—the trees will slow it down and give us a fighting chance."

We took off. Aiden's form shimmered briefly, but he didn't shift into his wolf. Instead, he twisted around, grabbed my hand, and pulled me on. My feet flew over the ground, matching his for speed, the threads of wild magic tumbling around us, urging us to hurry, to find shelter, to escape.

Katie didn't think our magic was going to be enough, either.

The ground trembled as the basilisk drew closer. Wild magic twisted around my fingers, mine and Katie's combined. I dared not unleash it. Not yet. Not while we were out in the open. Aiden was right—our best chance to snare this thing lay in the trees.

"Once the basilisk is a few meters in the forest," Ashworth shouted, "unleash net spells. If we layer them, the combination should hold the bastard long enough to deal with him."

Net spells, not cage. Perhaps he feared, as I did, that none of us could make a cage big enough—strong enough—to contain this thing for long.

I risked a look over my shoulder, making sure I kept my gaze away from the upper portion of the basilisk's body. The dust caused by its undulating movements surged before it, a wave that shrouded its form and chased our heels. But that didn't hide the fact it was closer now than it had been only a few seconds ago. It was faster—far faster—than any of us. We might not even make the trees before it hit us...

The dust rolled over Aiden and me, a brown curtain that snatched the other men from sight and turned day into dusk. Fear sharpened but I ignored it, concentrating on the barely visible forest, on the need to just get there, get *in* there, before the basilisk.

It was going to be close, so damn close...

We ran past one tree, two, then deeper. We were a good twenty meters in when, as one, Monty, Ashworth, and Eli tossed their spells over their heads and kept on running. As their magic skimmed over our heads, I jagged to the left, pulling Aiden with me, needing to see the position of their nets before I unleashed mine. The three spells hit a tree, then spooled out to the right and the left, one spell layering across the other as they formed a U-shaped net.

The basilisk hit the tree line. My breath caught in my throat, my tension so fierce my whole body vibrated. Would it see or feel the trap? Some demons were magic sensitive, and given how little we knew of these things it was entirely possible.

But the sinuous, shadowy form didn't alter its trajectory, and it hit the layered nets with enough force that it ripped the first spell to shreds.

But the other two held.

I sucked in a relieved breath, then cast my spell, sending it to the rear of the basilisk to close off the trap. The basilisk reared up and hissed, a deep sound that echoed through the silence, then began to lash its tail back and forth, testing the boundary of its cage, trying to force a break.

"What now?" Aiden asked.

"I don't fucking know." I glanced around, frowning, as Ashworth, Monty, and Eli appeared. "Where's Joel?"

"We sent him on, just to be safe." Ashworth stopped a few yards shy of the net and thrust his hands on his hips. "We need to send this bugger back where it came from, and quickly."

"But how?" I asked. "When we sent the rusalka back, we had the pentagram to protect us—"

"Because we were summoning it to us. As long as we

don't look into its eyes, the banishment spell should work just fine."

"Whatever we do, we need to do it now," Monty said, "because the nets aren't going to contain it for long if it keeps thrashing about like that."

Ashworth nodded. "Liz, you'd best stand behind your section of the netting—which is likely to be the strongest given the wild magic woven into it—and take the lead. You do remember the banishment spell, don't you?"

"Yes." I grabbed my knife and a couple of bottles of holy water from the pack, then dropped it onto the ground at Aiden's feet.

After dropping a quick kiss on his cheek, I ran down the side of our trap, passing Monty as I headed toward the rear. The basilisk hissed and lunged toward me, its black teeth scoring the netting between us, causing the magic to ripple and shift. Another lunge: this time the netting bulged out, bringing the basilisk's dark and dangerous fury altogether too close. I leapt sideways, increasing the distance between us, but it kept hitting the net, determined to get through, determined to get me.

Which at least took its attention from everyone else.

I ran around the tree that anchored my spell, then stopped at the middle point. The basilisk didn't attack my section of the netting, thanks no doubt to the wild magic running within it, but it slithered back and forth along its length before attacking one of the junctions where my magic latched onto the others. Another thread tore and slowly began to unravel.

We had to get this done. We were running out of time.

I flexed my fingers against the hilt of my knife, then shoved one bottle of holy water into the waistband of my jeans and popped the cork from the other. I hoped they wouldn't be needed, but feared that they would.

I swallowed heavily and then said, "Okay, ready."

"Go for it," Eli replied.

I started the spell. As my magic rose, the basilisk reacted, throwing itself at the barrier on Monty's side—the side that was still unraveling—causing the magic to pulse and shimmer at a faster rate.

The certainty that things were about to hit the fan in a big way rose, but I ignored it and continued spelling. There was nothing else I could do.

The basilisk hissed, a long, low, furious sound that vibrated through every inch of my being. It was not a good sensation.

I finished my part of the spell, stepped back, and glanced at Monty. He immediately took over, his words loud and sharp against the high-pitched noises being emitted by the furious basilisk.

The vibrations increased and the nearby trees quivered, leaves falling like rain all around us. There was a crack, and a branch came down, missing Monty by several meters.

The basilisk. Somehow, the sound it was emitting was causing the trees to shatter and break.

Another limb fell, larger and closer to Monty. I swore and cast a protection spell. As the magic settled around him, another limb fell, this time directly over his head. It hit the protection spell and bounced away, drawing dust as it hit the ground.

The basilisk screamed—a sound so odd with its snaky form—and returned its attention to the fracturing net, tearing at it with its fangs and then hitting it with its tail. No netting spell, no matter how strong, could withstand such an assault for very long.

As Monty wound up his portion of the banishment spell and Ashworth started, a large section of the netting completely fractured. The basilisk lunged at the gap, raised its teeth, and sprayed a dark and bloody liquid at Monty with venomous force.

But it wasn't venom. It was acid.

It hit the protective spell hard enough to send Monty stumbling back as it dribbled down the surface of my spell and hit the ground with loud splashes that instantly began to bubble and steam.

Monty's foot caught a tree root and he fell awkwardly, his glasses flying from his nose as he yelped and grabbed at his ankle.

"Monty," I yelled, even as he squeezed his eyes shut, "stay down and protect yourself. The basilisk won't attack my magic."

And hoped, even as I said that, that it remained true.

Monty's magic rose, and a dark orb formed within mine. A shielding spell—one dark enough to stop light entering and, hopefully, mute the basilisk's stone-turning ability.

As Ashworth continued the banishment spell, the basilisk lunged again for the break in the net. Its teeth scored the remaining spell threads, tearing multiple lines. It was going to get out...

And Monty was directly in its path.

Believing my magic would protect him was one thing; standing back and watching it being tested by the sheer force of this thing was another. I couldn't take the risk. I swore and sprinted toward him. The basilisk's head snapped around and, just for an instant, its gaze caught mine. Magic ran over me—much diluted thanks to the sunglasses, but still powerful—and an odd sort of ice began to creep through my body. It slowed my movements, thickened my thoughts.

Wild magic rose within me, but it couldn't battle the lethargy. I would freeze, just as the basilisk's other victims had, if this thing wasn't banished or killed.

But I wasn't frozen yet, and this bastard was not going to get me. Not while I still had breath in my lungs and movement in my limbs.

It lunged at me, its head so large it was all I could see. I didn't stop, didn't slow, forcing every ounce of speed and strength into my faltering legs. The basilisk's mouth opened wide, ready to consume.

I drew my arm back and threw the holy water into its throat.

Its response was instantaneous. It reared up, shaking its head violently from side to side, smoke streaming from its mouth. I doubted there'd been enough holy water to kill it, but it sure as hell was making it uncomfortable.

Eli's voice rose above the din. The final section of the banishment had begun.

The basilisk showed no awareness of the danger it was in, and we needed to keep it that way.

The high-pitched keening increased and the trees around us reacted violently, leaves and limbs thumping around me. I called my inner magic, but before I could raise any sort of protective spell, the basilisk dove for me.

I swore and threw myself sideways, hitting the ground and rolling back to my feet in one smooth motion. The basilisk's tail whipped around, catching me off guard, sweeping me off my feet and sending me tumbling through the air. I hit a tree hard and slid down its trunk to the ground.

Ground that was trembling. The snake was free and coming at me.

I scrambled upright, but my movements were slower, every muscle ached, and I wasn't sure if the cause was hitting the tree, the freezing magic, or a combination of both.

It didn't matter. Nothing would if I didn't fucking get out of the basilisk's way.

As I stumbled around the tree, magic rose. A heartbeat later, a sphere erupted from the darkness that hid Monty. It curled around the basilisk's neck, then split in two and sped off in opposite directions, each end lashing itself to several trees.

The basilisk reacted violently to being roped, thrashing itself back and forth, its keening reaching fever pitch. The trees holding the leashes shivered and shook, and limbs exploded, sending deadly wooden shards spearing through the air.

This time, the trees would break before the magic did.

I swore, knelt, and called to the wild magic. The earth magic, rather than mine. It swept up from the ground and coursed through me, judging my need between one slowing heartbeat and the next.

Then it leapt away and flooded the trees with its strength. The shattering stopped, but that only increased the basilisk's desperation. Once again, the magic that leashed it began to tear apart.

Eli's voice was rising. The banishment spell was close to culmination. We just had to hold on. Just had to give him time.

Movement, fast movement, from my left.

Aiden, coming in fast, holding a long, thick bit of metal as if it were a javelin.

The basilisk's head snapped his way, teeth bared, but I jumped up, shouting to gain its attention. The acid meant for Aiden streamed my way, and I leapt back behind the tree, a protection spell falling around me but not quite fast enough. A thin stream of dark liquid began to eat into the leather of my boot; I kicked it off and flung it away. The basilisk's head followed the movement, and Aiden was in the air, the metal held high above his head. I watched, heart in my mouth, magic buzzing around my fingertips, as he landed on the creature's thick neck and plunged the metal straight through the basilisk's brain.

It reared up and shook its head violently from side to side, tossing Aiden from its back. He tumbled through the air but landed on his feet, running hard as the basilisk tried to squash him with its tail.

Then Eli finished the banishment spell.

The basilisk's body began to vibrate, its scales rippling, shifting, separating, becoming smoke that was swiftly sucked into the void the banishing spell had created behind it. It drove its fangs into the ground in a desperate effort to hang on, but the disintegration continued unchecked, sweeping up its body, tearing it apart scale by scale, until there was nothing left but fangs stuck in the ground.

Then they too were gone, swept back to whatever hell it had been called from.

I dropped my head to my chest. We'd done it. We'd survived.

Soft steps approached, and I knew without looking up it was Aiden. He squatted in front of me and grabbed my hands, his gaze sweeping me, full of concern. "Are you okay? I thought for a moment that the basilisk might have caught your gaze."

"It did, but the sunglasses successfully diluted the power of it." I reached up and tugged them off. "I'm fine."

He didn't look convinced. I smiled and touched his cheek with a grubby hand. "When the basilisk disappeared, the effects of his gaze did also. I really am fine."

"Good." He paused. "Does this mean everyone else who survived its gaze will similarly recover?"

I nodded and held out a hand. "Help me up."

He clasped my hand, pulled me upright, then tugged me into his arms. He smelled of sweat and caring, and it was the sweetest scent ever.

"You do realize," he said, "that you scared the goddamn life out of me when you stood in front of that basilisk armed with only water."

"Not *only* water. I did have a knife."

"Which you didn't use."

His voice was dry, and I smiled. "That knife would barely have gotten through its scales. Besides, using it would have meant getting even closer, and I didn't think that advisable."

"Common sense." He lightly touched the back of his hand to my forehead. "No temperature..."

I laughed and knocked his hand away, then glanced around as Monty approached. He was limping quite badly and had torn his shirt in several places, but other than that, seemed fine.

"That was a movie-worthy move you made there, Ranger," he said, clapping Aiden lightly on the shoulder. "I was mightily impressed."

"It gave the basilisk something else to think about other than you two," he said. "Let's get back to the trucks—"

"And over to Lola's," Monty said.

Aiden frowned. "Do you think that's wise? Dealing

with the demon would have drained you magically, wouldn't it?"

"Aye, Ranger," Ashworth said, as he and Eli approached. "But if we don't go now, we lose all chance of finding them."

Both of them were sweating, and there was a nasty-looking scrape across the top of Ashworth's bald head, but otherwise, they too had come through the ordeal relatively unscathed.

We'd been lucky.

Extremely lucky.

But that pessimistic part of me couldn't help but wonder how much longer that luck would hold. Our vampire mages now knew what we were capable of and would adjust their attacks accordingly.

"It *is* likely any chance we had has well and truly left the building," Monty said. "But we need to try. Who knows, they might have left something behind to trace them with."

I rather suspected the chances of that happening were basically zero, but didn't voice my doubts. There was little point when we'd find out soon enough.

We made our way back to the trucks and drove across to McKenzie's Hill, which wasn't all that far away from the old stockyards.

Aiden pulled to a halt down the road from the building and undid his seat belt. "Stay here while I do a quick scout."

I nodded. "If the charm around your neck starts to warm, it means you've either hit a spell or there's a spell aimed your way."

It would also react if a vampire approached, but it was still light, so that really shouldn't be a worry.

He nodded and lightly ran a finger down my cheek, his touch sending warmth skittering through me.

"If that happens, I will hightail it the hell out of there."

"Good." I climbed out of the truck and moved to the rear, watching as he ran across the road and shifted to his wolf form once in the trees.

Monty, Ashworth, and Eli walked up and stood beside me. "Any of you sensing any magic?"

Ashworth shook his head. "But it's possible we won't. They might not have had time to set any traps."

"They had all the time in the world, given we've only just arrived."

"I doubt they would have risked laying traps or protections earlier," Eli said. "They were obviously aware there were a number of royal witches within the reservation—they wouldn't have wanted their magic being sensed."

I'd thought the same, but as he'd already noted, these people were playing by their own rules and anything was possible.

Aiden reappeared about ten minutes later. "Nothing," he said grimly. "No fresh scents, no sound of movement, no van, and absolutely no reaction from the charm when I paced the exterior. They're either asleep or gone."

"We still need to check, just to be sure," Monty said.

Aiden nodded, opened the back of his truck, and retrieved his spare boots. "These will be too big, but better than you walking around with one bare foot."

I accepted the right boot and pulled it on. My foot absolutely swam in it, which would be problematic if we had to run anywhere fast. Not that we would have to, given our vamps appeared to have fled.

And I crossed all mental fingers that I hadn't just jinxed us.

Aiden turned around, leading us across the road and

through the trees, meaning we approached from the rear rather than the front.

The building—a Victorian-style, two-story place—was in a sad state of repair, its paint peeling, the gutters full of weeds, and possessing a decided lean toward the front of the building, suggesting the stumps in that area had sunk.

What I *wasn't* seeing or feeling was any indication of life.

"It does seem likely that they've fled," Eli said, "But I think Ashworth, Aiden, and I should remain out here to keep guard, while Monty and Liz go in. Her magic has proven the most potent against these people."

Well, against the basilisk, at any rate.

Monty glanced at me, then at my nod, moved forward. The steps up to the rear deck creaked under our weight, the sound scratching at my nerves. The back door was unlocked. Monty warily pushed it open but didn't immediately enter, his gaze searching the interior shadows.

There was no sound, no movement, no obvious spells. The air drifting our way was warm though, so perhaps the fire remained lit.

We went in, checking each of the rooms before moving on. There was plenty of evidence of a hasty retreat, but absolutely no sign of vampires or vampire traps.

By the time we reached the bar area I'd seen through the stones, it was pretty obvious they'd fled. Maybe in killing their snake, we'd weakened them.

Or maybe they simply weren't ready to sully confront us yet.

"Damn," Monty said. "Missed them."

"Yeah." I walked across the room to the small table. The hand was no longer there, but the stones remained, sitting on top of a hastily written note.

You win this time, little witch, it said. *But I have your measure now. Send my best wishes to my mother and tell her I will see her suffering soon.*

It had been signed with a couple of Xs.

I checked the note for magic then picked it up and handed it to Monty.

"Well, the game remains afoot, Watson," he said after a moment. "I can't say I am in any way disappointed."

I snorted and shoved him toward the rear door. "You're certifiable, you know that?"

"Maybe. Thing is, I've got a feeling this is the big one. The last swansong of evil being called here by the well-spring's fading waves."

"I hope you're right."

He glanced at me, eyebrows raised. "Even as you know I'm not?"

"Fears you're not," I corrected.

"Ah, that's a very different thing, my dear cousin. We can do this. We can beat these bastards and settle down into a more peaceful life."

"I thought you didn't want a boringly peaceful life?"

"I'm going to marry Belle. Life will never be boring." His grin flashed. "Besides, I have a book on beasties to write."

I laughed and shoved him out the door.

Darkness might be plotting against us even now, but for the moment, we had time and space to regroup and plan our response.

And that was a win in my book.

EPILOGUE

Once again, I stood beside Aiden in the middle of the O'Connors' great hall. This was it. This was decision time. The moment we found out whether or not we'd be allowed to stay within the compound—whether our child would be allowed to run under the moonlight with the rest of the pack.

Aiden had made his case. His mother had made hers. To my surprise, what she'd concentrated on was not so much how dangerous my magic could be—a hard sell, given that same magic had saved the lives of many in this room— but rather the danger of allowing one outsider in and the snowball effect it could have in the future.

Which, in many respects, was a reasonable argument.

Karleen was many things—and she and I would never be, in any way, friends—but she wasn't stupid.

But this decision wasn't just about where we lived. It held ramifications for our daughter and what she would become. I couldn't just stand here mutely. I wasn't a wolf; I had no rights in this place—and maybe never would—but I nevertheless had to take a stand. I was to be an alpha's wife. I needed to start acting like one.

I squeezed Aiden's hand and then released it and stepped forward. I felt rather than saw the flash of concern, but he made no attempt to stop me.

"I would like to say something before your decision is made," I said.

A murmur ran around the room, then Larkin—who again seemed to be leading the discussion—said, "Please, feel free."

"When I walked into your wellspring, I walked into another world. One not only filled with power but also all the ghosts of the Fenna who had walked this earth eons ago."

My gaze swept the partitioned areas in front of me. There was no hostility that I could see, but there was disbelief. Few of those in this room knew anything about magic or the supernatural world, simply because few wolves were capable of sensing such things.

"Those ghosts," I continued, "accepted our daughter into the fold, making her the champion and protector of your wellspring. But they cannot teach her all that she needs to be taught. I can teach her magic, but I cannot teach her the ways of the pack—"

"This is presuming she survives until birth. Many half-breeds do not," a woman I didn't recognize said.

"That's a reasonable fear with *any* birth, not just half-breeds, especially in the first trimester. But she will. I've not only seen it, but the Fenna have confirmed it."

Another murmur ran around the room, this time filled with disbelief. But then, they had for centuries been told half-breeds rarely survived. It would take far more than the word of one witch to shake that belief.

"Aiden is her father," a woman to the right of Larkin said. "He's more than capable of helping her control the inner wolf."

"Yes, but to be a lone wolf is to suffer. If there is no pack, there is no community. There's no sense of belonging, no warm earth to feel between your toes, and no chorus to join when the moon blooms full. The Fenna died out because they forgot these things. Because they valued the security of the spring over the security and well-being of those chosen to serve. My daughter needs to be here, close to both the wellspring and the pack. She has been accepted, but she cannot serve and protect either if no connection is formed."

A soft murmur ran around the room. People shifted, sharing glances, but it was hard to gauge the mood. Which was frustrating when it was supposedly one of my talents.

"Very well," Larkin said. "Please step outside while we discuss the matter. Karleen, you are also to exit."

Her surprise was spear sharp. I resisted the urge to look around at her and somehow restrained my smirk. The doors closed behind the three of us. Karleen didn't say anything. She simply strode across the clearing, presumably to talk to some of the people gathered there.

"Whatever happens," Aiden said softly, "know that I don't care where we live as long as I'm with you. But if being here is so important to our daughter, then I will make it happen, no matter how long it takes."

I smiled, rose on to my toes, and kissed him, long and slow. "I do love you, you know. Madly, deeply, irrevocably."

"And I you, even if your fearless disregard for your own safety is likely to send me into an early grave."

I laughed. He wrapped a hand around my neck and drew me close again. Awareness of everything else fled, because there was nothing more important than this man and this kiss at this moment in time.

The doors finally opened, and we were ushered inside. I gripped Aiden's hand tightly, tension rolling through me. I couldn't read the expressions of most, but my gaze met Ciara's and she nodded, a small movement that nevertheless had hope leaping.

Larkin rose. "A decision has been made, though it was not unanimous."

No surprise there. Karleen might not have been present, but her faction would have had their say in her place.

"And what is that decision?" Aiden asked evenly. His tension was as fierce as mine, but there was little sign of it in his expression or stance.

The alpha was in full control.

"That you and Elizabeth may stay and bring up your children within the reservation."

My heart leapt, but Larkin wasn't finished yet.

"However," he continued. "She cannot represent the wider pack at council and will not take lead in decisions made within the pack. Karleen—"

"Karleen," I cut in, probably unwisely, but fuck it, "has already proven unreliable in many aspects of late. Her actions have endangered this reservation multiple times. I do not dispute my unsuitability when it comes to pack decisions, but surely as the wife-to-be of a pack alpha, I have the right to at least choose who shall represent me."

Larkin raised an eyebrow, his amusement evident. "What say the pack? Yea or nay?"

"Why the fuck are we even voting on this?" Karleen growled. "I *am* the senior female alpha of our line. She cannot take that position, so it remains mine."

"It remained yours for as long as your son remained

single. That is no longer the case." Larkin's voice hardened. "Sit down, Karleen. Now."

Her low growl sent chills down my spine. Our relationship had just been soured beyond any redemption. She might have eventually forgiven me for stealing her son, but she would never forgive me stealing her position.

"What say the pack?" Larkin repeated.

Against all the odds, the yeas won. Not by much, but that didn't matter.

Larkin's smile grew. He was on our side, I realized. "Do you need time to consider your replacement?"

"No." I turned and looked at Ciara. Surprise flitted across her expression, then she smiled and gave a short, brief nod. "I name Aiden's sister, Ciara."

I glanced at Karleen as I said it. Her gaze narrowed, and her aura was a seething mess of differing emotions. I'd been right. She wouldn't ever forgive this.

Let the battle begin anew, I thought, but for just this moment, didn't really care. The magic in this place would protect me from any physical attack, while rumors, lies, and verbal attacks could be countered by my actions. By living amongst the pack and letting them see *me*.

Larkin dismissed the meeting, and Aiden led me from the building so quickly I was almost running to keep up. "Why the hurry?" I asked with a laugh.

"I've something to show you," he said. "Something I've been working on for months now."

"Oh yeah?" I said. "What?"

"Wait."

"I hate waiting."

He chuckled. "So I've learned."

We walked past several gorgeous old longhouses and stopped in front of one with a scarlet red door, white picket fence, and a small front yard filled with wildflowers as bright and as lovely as the ones that bloomed across the earthen roof.

My heart caught... I once told him that I wanted the whole white-picket-fence ideal. This couldn't be... surely he hadn't been planning our marriage for so long that he'd had time to do all *this*.

His eyes shone in delight as they met mine. "What do you think?"

"It's gorgeous, but what has it to do with you and me?"

"This, my dear witch, will be our house." He paused. "Unless, of course, you hate it. Then we'll find somewhere else within the reservation. It might be normal for the alpha to live near the hall, but given we're breaking rules left, right, and center—"

I laughed, leapt into his arms, and kissed him. "It's perfect. Absolutely perfect."

"You haven't seen inside yet. It's a mess and definitely needs a woman's touch."

"I don't care."

"Good." He bent and swept me into his arms. "Then, my dear wife-to-be, let me carry you over the threshold so you can inspect your future home."

We not only inspected, we christened.

It was the perfect way to start our life in the compound.

ALSO BY KERI ARTHUR

Relic Hunters Series

Crown of Shadows (Feb 2022)

Sword of Darkness (Oct 2022)

Ring of Ruin (June 2023)

Shield of Fire (March 2024)

Horn of Winter (Nov 2024)

Lizzie Grace Series

Blood Kissed (May 2017)

Hell's Bell (Feb 2018)

Hunter Hunted (Aug 2018)

Demon's Dance (Feb 2019)

Wicked Wings (Oct 2019)

Deadly Vows (Jun 2020)

Magic Misled (Feb 2021)

Broken Bonds (Oct 2021)

Sorrows Song (June 2022)

Wraith's Revenge (Feb 2023)

Killer's Kiss (Oct 2023)

Shadow's End (July 2024)

The Witch King's Crown

Blackbird Rising (Feb 2020)

Blackbird Broken (Oct 2020)

Blackbird Crowned (June 2021)

Kingdoms of Earth & Air

Unlit (May 2018)

Cursed (Nov 2018)

Burn (June 2019)

The Outcast series

City of Light (Jan 2016)

Winter Halo (Nov 2016)

The Black Tide (Dec 2017)

Souls of Fire series

Fireborn (July 2014)

Wicked Embers (July 2015)

Flameout (July 2016)

Ashes Reborn (Sept 2017)

Dark Angels series

Darkness Unbound (Sept 27th 2011)

Darkness Rising (Oct 26th 2011)

Darkness Devours (July 5th 2012)

Darkness Hunts (Nov 6th 2012)

Darkness Unmasked (June 4 2013)

Darkness Splintered (Nov 2013)

Darkness Falls (Dec 2014)

Riley Jenson Guardian Series
Full Moon Rising (Dec 2006)
Kissing Sin (Jan 2007)
Tempting Evil (Feb 2007)
Dangerous Games (March 2007)
Embraced by Darkness (July 2007)
The Darkest Kiss (April 2008)
Deadly Desire (March 2009)
Bound to Shadows (Oct 2009)
Moon Sworn (May 2010)

Myth and Magic series
Destiny Kills (Oct 2008)
Mercy Burns (March 2011)

Nikki & Micheal series
Dancing with the Devil (March 2001 / Aug 2013)
Hearts in Darkness Dec (2001/ Sept 2013)
Chasing the Shadows Nov (2002/Oct 2013)
Kiss the Night Goodbye (March 2004/Nov 2013)

Damask Circle series
Circle of Fire (Aug 2010 / Feb 2014)
Circle of Death (July 2002/March 2014)
Circle of Desire (July 2003/April 2014)

Ripple Creek series

Beneath a Rising Moon (June 2003/July 2012)

Beneath a Darkening Moon (Dec 2004/Oct 2012)

Spook Squad series

Memory Zero (June 2004/26 Aug 2014)

Generation 18 (Sept 2004/30 Sept 2014)

Penumbra (Nov 2005/29 Oct 2014)

Stand Alone Novels

Who Needs Enemies (E-book only, Sept 1 2013)

Novella

Lifemate Connections (March 2007)

Anthology Short Stories

The Mammoth Book of Vampire Romance (2008)

Wolfbane and Mistletoe--2008

Hotter than Hell--2008

ABOUT THE AUTHOR

Keri Arthur, the author of the New York Times bestselling ***Riley Jenson Guardian series***, has written more than fifty-five novels–35 of them with traditional publishers Random House/Penguin/Piatkus. She is now fully self-published. She's won six Australian Romance Readers Awards for Favourite Sci-Fi, Fantasy, or Futuristic Romance & the Romance Writers of Australia RBY Award for Speculative Fiction. Her Lizzie Grace series won ARRA's Fav Continuing Romance Series in 2022 and she has in the past won The Romantic Times Career Achievement Award for Urban Fantasy. When she's not at her computer writing the next book, she can be found somewhere in the Australian countryside taking photos.

for more information:
www.keriarthur.com
keriarthurauthor@gmail.com

facebook.com/AuthorKeriArthur
x.com/kezarthur
instagram.com/kezarthur